DAN SCAMELL

WALNUT RIDGE

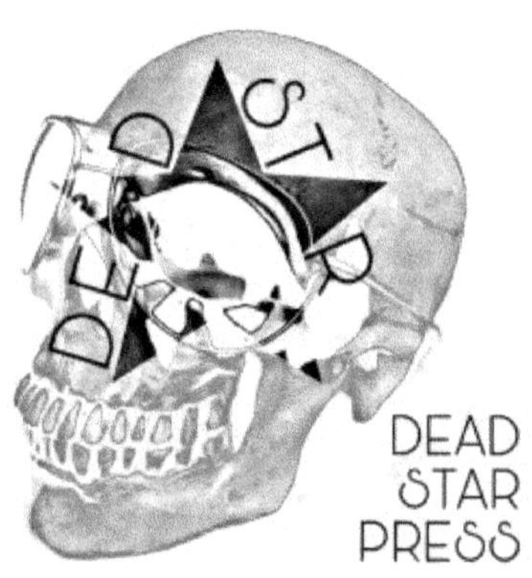
DEAD
STAR
PRESS

ACKNOWLEDGMENTS

I would like to thank Brandy for pushing me so hard in my writing. Her constant query, "Did you win at writing yet?" helped prod me to work through the lulls and get words onto paper. Without the coffees, the walks, the Insta-pot macaroni & cheese, and, most importantly, her companionship, this journey would have been far more of a struggle. I am also grateful to my beta-readers, Chris Mele, who helped greatly with editing and feedback-Bettergetaneditor.com, Heather, Dave, and especially my mother, who did a wonderful job taking the initial pass over this manuscript for copyediting. Secoura was generous with their wealth of knowledge about the inner workings of a Taco Bell kitchen, and for that, I am incredibly grateful.

Special thanks are also in order for Hank for granting me residence in his home, Mom (again), Jerry, for being an amazing friend and providing me a home-away-from-home, Nate, for bullshitting with me about everything practically every day, Chelsea, for opening and swapping old trading cards with me, Matt and Carrie, for their continued love, and anyone else who has or continues to put up with me on a regular basis. Also, Bill and Bob.

A huge thank you goes to the goons at Dead Star Press. Their belief in my work, and by extension me, is truly humbling. When I saw their ad and decided to send in my manuscript, I never really thought it would come to anything. Imagine my surprise when the reply I quickly received was not a form rejection! This has been an exciting and enlightening journey, and I'm still awed and bruised and pleased and reeling from it. The effort you've put into working with me and working on my dumb little book is tough for me to comprehend. Thank you for giving me a chance, Joe.

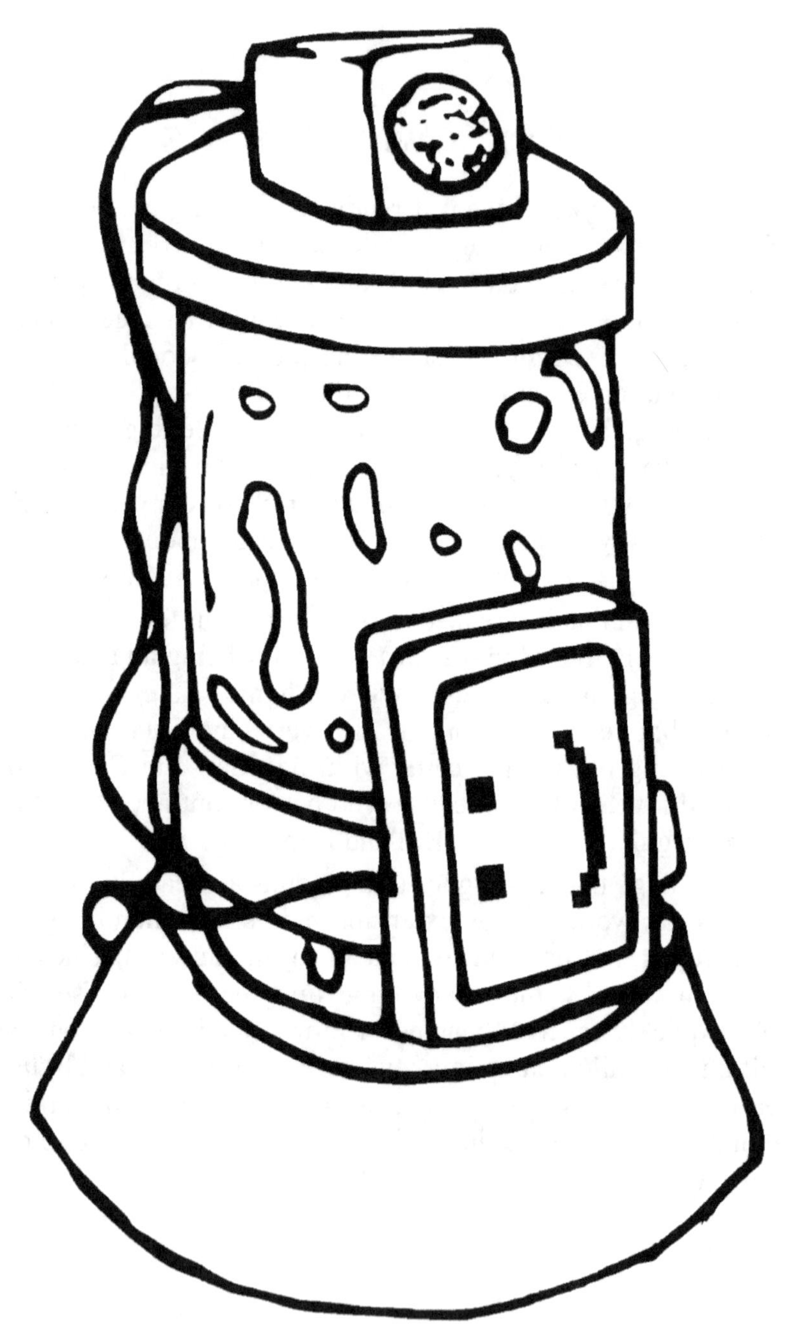

1.

One of the Angels walked past the group meeting room. It was not, of course, a real angel in biblical terms. It was a visual approximation of an angel, and that was what they liked to be called, Angels. Leo Salmon only saw it walk by because he was not paying much attention to what was going on in the group meeting room. He rarely did. Sharing sessions seemed senseless and repetitive to him most of the time nowadays. He tried to give them a shot, but man, could they be boring.

In addition to the woman running the meeting, the *tech*, all the lodgers still residing at the facility were currently in the group meeting room. Their numbers amounted to nine now. When Leo first entered the facility, it was at full capacity with those in need of re-programming. The mood at that time was light and airy and full of hope. The facility was a necessary stop on the way to the utopia the Angels were offering. Now, it seemed to Leo, all the glamour had been sapped from the atmosphere. That was more or less okay with him.

"Have you been putting effort into your homework?" asked Miranda, the tech running the meeting. She was a human, not an Angel, in her late thirties. She had likely been chosen for the job as much for her knowledge and background in psychology as for her appearance and warm demeanor. Most lodgers tended to trust her quickly and deeply despite knowing virtually nothing about her. Her question was addressed to George, a man who had been living in the facility almost as long as Leo.

"I always do my 'homework,'" he said, harassed. "Though if it's homework, I'd like the opportunity to actually work on it at my home."

Miranda sighed. This was an old and often retreaded subject with long-term lodgers who came through the facility. "As you well know, you are welcome to leave and return to your homes at any time."

"Right," George scoffed. "I know. I can walk out the front door and drive myself right back to my house. I can buy a hundred pounds of steak at the supermarket that's closed down and have a great big cookout with all my friends who have abandoned their houses to board the cross-ships." He paused before adding, "That is, if I can find a gas station that's still running between Vermont and New Jersey. If not, I might just break down and starve to death on the side of the road. Of course, then I'd be a ghost. I guess that wouldn't be too bad. They don't seem to give a shit about anything anyway." It was an insensitive thing to say, given that there were three ghosts in the meeting.

The television was on but muted in the corner of the room. Playing was a rerun of a late-night talk show from sometime in the past year or so. There were only about three stations still broadcasting anymore. They were all computer-run and played old programming. The screen showed a man in a gray suit sitting at a desk, addressing the skeletal, humanoid robot who sat on a nearby couch. The host spoke with a grin and then awaited responses from the robot, which hardly even moved and had only a speaker for a mouth. Clipped to the barrel-like torso of the robot was a nametag reading "Chris." This was common practice since most of the robot shells were identical and each typically contained dozens of deceased and decanted souls.

As George continued to vent his frustrations to Miranda, who took them with good humor, Leo tried to figure out who the robot on the television might be. It would obviously be someone dead whose soul had been loaded into the vessel, but who? A long-deceased writer? A comedian who had lived fast and died young? Maybe a member of a musical group whose life was cut short?

When Leo returned his attention to the meeting, George had finished sharing and seemed to be feeling a little more relaxed. George knew the reality of his circumstances. He knew that he'd eventually be decanted and carted onto an Ark, one of the large cross-shaped space vessels bound for eternal paradise. He just wanted to be cantankerous and autonomous for a while longer. Miranda was now hearing a share from a woman named Lois. Lois had been in the facility even longer than Leo.

Miranda listened and sadly smiled as Lois prattled on about memories and old friends. Most of the time, it seemed as though Lois was not aware of what was going on or why she was in a strange complex with strange people. She acted almost as if she were simply in some kind of poorly run resort and didn't remember, nor care, how she got there. In what seemed to be her moments of clarity, which were few and far between, she became disturbingly quiet and withdrawn.

Leo couldn't remember who had already shared, and he knew that he would have to speak at some point. He used to embrace the fact that the group meetings were limited on time, but now, with so few left in the facility, let alone the individual group, he could no longer count on the clock running out.

During a pause in the inanity that was Lois's share, Miranda cut her off to announce that there would be a new lodger at the PDF, or Pre-Decantation Facility. This information had just come in on her tablet computer, which was always cradled in her arm. She gave the group the familiar spiel about accepting the new lodger and making them feel welcome. It was an innocuous and impersonal reading designed to keep new lodgers from being accosted or overwhelmed in their initial days.

"We ask that you welcome"—Miranda checked the information on her screen—"Frances to Walnut Ridge." Walnut Ridge was currently the official name of the facility. It was an intentionally disarming name like those given to nursing homes or drug treatment centers—places you put sick people who you didn't want to see being sick. "Please open your hearts and help her integrate into our community while also respecting her boundaries. As a fellow child of God, she is your sister—"

"Ain't never knew I had no sisters, Ma!" shouted George. He shouted this exact statement every time a new lodger was announced in his presence. He seemed to find it hilarious. Sometimes, a newer lodger would chuckle at his interruption, but mostly, everyone just ignored him. He seemed ecstatic that he was afforded one more chance to fire it off. There had been no new lodgers for weeks, and none had been expected.

"—and we appreciate your help and patience in welcoming this lost sheep into our flock," finished Miranda.

To Leo, all the religious, God-stuff felt a little shoehorned in. He had never really come around to the way the Angels liked to push the Christian aspect of their appearance into the nature of their mission. Maybe, Leo thought, the lodgers' acceptance of the confused, quasi-religious mumbo-jumbo was an integral part of the pre-decantation process. It wasn't worth questioning it at this point. With few exceptions, those who came to Walnut Ridge, no matter how ornery or insane, inevitably transformed into loving and tolerant creatures with seemingly infinite optimism. Sometimes, the change was obvious. Other times, it was simply a personal observation. Whatever mysterious machinations the Angels had devised, whether brainwashing or true enlightenment, appeared to work like a charm.

Quiet filled the room for a while after Miranda's speech. When Leo adjusted his legs in his chair, the sound of the faux-leather upholstery sliding against the cotton of his pale-blue medical scrub pants seemed very loud. He stopped mid-movement and wound up with one leg awkwardly hanging half-crossed over the other, not wanting to make more noise.

"Leonard," Miranda said, "how are you feeling today? We haven't heard from you in a while."

Leo shot a glance at the clock on the wall—five minutes until four. He had almost made it. "Well," he started, staring down at his socks, one of which had turned itself upside down on his foot, "I suppose I'm feeling about the same as usual. Just, um"—he paused—"usual." Against his better judgment, he looked up at Miranda. She was smiling serenely at him. He averted his gaze as he tried to think of something to say—something with any shred of substance.

"I guess I've been, just"—*Say something*, he thought. *Anything!*—"excited. About getting decanted and, and joining all those people on the ships." There, he thought, that ought to work for now.

"Oh?" said Miranda, with slight concern. "I'm glad to hear that. Though, your rhythmic feedback hasn't shown any marked changes." She swiped her hand across her tablet's screen, seemingly checking for information about Leo's false enthusiasm.

"Well," Leo stammered. "That is to say, guarded excitement, of course. Or else I wouldn't still be here." He gave a painfully fake laugh and looked around the room for something. Reassurance? Permission? A smile?

He hopelessly surveyed the room from one corner to the other, taking in all that there was to see, searching for some unseen salve for the discomfort of having to continue sharing. He saw George zoning out and staring at a wall. He saw Lois doing her needlepoint and mouthing words to herself. He saw, sitting on an end table, a jar of translucent blue fluid, which was Alphonse, a decanted human who had been sent back to the PDF for reasons not entirely clear. He saw Rhonda staring at the muted television. He saw the window high on the wall. Through the window, he saw the sky, which was purple. He saw Brock looking at both Leo and Miranda since his eyes never pointed in the same direction. He saw the robot shell that currently housed the three remaining ghost lodgers at Walnut Ridge. None of what he saw offered any clues as to what his next move should be.

"I'm," Leo started again, thinking of something true to say. "I'm glad that we'll be having peach cobbler with dinner tonight."

"Thank you for your share, Leonard," Miranda said mercifully. "I like the peach cobbler as well."

Leo looked back out the door to the hallway and caught sight of two Angels leading a female to the technician's station. She was dressed in a black T-shirt and a purple skirt over black and purple striped leggings. The entire ensemble was torn up and caked with mud. From where Leo sat, it looked like the woman had broken twigs in her hair and scratches on her face and arms. George, who still smoked despite being on detox meds like the rest of the lodgers, coughed loudly. The woman at the desk turned sharply and looked into the group meeting room. Her eyes met with Leo's. He felt paralyzed. Her gaze had locked him in place, and he was powerless to turn away or blink. Her face was unreadable to him. Disgusted? Determined? Dejected? At length, she turned back to the papers she had to sign at the desk.

Leo seemed to regain control over his muscles again, and his body relaxed almost entirely. Though, after a moment, he realized with horror that for the first time since arriving at Walnut Ridge almost nine months ago, he had an erection. He wished more than anything at that moment that he was wearing jeans instead of scrubs.

2.

"Is she fine?" asked Brock. Leo had told him about seeing the new girl checking in during the group meeting. This was the first and, apparently, the most important question to enter Brock's mind.

"She's," started Leo. He was sitting across from Brock in their small, shared bedroom. Although there had been plenty of room for all lodgers to have their own quarters for months, the Angels preferred keeping two to a bedroom. Leo had shared bedrooms with dozens of other lodgers during his time. Brock had been at Walnut Ridge for about five months and roomed with Leo for the past two—the longest he had any roommate. "She's pretty, yeah."

"Nice," Brock replied, grinning, his eyes pointing in different directions.

In reality, Leo couldn't remember if the new lodger, Frances, was "fine" or not. He couldn't really remember what her face looked like. She was white or light-skinned. Her hair was filthy but was probably blonde or light brown. She had two eyes and a nose. Probably a mouth, he couldn't quite remember. She did have scratches on her face. That, he did recall.

"So, you been here a while," Brock said in his thick-tongued drawl. "You get a lot of trim?"

"I'm sorry?"

Brock laughed. "Chicks. Ladies. Females." He grinned, "Pussy! You know? How many girls you had?"

"Oh," said Leo, still trying to dredge the new woman's face from his fuzzy memory. "I guess, a few," he lied.

"My man," Brock said, clapping a large dark hand over Leo's knee. "Grundy's a freak." Brock insisted on calling Leo "Grundy." He was unable to grasp the fact that Leo's last name was Salmon, like the fish, and not Solomon. He explained that Leo had the same name as a character from the old *Super Friends* cartoon he watched as a child. This name was Solomon Grundy. As roommates went, Brock was a decent one.

Most of the lodgers who came through Walnut Ridge transitioned quickly and without incident. Others did not. One particular roommate of Leo's named Rupert had jumped on Leo in the middle of the night and clawed at Leo's face until security could stop the attack. It was a brief but jarring affair, and afterward, Rupert was taken to a separate wing for intensive transitive therapy. Leo was also given extra therapy sessions in private, but they were short-lived. The incident had not affected him as much as the Angels had feared.

A part of Leo wondered if the attack had been a setup. He questioned if the Angels had, perhaps, allowed a dangerous person to come in contact with him to jumpstart or alter his progress in pre-decantation, which he was told was "somewhat slower than usual." It was a moot point to think about, though. Whether it had been an intentional tactic or not, it had not hastened Leo Salmon's pace toward whatever goal the Angels had in mind for him.

Just as Leo lay back onto his mattress to relax, the electronic chimes indicating medication dispensation flitted over the PA system. It was time for evening meds and homework assignments. Leo lay for a minute longer as Brock stood and trotted into the hallway to get himself a good spot in the line, which used to be long. Before joining the rest of the lodgers in the queue, Leo changed from his thin cotton scrubs into blue denim jeans. This was in case Frances was in the line and there was a repeat of the earlier incident. He was pretty sure that no one had noticed in *"group,"* but doubt lingered in his mind.

By the time Leo got to the counter where medication was dispensed, almost everyone had gotten their pills and their sheaf of papers for the night. As usual, Brock was talking with a few techs at the nurse's station. In his hand were two papers. Most lodgers only got a few sheets for their homework, and in Lois's case, she had no assigned questions to answer. She was simply to write in a diary and present it to a technician a few times a week.

Leo bellied up to the counter to receive his paper cup of pills. He had the standard lot—detoxification pills, vitamin tablets, and a green and white capsule called "olive branch." This was something the Angels had devised for use on humans to relieve tension and ease emotional and mental resistance to the admittedly odd circumstances of the current world. Leo wasn't sure if they did anything, but he was also afraid not to take them. There were also intravenous versions of the medications, but Leo had never needed to have them administered. They were usually reserved for newer, less willing lodgers. Leo had seen a few people stuck with needles, but not for months.

"How are you, Leonard?" asked Doris, the evening nurse who gave out medications.

"I'm fine. Thank you, Doris," he replied. He gulped his pills down with the water he had carried in a paper cup from the cooler and opened his mouth to show that he had indeed swallowed his medication. This was sort of a leftover habit from his earlier days in the PDF when he was on far more medications. The Angels, like the proprietors of any treatment or therapy center, were concerned with the well-being of their patients, or lodgers, as was the preferred nomenclature.

When first called to Walnut Ridge, Leo was on a handful of medications for various problems, including, but not limited to, depression, anxiety, cholesterol management, heartburn, high blood pressure, and insomnia. Over the course of a few months, many adjustments were made, and eventually, Leo went from two paper cups full of colorful pills to his current regimen of three single pills. He had to admit that he felt better than he had before entering the facility.

Leo looked around the hall. "Is the, uh, new girl around?" The words sounded stupid and juvenile, and he immediately wished he had kept his mouth shut.

"She's meeting with Haniel at the moment. It's a big adjustment for her, and she's not ready to mix with you lot yet." She paused as though she had said something she shouldn't have. "Here's tonight's load. Enjoy, sweetheart." Doris slid a stack of paper across the counter to Leo. It was around thirty pages held together with a small binder clip. Since arriving, Leo had routinely been given at least ten pages of homework a night. Often, he received much more. Though some lodgers would occasionally get stacks as thick as Leo's, his were consistently hefty.

The purpose of the nightly assignments was thought to be that of a progress report—something the doctors, nurses, and Angels could use to assess and gauge a lodger's status. During his stay at the facility, Leo had poked numerous holes in this theory, plugged them with rational reasoning, ripped out the plugs, made new holes, and, eventually, stopped thinking about it altogether. People and aliens wanted him to answer questions and write out thoughts and feelings about things, so he decided he would do it without thinking too much. He didn't always finish the assignments, but he usually made an effort.

As Leo padded on socked feet back to his bedroom, George called out to him. "Hey, Leo!" Leo tried to get by with just a falsely enthusiastic wave to the man, but George beckoned him over.

"What's up, George?"

"I heard you saw the fresh meat. What do you think?" asked George. He had been talking with Rhonda, another of the remaining lodgers, and now it was a three-way conversation.

"About what?" asked Leo. "I only just saw her checking in."

"Does she seem nice?" asked Rhonda.

Leo remembered the unreadable, unbreakable stare. "I don't, I don't know. I just saw her for a second."

"I'm just glad that she's another one of us," George said, then paused, seemingly startled. "She is, you know," George said, lowering his voice, "one of us. Right?"

"One of...?" Leo thought for a second. "Oh right, yeah. She's a human. With a body, I mean. You knew that."

Rhonda's smile faltered. "I thought it might be sort of nice for Alphie to have someone like him—someone he could relate to." She was referring to the lodger named Alphonse, who was a human who had been decanted. This meant that he had his body, memory, and consciousness mysteriously dissolved and congealed into several ounces of sentient, viscous, blue fluid. The entirety of everything that had ever been Alphonse was now contained in a large glass beaker attached to a pocket dictionary-sized computer. The computer allowed him to communicate visually through text and images or a speaker and a voice synthesizer.

"You're just worried you won't be the prettiest girl on the wing anymore!" George said, chuckling.

"Shut up!" Rhonda said with a returning grin. She punched George lightly on the shoulder, then quickly re-crossed her arms and grasped her wrists. She did this out of habit to avoid being asked about the crisscrossing scars on her wrists and forearms. No one left at Walnut Ridge ever asked about them. "Don't you ever feel bad for him? We have each other, and the ghosts all share that same body, but Alphie is the only one who's been decanted. He's the only one who knows what that's like, and he can't talk about it with anyone."

"You're right," Leo said. "It would be nice for him to have someone else around like that." Leo thought about the prospect of another decanted human in their midst—or five more, or ten. In reality, it upset him. Every time he thought he had come to terms with the concept of decantation, he would see Alphonse in his jar. He would think about what life must be like in such a state.

Presumably, it was preferable or, at least, comparable to the life that humans had lived up to this point. Why else would so many be willing, excited even, to have the procedure? When he thought about it, Leo was reminded of French toast. In childhood, he had seen his friends eat it while he ate cold cereal. He had watched his father eat slice after slice—had smelled the pleasing aroma of the bread being cooked. But he refused to eat it. He had seen his mother making it, dipping old bread into a slop of milk and eggs and vanilla and spices. Wet bread. The way the mixture dribbled off the corners of each square of bread made his gorge rise, and he found himself never wanting to eat the stuff.

Leo loved syrup, butter, fruit, jam, cinnamon, sugar—all the things that went along with the dish. The scent of the brown, fried slices of toast made him salivate. He knew that it was moist and crispy and delicious. He knew he would love it. But he could not make himself eat it without thinking of the vile, messy way it was prepared. It was similar with decantation. He knew in his heart that it was better—that it was the means to a more pleasant, a more comfortable end. But he could not fully commit to it—could not clear the hurdle. It was his own failing, and seeing Alphonse brought that to the forefront of his mind.

"Yeah, I mean, I don't have any problem with the guy," said George. "He's nice enough, and yeah, it must be weird being the only one like..." he trailed off.

"Well, we probably won't even see much of the new girl," said Leo. "She'll most likely be in and out of here in a day or two." He turned to Rhonda. "And she'll be nice enough if she does stay around. Everyone is, after they've been here for a little while."

"Not me!" George bellowed, predictably.

"Shut up. You're a big teddy bear," Rhonda teased.

"Sweetheart, I could tell you some stories that would curl your toes and leave you speechless."

"I could do the same, big man. But stories are just stories. You aren't like that anymore. I know you aren't. *You* know you aren't."

George sighed, conceding, "You're right."

Walking back to his room, Leo thought about what Rhonda had said. Within a few days or weeks or months, no one who came to the facility was the same as they used to be. Not really. They all came to terms with the truth of themselves and moved past it. They didn't lose their individuality. It was more like they amended it. Leo wondered how different he was from when he first came to Walnut Ridge. He wondered how different he was at the basest, core level of his being.

As he pondered this, he entered his room and sat on his bed. He took a pencil from his nightstand and, without looking, answered the first question of his homework assignment. It was always the same question. "Between one and ten, one being severe sadness and ten being total elation, how happy are you today?" Leo's pencil moved almost without his guidance over the circle containing "5" and filled it.

3.

Frances sat in an office on the third floor of Walnut Ridge. A large desk made from particle board provided a comforting space between her and the thing sitting across from her. That thing was an Angel. Frances was only now getting a good look at her perceived captors. Up until this point, she had seen only glimpses of them. Since she'd been inside the facility, she had kept her head defiantly low. She was now beginning to accept her fate as a prisoner of this place—at least for the time being.

She tried not to look at the thing across from her. She didn't want to give it the satisfaction of her attention, but due to its size and the spectacle of its appearance, it was hard to look away. It was a big fucker, but she already knew that much from having tangled with its kind before being caught and from being led around this strange building with them. The figure across the desk, as well as the others she'd seen like it, were between six and eight feet tall.

The face that stared back at her now looked generally human, though somewhat unfinished. It seemed to be made up of several plates of a very thin material—some kind of metal or plastic, which gave it the look of a doll or, perhaps, a dummy. This allowed the face to effectively emote while retaining an unnerving, inhuman quality. Frances did not like it. At all.

From the top of the head sprouted flaxen hair which fell in soft curls to the robed shoulders of the being. Inexplicably suspended about eight inches above the hair was a golden ring—a halo. Frances looked between the head and halo for some kind of wire or brace—something that would explain how the seemingly solid object remained floating, but she could see nothing. Large, folded wings coated in white feathers sprouted from its back. Loosely hanging from the being's shoulders, which were also made from thin, Caucasian flesh-tinted plates, there were robes of white and burgundy. Its chest was upsettingly exposed.

It became clear to Frances that the... whatever it was sitting before her fancied itself an angel, an angel which appeared to have been created for an animatronic theme park ride that ran out of funding, but an angel, nonetheless. Frances looked over at the human woman standing to the side of the desk to gauge the barometer of her personal reality. It helped slightly.

The Angel opened its doll mouth, and speech emitted from a speaker within its throat. "I am called Haniel. We sincerely hope that you are well and comfortable. We wish to welcome you to Walnut Ridge Pre-Decantation Facility."

Frances was taken aback by the way the creature before her had spoken. It had seemed synthetic before, but now, there was no doubt in her mind. "Why does your voice sound like it's coming through a rotary phone inside of a garbage can?" she asked.

"We utilized the technology we thought would be adequate for our mission. We had not anticipated the technological advances that would occur on this planet." The Angel was unfazed by what Frances had hoped would seem like an insult.

"Could you explain a little about what is going on? I know some of your friends tried to before, but I really wasn't listening. Who are you? What's with the whole angel... thing? Where am I, and why?" Frances raised her arm, bandaged from the ordeal leading to her capture, to casually run her hand through her hair, having forgotten that she had told the intake nurse to shave it off. It was a funny feeling. Her head felt bumpy and scratchy.

"My comrades and I are on a mission. Eons ago, our race, in an effort to expand our colonies, set out in search of inhabitable bodies. During this search, we discovered a doorway, a sort of gate that led to a space existing between dimensions. It is not strictly a physical space as you know it. It is a paradise there—a peaceful utopia of eternal bliss. The vast majority of what has ever existed and will ever exist in our realms, yours and mine, exists there. It is timeless, and residents can choose to experience any of it for any duration at any moment.

"We have traversed the galaxy, searching out lifeforms, races, civilizations that are compatible with this existence and ferrying them to this paradise. Several hundreds of your years ago, my race discovered Earth. We were delighted to find that your human consciousness—your very souls were of the kind most receptive to this heavenly existence—this *Caldo*."

"Caldo?" asked Frances.

"Caldo." The Angel, Haniel, despite his somewhat primitive features, gave a look of sheepishness so contrived it made Frances roll her eyes. "It is of a language spoken mostly in the area of your planet called Italia—Italy," he corrected himself. "In English, it means 'warm.' This is the feeling which most closely approximates the sensation of being in the paradise I have described to you."

"So, basically," started Frances, "you go around space, kidnapping aliens and forcing them to go to this wonderful place they've never seen? Is that about right?"

"We would never force any sentient being to do anything against their will."

"That's a funny kind of thing to say after you guys just finished chasing me through the woods for hours. Did you just think I wanted some exercise? How do people normally react when they're accosted by giant... whatever-the-fuck you're supposed to be? I thought you were some kind of mutant bear or something. But bears, in my experience, don't tend to wear tacky robes."

"I apologize for the distress we caused you. The size and appearance of our Terran vessels are results of a miscalculation on our part. During our scouting mission, those we judged to be the most advanced members of your civilization, men and women living in Rome, France, Germany, and Spain, seemed to be moving toward a greater commitment to the Christian movement. We based our appearance on what we assumed would instill the greatest sense of trust in humans at the time." The massive, white-feathered wings coming from his back extended and covered three walls of the office. "We hypothesized that by this time, humans would be of a fairly central mindset on Christianity, allowing you to accept angels into your lives."

Frances fought against the awe she felt at seeing the large wingspan of the counterfeit angel before her. She did this with profanity. It worked well for her. "Well, you fucked up there, honey." She felt more centered. "Most of the people I know don't even own a bible anymore. And my school didn't even offer classes in Italian."

"Had our scouts waited another one hundred years, perhaps we would have been able to better forecast the trajectory of your cultural and physical evolution. However, we lacked patience in our desire to offer Caldo to your people." Haniel's wings were now retracting.

"As I've mentioned, we designed our physical bodies based on our studies. Utilizing our calculations and research on other races similar to Homo sapiens, we were certain that the average human being would, by today, stand at an average of eight feet in height. We had hoped to appear non-threatening in our short stature."

Something about this idiotic gaffe softened Frances's heart, but only momentarily. "It didn't feel particularly 'non-threatening' to have you giant freaks chasing me for all that time," she said.

"That," Haniel said, bowing his head, "is an unfortunate reality of our mission. You seemed confused and disoriented. In that case, it is our duty to help a being, a person, get to a safe place where they can receive the help they need."

"So, that's where we are now? This is the safe place?" She gestured with her hands. "This old folks' home?"

"This is one of many safe havens we have established on this planet. You are safer here than you would be anywhere else. You also reap the benefit of learning the state of affairs—the reality of your existence. You can now be given all the information you require to make the choice that all sentient souls on Earth have made or will soon make."

Frances looked to the human, who still stood obediently near the desk. It was Miranda, the head psych-tech on the floor. She nodded at Frances reassuringly. "If it's okay with you, Mr. Angel-man," said Frances, "I think that's about all I can take for one day."

"Certainly," replied Haniel. "We would not like to overwhelm you too much. My sincerest apologies for what you have been through today. Miranda, would you show our guest to her room?"

4.

Miranda led Frances to her bedroom. It was unoccupied and at the opposite end of the hall from where the other lodgers were staying. Rhonda and Lois shared a bedroom, so Frances would have no roommate. It had been a long time since Miranda felt uneasy about a new lodger. Her conditioning before and since entering employment with the Angels had made her very accepting of people and their unpredictability. Frances put her on edge, though.

While the two walked to room 411, where Frances would be staying, Miranda attempted to make small talk. "You can have your clothing back after we've had it laundered. One of the Angels here, Sariel, enjoys sewing. He would be happy to fix some of the tears you got in your skirt." This seemed almost immediately like a stupid thing to say. Miranda flushed.

"That's fine. I don't want them. I'm good with scrubs." Frances spoke absently. She played with the bandages stuck to her arms and shoulders. There were more on her legs. She had needed only a dozen stitches in total, which was not a lot considering she'd gotten herself tangled in a barbed wire fence while trying to evade the Angels. The tetanus shot was the worst part.

Miranda entered room 411 and turned around. "Here we are. You don't have a roommate yet. I hope you don't mind. You can pick whichever bed you prefer."

"This one looks good," Frances said, sitting on the nearest mattress.

"There are towels and washcloths in the bathroom, extra shirts and pants in the dresser over there. You'll hear chimes and announcements for meals, medications, and group meetings. I'm not certain if they'll have you starting group tomorrow or the next day."

"Sounds pretty simple," said Frances, looking around the small, sparse room. She felt slightly agitated since leaving the office. She was also surprised at herself that she hadn't given the stupid robotic alien-thing a harder time. She had told herself that when she met the people who chased her down and brought her to this place against her will, she would rip them all new assholes. The feeling had abated while talking to the Angel, but it was now returning.

"I hate to bother you more. I'm sure you want to rest," said Miranda. "Would you mind if I just asked you a few questions for our records?" She felt genuinely guilty about not being able to leave this poor girl to her solitude.

"Shoot. I've got nothing planned," Frances said, lying on the mattress, testing its firmness. Its comfort level fell somewhere between that of a bag of sawdust and a pile of wire coat hangers. She noticed the shiny black panel mounted to the ceiling above the bed. *Mirrors on the ceiling*, she thought to herself, *kinky*.

"We'd just like to know a little more about you, is all. We can stop whenever you like," said Miranda. "Your full name, age, and address to start."

"Frances Grace Brown. I'm thirty-three. My address is pretty much just where the Angels found me. I've been living off the grid for about two years, I guess. Oh, and for the record, I prefer Frankie. I never liked Frances."

"Oh, of course," Miranda brightened. This seemed like a step in the right direction. "So, you've been out there for two years? Were you, well... aware of any of what's been going on in the past eighteen months or so?"

"Aliens? Giant robot-angels? Mystical paradise? No. I'm afraid not. Grady told me that when shit went down, just go to one of the hiding spots and lay low. No phones, no TV, no internet. Wait for personal contact. I've just been in the shelter reading comics."

"Grady? Is he a friend of yours?"

"I don't know. I guess. I met him, like, ten years ago, and he introduced me to all this conspiracy stuff. I used to live with him in his shelter when he told me the government was going to start taking the guns away. That didn't happen, and I didn't like being stuck underground as a combination housekeeper slash fuck-toy, so I bolted. We would kind of get together every few years after that." Frankie stopped, surprised to hear herself sharing this, surprised to be speaking to someone after so long. "I guess that's pretty dumb."

Miranda wanted to comfort her but felt it would be more prudent to continue the questions. "Ah, so, this last time you were living alone?"

"Yeah. Like I said, Grady and I were on-again, off-again. We were on-again about two years ago. He was into all that tinfoil-hat, alien shit," Frances paused, "which I guess doesn't seem as weird now. Anyway, he was always going on about all the terrible shit that the government or the extraterrestrials were going to do. The drugs didn't help. He was into some pretty bad stuff at the end. When the meteor came down that day, Grady was... he was in a really bad way. He started screaming a bunch of shit I couldn't understand, then he... shot himself."

"I'm so sorry," Miranda's reply was automatic and sounded heartless to her own ears. She perked up, thinking of something. "Oh, but if he's dead, it will make him much easier to find!"

Frankie glared so intensely that Miranda could almost feel two laser beams boring through her skull. "Yeah," Frankie spat, "I guess corpses are pretty easy to track down. They don't tend to move around that much. Not a lot of Uber drivers willing to cart dead bodies around, you know?"

Miranda put her palm to her forehead. "Oh my God! I'm so sorry. I forgot. You don't know everything that's been going on. I'm such a moron." She took a moment to compose herself. "The Angels, they aren't just taking living human beings to Caldo. When they came, they had the technology to communicate with the souls of those who had died on this planet. They bridged the chasm between the living and the dead. I'm so sorry. You didn't know."

"What?" asked Frankie. It was a reasonable question.

"Ghosts—the souls of the dead, the Angels have a way that allows them to be found, isolated, and given a voice. The Angels don't want to leave any souls behind. They never do. The ships that the Angels will use to take us away, the Arks, they contain a sort of soul storage unit. We call it the Ether-base. For a while, some ghosts were given physical bodies, robotic ones, so the living could come to terms with the reality of the situation. We currently have three ghosts on this wing."

"So, you can talk to dead people now?" asked Frankie.

"Yes. Those who we have lost are no longer gone from us forever. Although,"—Miranda paused—"the effect of crossing over into the next plane has altered them slightly. To be honest, they're all sort of bland and cagey. I shouldn't say that. What I'm getting at, though, is that you can reconnect with Grady if you want or need to. The Angels sometimes arrange meetings between lodgers and ghosts as part of the pre-decantation process."

"Well, fuck," said Frankie. "I don't really want to talk to that asshole." She crossed her arms and closed her eyes where she lay. "You had some more questions?"

"Yes," Miranda said. "You mentioned a meteor just before."

"We were out, Grady and me. He was trying to show me how to set up snares to catch small game, and I was trying to ignore him. It was the middle of the day. This... thing, it looked maybe the size of a basketball, fell out of the sky. It snapped a bunch of branches on its way down. Made a hell of a lot of noise. It slammed into the dirt, and before I knew what was happening, Grady was shouting a bunch of gibberish about how it was some radiological attack and we were all fucked. Then he pulled out his pistol and... blew his brains out."

Miranda made a note of the meteor. "I'll speak to the Angels about that," she said. "Perhaps it was a meteor or a piece of debris from the impending arrival. The timeline would match. There was a lot of debris falling through the atmosphere two to three years ago."

Frankie seemed almost to have not registered what Miranda said. "After he, you know, I just kind of freaked out and ran back to the shelter. I stayed down there for a few days. Then I came back up to," she stopped momentarily.

"We don't have to continue."

"To bury Grady's body. Something had already gotten to him. A bear or maybe a bunch of smaller animals, but I had to do it. I couldn't leave him out there. I had to laugh, though, thinking about some bear munching on him and then it having a massive freak-out from all the junk Grady was on. Some bear sitting in his cave, rocking back and forth, listening to Pink Floyd, and counting his toes." She laughed harshly. Miranda tried not to react.

"I picked up the chunks of the meteor, too. It had cracked apart, I guess. I buried them with him. I thought he might want it that way—to be buried with some kind of proof for his paranoia. Or not. I don't really know what he would have wanted. Maybe I'll get a chance to ask him soon. Or maybe I'll just tell him to go and choke on his own ghost-cock.

"Anyway, I stayed down in the shelter for a while after that, just eating soup. Somehow, Grady got his hands on a pallet of Campbell's Chunky soup. A fucking *pallet!* When I came back out again to check—when I had just decided that it was all bullshit and I was being paranoid and crazy, that's when I saw that the sky was purple." She looked directly into Miranda's eyes. "The sky is purple."

Miranda couldn't tell if it was a statement or a question. "Yes. The Angels, they used a gaseous vapor when they first arrived to keep humanity calm—to keep themselves from being attacked. It gave the sky a lavender hue. It was thought only to be temporary, but it seems to be rather long-term. I more or less like it now. It's a nice color."

"It is a nice color," replied Frankie. There were tears welling in her frustrated eyes. "I fucking hate it."

5.

Somewhere, millions of miles above the now purple sky, floated a satellite. The satellite was a transportation gate set up by an alien race of sentient rectangles who had been tracking the Angels for an excruciatingly long time. The satellite also received data from a biological transmitter it had launched to Earth, and it sent that data to the alien race that had built it. That biological transmitter had implanted itself into Frances Grace Brown nearly two years ago.

Messages and information were being sent to the race of sentient rectangles, who called themselves Strappons. The similarity in pronunciation to a human word in the English language, indicating an apparatus for use in sexual intercourse, was purely coincidental. The humor of the coincidence would have been lost on the aliens. Sexual intercourse was so foreign a concept to them that it was not even worth trying to understand.

Now, the data transmitted to the Strappons was both miraculous and difficult to bear. It told them that they had, at long last, located the race they were hunting down. They had located the ambassadors who offered Caldo. However, it also told them that time was terribly short before those ambassadors, guised as angels on Earth, would fly off into the cosmos again. The Strappons had no way of tracking them back to Caldo or whatever planet they would be visiting next. It was all they could do to set up autonomous observation satellites and shoot beacons onto planets that may one day be visited.

If the Strappons wanted to meet up with the angelic ambassadors, they would have to do so while the ambassadors were visiting this "Earth" planet. And if the information they were receiving was correct, they had far less time than they had hoped. The intention of the satellite beacon was to stake out a potentially visited planet long before the ambassadors ever showed up. Their beacon had incidentally arrived on Earth just in time, but the creature to which the beacon had attached itself had gone into hiding. This made it impossible for the creature carrying the beacon to observe and interpret information to be sent back to the satellite transmitter. The information being gathered now stated that the Angels were on the planet and were very close to leaving again.

Many, many Earth-years ago, the Angels visited the planet Strappon with the intent of taking all its residents to their paradise. They did not look like or call themselves Angels at that time. They had manufactured tangible vessels that would elicit more trust from the Strappons. The Angels appeared to them as triangles of roughly the same surface area as a Strappon rectangle.

They conveyed the news that the Strappons would be granted access to Caldo, though, in the language of the Strappons, the paradise, of course, had a different name. For the Strappons, the Triangles referred to the promised utopia as "Octacontaheptagon." This meant a two-dimensional shape with eighty-seven sides. The rectangles thought of it as one of the most pleasing shapes there could be. The Strappons rejoiced in their good fortune and held a massive celebration.

During the course of this planet-wide celebration, which took place before any conditioning or traveling preparations were made, one of the leaders of the Strappon rectangles asked one of the leaders of the visiting Triangles to join it in a round of a game that was popular on the planet. The game involved arranging random two-dimensional shapes together in such a way that there would be the least amount of empty space between them. It was, incidentally, called "Handjobb." After much prodding, the Triangle acquiesced, and the game began. To the surprise of all the rectangles, the Triangle was exceptional at this game.

Round after round, the Triangle would arrange its shapes so closely together that there would be virtually no empty space. The Triangle won a few rounds of Handjobb and asked to take its leave. The rectangle leader would not have this. It wished to continue playing until it could beat the Triangle and redeem itself. It made many excuses for itself—said it had not played in a long time or that its senses were dulled by the intoxicating *hendecagons* it had imbibed.

The rectangle grew increasingly frustrated, and the Triangle repeatedly tried to cease the game.

More and more Strappons were brought in to try to beat the Triangle. Champions of worldwide Handjobb leagues were summoned to face the extraplanetary visitor, and each one was bested. Again, the Triangle did its best to remove itself from the situation and was not allowed.

Eventually, the Triangle intentionally lost a game, stating that it had finally been bested. It was clear to all the rectangles watching that the game had been thrown on purpose. This infuriated them more than losing fairly. In their ire and jealousy, the Strappons told the Triangles that their race had no desire to accept a paradise given by such arrogant and selfish beings. They chased the Triangles away, sometimes using force and violence. And just like that, the Strappons lost their paradise.

Some time later, after the Triangles were gone, tempers cooled. The sense that the rectangles had shown their pride and defended the sanctity of their race began to give way to the sinking feeling that they may have made a mistake. They had been given access to something very few beings had heard of, and even fewer had been offered. They threw all this away in the name of ego. They would likely never be able to receive the paradise they had denied.

Perhaps, some of the rectangles thought, if they could find the Triangles, track them down, and explain their mistakes, they would get another chance to go to Octacontaheptagon. Unfortunately, they had no leads on where the Triangles had gone, but prior to the Handjobb incident, they were made aware of a few other planets on the shortlist to be offered paradise. One of the Triangle ambassadors had confided the names and general locations of other planets where the Triangles would be traveling after they finished with the Strappons.

The best scientists, astronomers, and physicists among the sentient rectangles began plotting ways to find the Triangles again. They sent tracking beacons and research satellites out into space to discover how far and in which directions these unknown worlds were. Their chances of finding any of the planets disclosed by the Triangles with the information they had were so low as to be nearly nonexistent. They did, however, eventually find the Solar System and its planet called Earth. This discovery had taken such a long time that the Strappons had no way of knowing whether the Triangles had already been there or not. There was life on the planet, but they could not be certain it had not come to be after the Triangles had already been there.

Their beacon shot a transmitter at the planet and immediately started sending information. Somehow, though, the data had gone from indicating no presence of the Triangles for almost two Earth years to indicating that the Triangles, in another physical form, were there and could be leaving again at any moment. Time was short if the Strappons were going to catch the aliens they had shunned so long ago. They were scrambling to ready their ships for travel between the portal they had built just outside their own planet's atmosphere and their satellite gate in Earth's system. The plan was to load as many members of their race onto a transport ship as possible and meet up with the Triangles. They meant to regain access to Octacontaheptagon either by begging and pleading and apologizing or, if necessary, by force.

There was no time to send a scout ship to assess the situation on Earth. The data from their beacons and transmitters could be sent instantly across space. Their ships could not. It would take time for their transports to travel between the gates of their intergalactic portal. The Strappons were racing now at breakneck speed. Or rather, they would be if they had necks.

6.

Night had fallen on Walnut Ridge, and Leo Salmon lay on his rubberized mattress staring up at the large, flat panel mounted above his bed. Similar ones were mounted over all the beds in the facility. They were not lights. Each one was a sort of sensor used to take readings on the brains and bodies of the lodgers sleeping beneath them. Perhaps they even took readings on the souls trapped within those bodies. Only the Angels knew for sure. They were called Rhythmic Feedback Analyzers, or RFAs. They emitted a low hum to help lull lodgers to sleep at night.

Leo looked at his reflection in the glossy finish of the RFA. He looked ghostly in the green glow cast by the nightlights sticking out of the electrical sockets. He saw, lying on top of the sheets, the body that was to be liquified and put into a jar to travel to an unknown paradise. The body was thin and weak. He had never felt much adoration for it, but it was his, and he had had some fun with it throughout his life.

A thought crept into Leo's mind. It was a thought that visited occasionally. The thought was that he would never be decanted. That he would remain the sole human on the planet as the Angels' ships flew off to everlasting bliss. He supposed the thought ought to bother him intensely. It did from time to time, but not often. Part of him wanted so much to give the right answers on his homework—to share frankly and completely in group meetings—to be offered and to accept the Angel's Promise like billions of others. Another part of him was tired and scared and longed for the return of a blue sky.

Unable to sleep, he rose and walked into the hallway. Typically, being out of bed after lights-out was frowned upon, like in any kind of hospital or treatment facility, but now that there were so few lodgers remaining, the rules had relaxed. Leo slid his socked feet across the linoleum tiles, doing a sort of slow cross-country skiing down the corridor. He passed bedrooms, some occupied, most empty, all with their lights out.

On the wall near the intersection leading to the right, where the nurses' station was, hung a painting of a woman with curly gray hair. Prints of the same painting hung on every floor and in many offices around Walnut Ridge. The woman in the painting was Denise Elkins. She founded Walnut Ridge as a drug and alcohol treatment center in the 1970s. Back then, it had been called the Denise Elkins Addiction Treatment Home. This name was used for about three months before one of the first patients to be admitted to the facility noted that all the stationery in her room had the word DEATH ornately printed in the corner. Somehow, none of the smart and empathetic people who founded the treatment center had noticed this or thought it was worth mentioning. Shortly after this, the name was changed to Walnut Ridge, but the story had gotten out, and jokes were already being made.

Colloquially, persons mandated to attend the treatment facility were said to be "sentenced to DEATH." Leaving Walnut Ridge early or getting kicked out for bad behavior was said to be "a fate worse than DEATH." After being converted to a pre-decantation facility, most of the jokes ended. They didn't make much sense to people who came from far away or didn't know any of the history of the place.

A few feet down from the painting of Denise Elkins, who had died and was now a ghost loaded into the Ether-Base on one of the Angels' cross-shaped space vessels, was a poster. It had been hung a month or two after Walnut Ridge was converted from a treatment center to a PDF. It showed an image of an angel, not the animatronic, uncanny-looking kind, but a real angel reaching its hand out toward whomever may be viewing the poster. Along the left, right, and top borders of the poster were printed words like "tolerance" and "patience" and "joy" and "freedom." Along the bottom border, in larger print, it read, "PROMISE."

The Promise was the means by which a human or ghost would fully accept the nature of reality and be deemed ready for decantation. For the first few months after the Angels had arrived, Promises were being made by the millions. Most people had never even needed to stay overnight in a pre-decantation facility. For many, the process took no longer than a dentist appointment. People were generally enthusiastic about getting off the planet. Boredom had been hewn into their genes. They wanted something fresh and new, and they felt that they had earned an eternity in paradise.

Leo had heard about the Promises made to others. For a while, there were stories attributed to decanted humans on television describing the wonderful process. For some, it was very stoic and businesslike. A person would meet with one or more Angels and have a brief talk. They would shake hands, and the deed would be done. Both parties would be fully synced in spiritual terms. Some Promises involved the use of music or movies or meditation or strenuous physical activity or sex or artwork or sleeping or crying or yoga or driving or any other personal concept that could connect a human soul to the collective consciousness of the Angels and all the beings in Caldo.

Stories were told of Promises being made after eating a delicious meal in an expensive restaurant. A surprising number of people were said to have made Promises following a strenuous two-week stint working on a peanut farm. One story involved a person accepting the Promise and coming to terms with everything about herself and what could possibly be after she spent thirty minutes in an inflatable bounce house in the company of baby goats. It took whatever it took, and eventually, everyone, even the most hardcore skeptics, came around to the ultimate truth. *Almost* everyone.

Leo had wondered how his Promise would look. He figured it would be something stupid and boring. He often imagined himself looking at some beautiful painting while listening to Pachelbel's "Canon," breaking down in tears and finally understanding everything in his life that had confounded him. No matter how silly or cliché his Promise would be, he desperately yearned for it to happen while, at the same time, dreading its implications and simplicity. In his time at the facility, he had spoken to scores of people who seemingly shared many of the exact same thoughts he had. They had all come around eventually. One way or another.

Staring at the poster made Leo tired. He felt that if he could walk back to his bed while maintaining this level of grogginess, he might even get some sleep, but he worried that moving an inch in any direction would perk him up. He couldn't sleep standing up in the hall, though. He turned around and began to head back to the room he shared with Brock. Turning, he noted that a door at the end of the corridor was cracked open. It was the door to room 411. Usually, room doors were required to be kept entirely open. The exception was during individual therapy or meetings when they were entirely shut. Leo figured it meant the new lodger, who didn't know the old rules, must be in there.

Despite his better judgment, Leo resumed his sock-skiing toward the door to 411. It was stupid. Why did he need to look in there? Was he going to just stare at a sleeping woman? That was really weird. He continued down the hall.

When he got to the doorway, he craned his head around the wood slab to peer into the dark room. He saw that someone was in the bed nearest to the door. He gazed up through the eerie, mint-green night-light aura and saw the woman from earlier, Frances, lying in bed. Her head was shaved. She faced the doorway—her eyes wide open. Leo was paralyzed again. His heart hammered in his ribcage. He had been caught. For five agonizing seconds that felt like an eternity, he stood, locked in the gaze of those glossy, goggling eyes. He wrenched his neck back around the door and jogged down the corridor to his room.

Leo crawled into his bed. He pretended to be asleep, certain that either the girl or some tech was going to come into his room and scold him. If it was the girl, Leo hoped if he acted groggy enough, she'd believe he'd been asleep. Maybe she would think she'd dreamt it or that her eyes had tricked her. He lay awake for a long time, periodically opening his eyes to see if anyone had come to reprimand or check on him. No one did. Sometime during the course of the night, despite his anxiety, he fell asleep.

7.

The seven-a.m. chime sounded for morning medication call and check-in. Every morning, the five human lodgers reported to the nurse's station to check in, have their pulse and blood pressure taken, and receive morning medication. Ghosts did not need to have their blood pressure checked, nor did Alphonse. There was a sixth human this morning. Leo had hoped against hope that she would not be there, but she was. Frances was introducing herself to the other lodgers when Leo made the trek to the nurse's station—his late night had made it hard for him to rise at the first chime. Brock had needed to go and shake him awake. "Grundy," he said. "You gonna be late. You sick? Don't give me nothing. I ain't been sick in years."

Eventually, Leo rose and attended the morning ritual. He was the last to have his blood pressure taken. For the first time in months, his reading was abnormal. His pressure was slightly high, and his heart rate was well over one hundred beats per minute. He sat for a moment, tried to calm himself, and then had the tech read it again. He was able to ease his panic enough to get his vitals to more acceptable levels on the second reading.

As much as he wanted to go back to his room, skip breakfast and socializing, and show up at a later group meeting, Leo knew that would only prolong his discomfort. He went to the counter to receive his morning meds, then joined the rest of the human lodgers near the water cooler. They were all making small talk when Leo got to them. He tried to avert his eyes from the new arrival. She was talking to Brock, who turned when he saw Leo.

"This is Grundy," Brock said to Frances, indicating Leo. "He's been here longer than anyone else, 'cept Lois. You feeling better?"

"Yeah," Leo said, looking at his hands. "I'm not sick. I just didn't get much sleep last night." His regret at saying this last part was immediate and severe.

"Me neither," chimed in the new lodger.

Leo's eyes snapped to her. She was looking directly at him. *She knew*. He was sure she knew he had crept to her room in the night and ogled her while she slept.

"I mean, I feel like I slept, but I don't feel rested at all. My name is Frankie." She extended her hand.

"Frankie?" asked Leo, tentatively taking her hand in his, hoping his palm wasn't terribly sweaty. He should have wiped it off, but she would have seen that and then known for certain that he had sweaty palms. It was better to take the chance that maybe she wouldn't notice if his palms were sweaty.

"Yeah," she said.

The handshake broke off. She did not wipe her own hand. Either Leo's palms were not too sweaty, or she was very polite.

"I hate 'Frances.' Your name is Grundy?"

From across the small circle of humans, George laughed.

"No, it's Leo," said Leo.

"It's Grundy where I come from," interjected Brock.

"It's nice to meet you, Leo," Frankie said. "I think I saw you yesterday."

Leo's guts froze. She was calling him out on his night creeping.

"When I was checking in, you were in that room down the hall."

Leo's innards thawed a little. In his horror, he had almost forgotten about seeing her yesterday afternoon.

"Oh yeah. You had hair then," Leo said.

"Oh my God! I love her hair," said Rhonda, turning to Frankie. "I love your hair! I would never have the nerve to cut mine so short."

"Thanks," Frankie said, running her hand over the fuzz on top of her scalp. "It's not a big deal. It's just hair. I cut it off sometimes. It was all tangled and full of twigs and shit when I came in. This was just easier."

Miranda called everyone to line up to go to the cafeteria for breakfast. The cafeteria was only open three days a week anymore.

The rest of the time, food was prepared and brought to the fourth floor to be eaten in the group meeting room. There were no longer enough non-decanted human employees to run the facility on much more than a skeleton crew. The six human lodgers followed Miranda, who was carrying the jar of ooze named Alphonse, and a few techs down two flights of stairs to the dining hall on the second floor. Before taking a seat at the employee's table, Miranda set Alphonse on the table where the lodgers ate. He no longer needed food as sustenance, but he enjoyed being in the company of the others.

Frankie was, of course, the big topic of discussion. Everyone was asking her about herself and how it was that she had not been called to a PDF yet. She explained about going into an underground shelter and not even knowing what was happening until the Angels captured her. Rhonda was especially interested in the chase part of the story.

"That sounds terrible!" Rhonda said while grinning from ear to ear. "They really chased you down and wrangled you into a van?"

"Well," said Frankie, "the wrangling part was pretty easy for them after I got tangled in the barbed-wire fence." She looked down at her arms and hands, which were covered in cuts and scrapes and bandages,

"You're like a superhero," said Rhonda, her eyes wild.

"Sure," said Frankie flatly. "Laceration-Girl."

Brock's head perked at this. "Oh, shit," he said. "Freaky."

"Settle down, Broccoli," said George. "She said *laceration.*"

The comment got a laugh from everyone except Brock, who didn't seem to have picked up on the wordplay. He frowned.

"I told you, man, don't call me that," said Brock, whose last name was Leigh.

"I still have a lot of questions," started Frankie. "You guys know pretty much my whole story. What's the deal with this place? Those giant freaks tried to get me up to speed, but it's a lot to take in."

"Leo's the guy to ask," said George. "He's been here forever."

"They'll probably show you a few videos to clear things up." Still afraid to engage this woman in one-on-one conversation, Leo avoided eye contact as he spoke. He elected, instead, to look at an imaginary point somewhere between her chin and left shoulder. "What is it you want to know? I don't really know much more than anyone else. There's Miranda..." he nervously trailed off.

"I'm not sure I trust her very much. She's tight with the Angels, and, well..." Frankie presented the cuts and bandages on her skin. "I'd rather hear from you guys." She sipped from a foam cup of coffee and looked down the table at Lois, who was drawing shapes with her finger in spilled salt. "I guess I'm mostly wondering why everyone is just so, I don't know, okay with what's going on."

"It was all kind of strange how it happened," Leo said. "One afternoon, the sky turned purple, and it seemed like everyone around got sort of mellow feeling. Like, we knew it was weird, but we didn't care all that much. I don't remember anyone really freaking out where I was. There were some news reports about instances of panic, but not nearly as many as you would expect. Then the ships started showing up all over the planet." He quickly added, "I'm not, like, an expert or anything. Sorry."

"It's okay," said Frankie, giving Leo a quizzical glare that almost made him issue another unnecessary apology.

"I wasn't gonna panic for nothing," said Brock, lightening up. "I was hella' baked, and that purple sky was real nice looking."

"So, everyone just, like, accepted that aliens were invading?" asked Frankie. "There weren't any planes trying to shoot them down or anything? Did, I don't know, the president make an announcement or, or a speech or anything?"

"No planes, no tanks, no S.W.A.T. teams," said Leo. "Nothing. You met with one of them, right?"

"Yeah, after they brought me here, I sat in an office with someone"—she stopped, then corrected herself—"*something* named Haniel."

"Did you notice feeling kind of peaceful?"

Frankie thought back to the meeting and the ride in the van with the Angels. Something made her lose the will to fight, which was very unlike her. Before she went into the office with Haniel, she wanted to find out who was responsible for the confusion and agony she felt and pound the crap out of them. Belligerence was in her nature. She got a rush from combat—from beating her fists against flesh. The sight of blood electrified her. Whether it was hers or her opponent's mattered little. In her thirty-three years of life, she had suffered dozens of injuries from fighting. She broke her nose two times that she knew of, lost three teeth, fractured her orbital bone, broke her left clavicle twice, had at least six concussions, and broke fingers and toes on numerous occasions. Yet, when she entered the small room with her tormentor, she lost the drive to launch herself over the desk and smash the thing's head into pulp. She didn't try to escape the van when they transported her to Walnut Ridge. Why not? She had rolled from moving vehicles before. It was not fear that kept her from attempting to get away. She simply hadn't felt her typical need to get away—to control and punish those who had or would wrong her.

Eventually, she spoke. "I did."

"I wanted to beat the shit out of those assholes," said George. "Or, at least, I thought I did. Any time I got the chance to, any time I really thought about going and trying to fight back, I just felt like it was a better idea to calm down."

Alphonse, who rarely spoke, piped up at this point. The voice synthesizer hooked to the jar in which he now resided sounded robotic, like something manufactured in the late 1980s. "Initially, I tried to fake them all out," he said. "I'd hoped I could act like I was going along with them while still remaining autonomous, but after a while, I—"

"What the fuck was that!" shouted Frankie. The techs and nurses at the employee's table looked over.

"That was just Alphonse," said Leo. "Shit. Did anyone introduce you to him yet? I'm sorry, I should have said something."

"Him?" asked Frankie, identifying the source of the earlier sound as the glass, goo-filled container. "That's a 'him?'"

"Don't make fun of your cousin," said Lois. "He's young. He'll get better at baseball if you teach him." Everyone ignored this.

"Alphie's cool as hell," said Brock. "We were talkin' when he first showed up. Turns out, we were at the same Prince show at the Garden in eighty-eight." He grinned. "Had a shitty seat, but I sweet-talked the cutie at the gate to let me down to the floor. My man was up in the nosebleeds. What are the odds we both end up here?"

"I'm, I just," Frankie stammered, "I'm sorry. They told me a little about decanting, and they told me someone here was decanted, but I just, I was caught off guard. I didn't know it talked."

"You get used to it," said Rhonda. She giggled inexplicably. "He's a really nice guy too. Quiet most of the time, but really friendly."

"Sorry, Alphie," said Leo. He felt sweat breaking in his armpits. "She didn't mean anything by it. Go on."

After a pause, the synthesized voice continued. "I apologize for freaking you out. I was just saying that I wanted to try to trick the Angels into thinking I was going along with them, then find a way out at the last minute. But when the last minute came, I found that I actually wanted what they had to offer. I had wanted it for some time. I came around to what made the most sense."

"That's pretty much what you hear from people," Leo said to Frankie. "It isn't like being mind-controlled or made to do or feel anything. It's sort of, like, a nice, peaceful consent that happens. I think that's why there wasn't any real resistance when they showed up. Whatever they give off, whatever they pumped into the atmosphere, makes you feel like you should just do what's good for you."

"That's fucked up," Frankie said.

Leo shrugged. "Yeah, it pretty much is."

"I don't like it," she responded. But despite herself, she kind of did.

8.

In an electronic cabinet on the fifth floor of Walnut Ridge resided the soul of Meng Ji. She had lived about nine thousand years ago in the eastern portion of what is now The People's Republic of China. Due to her exemplary intelligence and accomplishments while living, the Angels had singled her out among the souls of every human who had ever died on Earth.

She had done a great deal with her time on the planet. She developed no less than six written interpretations of her people's language. She correctly and independently inferred the nature of the Solar System, which led to a thought process that resulted in a quantified concept of time and a modified lunar calendar. She devised her own means of measurement, which she used to invent mathematical formulae. Her systems allowed her to quickly and correctly measure the heights of the trees and mountains near her home. She used her written languages to document her findings, though they would be indecipherable to most. Her intellect extended beyond math and science. She also wrote poetry and used pigments from plants, fruits, clay, and organic matter from insects and animals to create hyperrealist finger paintings.

Her life was short and humble despite her accomplishments, none of which were ever discovered or acknowledged. She died at age thirteen, having been beaten to death by a twenty-year-old male cousin who also amounted to a husband. He was angry that she did not have a meal ready for him after he returned from an unsuccessful gathering trek into the nearby mountains. She had been measuring shadows in an attempt to figure the circumference of the planet, which she knew was round. The task had enraptured her, and she had forgotten to fetch any water or cook any rice. After the murder, her body was thrown unceremoniously into a cave.

She spent her time in what the living call *the afterlife*, thinking. That was what most souls without a vessel did. In the millennia since her death, with access to knowledge she could not have hoped to attain in life, her philosophizing and theorizing were unbound. Other souls would sometimes seek her out for in-depth conversation in the ether. They all left confused or unsettled. Those who were famous while alive for their great minds were often skeptical when they first learned of the spirit of Meng Ji. She truly did not care.

The Angels chose her ghost to aid them in their task on Earth. She accepted their offer to cross the plane between life and death again. She had requested no mobile body like those given to many ghosts—a simple cabinet with a screen and speaker was sufficient. The Angels now conferred with her in their language, which she had picked up almost instantly. She was speaking with Haniel, who ran Walnut Ridge, and Raphael, who had chased Frances so fervently that she tangled herself in a barbed-wire fence.

"On this world," Haniel said in his native tongue, "we have, at this time, over thirty thousand remaining un-decanted. Our projections led us to believe that we would have been able to convert *all* humans here within four hundred revolutions. Unfortunately, our rate of success is far slower than we hoped."

From her tinny speaker, Meng Ji spoke. "When you first told me your goals, I was honestly unsure they were possible. I voiced these concerns to you. I am surprised that you have made the progress you have thus far."

"We have not had this level of difficulty on prior planets," said Raphael. "Well, aside from one complication a long time ago."

"This is not like that," replied Haniel. "There are simply qualities in humans that we had not looked at closely enough. And still, the bulk of the species has responded beautifully to our methods. They are eager and able to be decanted and enlightened."

"That is the largest surprise to me," said Meng Ji. "If you had asked me when you first came here, I would have given you, at best, a sixty percent success rate. There are so many variables in the human condition—physical, mental, spiritual, chemical, emotional, behavioral. We are instilled with a sense of free will—self-reliance. It can take time for us to come to terms with things—to accept reality. I see it in the freshly deceased very often."

"And yet..." Raphael started emphatically but paused to correct his tone. "We have had no trouble with the deceased of this planet."

"We cannot entertain that kind of thought," said Haniel. He still had his reservations, though. It was dangerous to spend too much time on any single planet. They were already beyond the projected time they had allotted themselves to be on Earth. There were races that yearned for what the Angels had to offer—those who had been denied or knew they would never receive their invitations to Caldo. There were age-old whispers throughout the universe, and any time the Angels stopped moving, they were in danger.

"I must offer my resistance as well," said Meng Ji. "A day does not go by that I do not think of my passing to this plane. It is a soul-changing experience to transfer from life to death for my species. As spirits—as ghosts, we mostly get by well enough. But even with the knowledge, the serenity, and the escape from all Earthly troubles that one comes to understand after the fact"—she paused for an uncomfortable amount of time—"I would not—can not recommend euthanizing any living human, even if the end justifies the means. I should know better than to say something like that, but I cannot resist the memory of my own experience."

"I can accept that," said Haniel. "I believe that with things going as they have been, we need to assume that there will be members of the human race who we will not be able to decant in a safe time frame."

"We can't leave life forms on the planet," said Raphael. "We never have, and it's not acceptable. It runs counter to our mission."

"I have to agree with Haniel," said the synthesized voice of Meng Ji.

Haniel spoke again. "I do not want to leave a single soul behind. I do not want that to stay with me for the rest of time, but I cannot justify taking so long here that we are discovered. That will happen, eventually, and we, every human we have decanted, all those who have not been decanted, and the entire mission will be at risk. We must think of the larger issue."

"I don't know if I can bear it," said Raphael. "We promised them, *all* of them, paradise."

"There was no way we could have known how impossible it would be to honor that guarantee," Haniel said. "We have done everything we can do here. It is a bitter fact. We need to set a deadline and adhere to it, or we risk everything."

There was a long silence before sound emerged from the electronic cabinet. "How much time do you think you have before it is too dangerous to stay here?"

"I do not feel comfortable being stationed here, even now," Haniel said carefully. "Every moment is exponentially direr than the last. I would dare not linger more than nine further revolutions."

"Nine days." Meng Ji paused to calculate. "At best, I would guess that there could be ten to fifteen thousand more decantations in that amount of time. That is if efforts around the planet were increased and hastened."

"That could leave over twenty thousand behind, maybe more," said Raphael.

"In addition to our efforts to decant the rest," Haniel said, "we must start thinking about how to leave those who can't accept The Promise in some kind of sustainable state. It will be minimalistic at first, but I think they will have a great opportunity to flourish if we can provide them with aid and parting gifts."

"I will start the process of letting our colleagues around the world know," Raphael said coldly.

"Ji," said Haniel, addressing the machine containing the ghost of the smartest human to have ever lived. "We will need as much help as you can provide us."

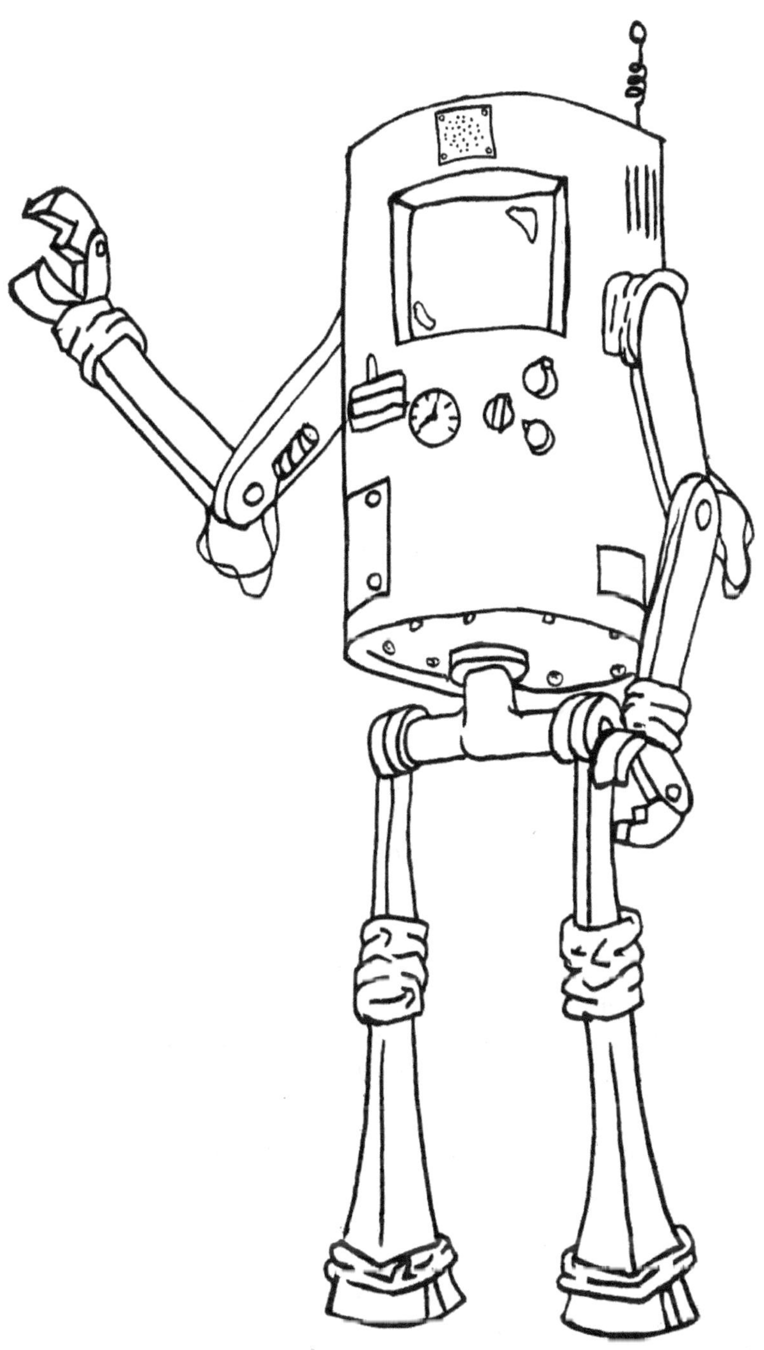

9.

After breakfast was finished and the lodgers were all back on the fourth floor, morning group was held. Everyone gathered in the group meeting room and waited for Miranda. She came in a few minutes later than usual, swiping across her tablet computer before sitting in her corner chair.

"Sorry, gang," she said. "Just getting a little new info from the Angels. We'll begin in a few minutes." In her chair, she stared intently at her screen, swiping up and down, seemingly reading and rereading pages of notes.

For a few minutes, everyone shifted and mumbled and chuckled to each other. Leo sat in his usual seat against the wall between the meeting room and the hallway, and Brock sat next to him. "Yo, Grundy," he said softly, "You didn't tell me the new girl was a dyke."

"What?" said Leo. It seemed the most appropriate response.

"Shit, man," Brock scoffed. His eyes were pointing in their typical separate directions, and neither one was looking at Leo. "Name like Frankie, and that buzz-cut? Not to mention she got a face like a boxer—all jacked-up and shit. She got that melancholy ear."

"Cauliflower," Leo absently corrected him and then sighed, realizing the futility of addressing any of the other ignorant nonsense spewed by his roommate. Leo hadn't even thought about Frankie's sexuality or even much about how attractive she was. Initially, he had been struck by her eyes, and they got him again last night during the night-stalker incident that she seemed, thankfully, not to remember yet. There was something about the woman, but he couldn't place it. There was something there—something inviting yet jagged. She seemed to know something that Leo didn't but desperately wanted to. She wasn't the type of woman Leo usually ended up with, but despite her "jacked-up" appearance, he realized that he certainly wouldn't mind sleeping with her.

While Leo was lost in thought, Brock had continued talking and was still going. "...I mean, Rhonda was married, yeah, but I bet I could hook those two up. I got a silver tongue, you know, Grundy? Don't worry, my man. If they invite me to watch, I'll make sure you get a front-row seat, too." Brock laughed to himself for almost a full minute before Miranda started group.

"I think we'll begin now," Miranda said. She looked flustered. "We're going to do things a little bit differently today. Instead of an open share, I'll supply a topic for discussion. Everyone will have to share today. The meeting won't end until everyone has spoken." This prompted a few groans from the group. "I know, I know. You can pass, but we'll come back to you after everyone else has shared. The topic for this session is a question. What are your thoughts on Caldo?"

There was a dull silence in the room. George finally spoke. "I've answered that probably twenty times in my homework. What more am I supposed to say?"

"We've never had a full group discussion about it, though," said Miranda. "Our goal is to ramp up the intensity of our sessions. We need to redouble our efforts to get you all ready for decantation. So, why don't you start us off, George?"

George folded his arms and gave an audible harumph. He actually said "harumph" as though it were a real word. "I don't know. What else could my thoughts be about a place they call paradise? The way they describe it, it sounds like some kind of dream, except you're in control of it. That sounds pretty great to me. Better than what I've got right now anyway."

"So, would you say you're excited about the prospect of going?"

"Sure. What else is there to say? It's hard to get too excited for something I barely friggin' understand, but since probably three days after getting here, I've been really itching to go. Goop me up, put me in a jar, and shoot me across space."

"Good. Thank you," said Miranda. While George was speaking, Miranda had been continuously glancing down at her tablet. There was some kind of reading or information on there, but no one could see it. "We'll just go down the line then. If that's all right?" She turned to Rhonda, who was sitting next to George.

"I just think it all sounds so cool," Rhonda said. "It sounds like something out of a fairy tale, and I love it. I thought it was too good to be true for a long time. I believed they were telling me the truth about it all in my head, but I couldn't feel it in my heart, you know?

"I saw everything they were, the Angels, I mean, and everything they could do, and I knew there was no reason not to believe that they wanted to help us and take us somewhere beautiful. For a while, I thought that we didn't deserve it. What have we done for anyone, you know? Humans, I mean. Maybe that was why I couldn't fully trust them."

"And now?" asked Miranda.

"Gosh, I'm ready to go now. I worry a little about what's taking so long—why I haven't been able to accept a Promise yet. I mean, they've offered, and I've tried, and it's been wonderful. They sat me down in this grassy field, and"—she paused—"well, it wasn't a real field. It was raining outside, so they did it with their virtual stuff, you know? Maybe that's why it didn't work. But most people take their Promises with virtual, um..."

"Equipment?" offered Miranda.

"Yeah, equipment. So, I don't see why that would be the issue. It was a few months ago. We sat down in this field with the sun shining, and I was naked and sitting there all warm. The Angel took out this huge book. It was like an old-fashioned one, like a wizard's spell book or something. And it had this story in it. I can't remember the story, but it was so beautiful. I felt so peaceful and happy, and I was sure that I was ready to take the Promise, but, for some reason, it just never happened. I must have"—she stopped, getting choked up. "I must have screwed something up."

Miranda reflexively handed a box of tissues to George to hand to Rhonda. "That's not how it goes, Rhonda. You know that. The time has to be just right for the Promise to be offered and accepted. I'm sure it was no fault of yours. It is an intricate process, and if everything doesn't go just right, it can result in a fractional distrust. Maybe there was an issue on the Angels' side, and they didn't want to risk doing something prematurely. There are hundreds of reasons it could have gone that way."

Rhonda sniffled. "I know. I just wish it could have gone right."

During Rhonda's share, Miranda had again glanced back at her tablet several times. She made a few small notes as well. "Well, shall we continue?" She looked to the chair two down from Rhonda's. In it sat a metallic humanoid creation. It was a large, gray cylinder with very thin, springy arms and legs protruding from it. There was a blank screen as well as some knobs and dials on the front of the cylinder. No one knew if the knobs and dials did anything. If nothing else, they gave a human something to look at while talking with or addressing a ghost housed within.

The Angel's ships carried thousands of these ghost-housing contraptions. Ghosts could be loaded into them to ease the shock a living person may feel when communicating with a deceased spirit. Ghosts had been essential in the pre-decantation and Promise processes. Their presence provided definitive proof for the living that what the Angels said was to be believed. Ghost vessels would sometimes visit living family members to reconnect. Sometimes, the vessels would do public appearances as the person housed within them to give speeches or do question-and-answer panels.

Most ghosts had no trouble going with the Angels. There were no intricate Promises to be made to them. They already knew everything the Angels had to say. Ghosts simply needed to make a choice. In the vessel, two chairs down from Rhonda, were the only three ghosts in the hemisphere who had not yet decided to be loaded into the Ether-base. Other ghosts were still on Earth, helping the Angels or finishing up odds and ends, but they had all made their decisions.

From a speaker near the top of the vessel's cylinder, a soft voice spoke. It was synthesized, of course, and the speaker's native tongue was automatically translated before being synthesized. "I have my doubts about Caldo," the voice said. Speaking was the spirit of a long-dead Native American Algonquian woman named Wapun. Each spirit could choose its own style of voice from a somewhat limited selection. "Although I have learned much in death—although my brothers and sisters have all solemnly sworn to me that the spirit of our planet lives on with every soul, living or dead, I have not been able to bring myself to leave her."

"So, your hesitation comes less from a distrust of the Angels and Caldo and more from a sense of duty—a sense of connection to this physical world?" asked Miranda.

"In broad terms, yes," spoke the voice of Wapun. "I want to know. I want to have what all who have boarded the Angel's ships have. I crave the desire to be taken to the existence I truly believe in and trust. Yet, I cannot retain my grasp on that desire. My family would not lie to me. These ambassadors would not lie to me. I cannot explain it. I have total trust in them, but I am tethered to this planet—to this land."

The group meeting continued with each lodger explaining their feelings on certain aspects of their circumstances. The two other ghosts housed in the vessel with Wapun, Cody and Sophie, explained their reasoning for not boarding the ships yet. Cody had, in life, also shared a vessel with other souls. He and six other souls, all Codys, had somehow wound up in a single human body. This happened from time to time on Earth, and the vessel housing the multiple souls was often deemed unwell or insane. Cody was convinced the six other Codys did not want him around, so he was bound and determined to stay on Earth as a way to finally "set them free."

Sophie was a deceased biologist who said she wanted to stay around on Earth and witness the evolutions of all the new species that would come about in the wake of humankind. She also did not want to be loaded into the Ether-base with her ex-husband. She felt very little desire to leave the planet. The warm embrace of Caldo, which had converted even the most stubborn martyrs and masochists, had no significant effect on her. Miranda rarely made notes while Sophie spoke.

Lois spoke for a while about unrelated topics, none of which made any sense. She talked about her sister in Florida, President Reagan, knitting, and, eventually, about a big upcoming trip. In her more lucid moments, Lois seemed aware that an important pilgrimage was approaching and that she was to be part of it. In the presence of an Angel—in the light of their truth and benevolence, others in unstable mental states had been able to achieve slight levels of trust in the visitors. However fleeting, this was enough for a Promise to be made at some point. The process was the same for newborns and those with severely debilitated mental faculties. A Promise was not precisely about facts or belief or a single perspective. It was more about accepting a truth that was both personal and universal.

There was something about Lois—something beyond her mere mental degeneration that prevented her decantation. No one had quite figured it out yet.

Frankie was next. The human lodgers all subtly adjusted themselves in their seats before she spoke. Even Alphonse seemed to react with interest. A gas bubble floated up through his jar.

"I don't know what to think about any of this yet," Frankie said after Miranda asked her the topic question. "The past few years have just been hellish, and now, to find all this out so suddenly is just..." She searched herself for strong enough words.

"Take your time," Miranda said compassionately. "You can be honest here."

"Christ!" Frankie spat. "How did I end up in this circus? And don't patronize me, please. I don't need sympathy. It's never done me any good."

There was silence for a moment. George smiled.

Frankie continued, "What do I think about—what is it? Caldo? Some eternal land of gumdrops and laughter? What am I supposed to say? You say it's paradise? Well then, who wouldn't want to have it?

"Do I trust the giant puppet-angels? Fuck no! Have you seen them? I crawl out from under the dirt after years of living alone, and the world is some kind of acid trip with barely any people left because they all decided to turn into bottles of goo. There are robots that supposedly have dead people's ghosts in them. You all got to see this shit happening. I just got pulled out of sleep from one nightmare to another."

"We typically wouldn't push so hard this early on," Miranda said. "But the Angels are insisting on—"

"Fucking *Angels*," Frankie interrupted. She rose from her seat and walked to the water cooler in the corner of the room. She pulled a paper cup from the dispenser attached to the side and held it to her forehead. "And I'm a unicorn." She crumpled the cup and threw it down, returning to her seat. "Angels," she said again. It aggravated her to realize that the mere thought of the Angels now seemed to subdue her growing rage.

"At this point, everything everyone is saying just sounds like bullshit." She smiled mirthlessly. "But I know it's all true, don't I? I'm here with aliens and a goo-person and robo-ghost over there. It's a lot of trouble to go to just to gaslight little old me... I guess I'm done for now."

"Thank you, Frances," Miranda said, looking up from her tablet. "We all appreciate your honesty. Brock, whenever you're ready."

Brock talked about what it was going to be like in Caldo for him. The description involved endless legions of highly attractive famous women and nonstop funk, soul, and disco music. Everyone, including the Angels, figured that his inability to take the Promise so far had been due to his attachment to familiar and material things like sex, dancing, music, and chit-chat. His homework questions were designed to help drive the point home that all these things were possible and even inevitable in his future in Caldo.

After Brock, Alphonse spoke of his confusion about being sent for more study or treatment or counseling after being decanted. He said it was obvious that he was fully prepared for Caldo and that he was excited to go there. He suspected there was some physical problem with his decantation and that the Angels were working on it. In fact, he was partially right.

He was decanted, but something had gone wrong with the process. His readings post-decanting were atypical. For some reason, his density and resiliency readings were such that it seemed he would not survive the trip across space. This had never happened before, and the Angels were trying to figure out how to deal with the situation.

Leo didn't hear much of what Alphonse had said. After Frankie's share, Leo's brain had shut down most of its functions. It was now primarily working on two levels—processing what the new arrival had said and worrying about what he was going to say when his turn came.

Suddenly, horrifyingly, it was his turn to speak, but during his silent mental frenzy, he'd forgotten what the question was. He waited to be prompted by Miranda, trying to fill his mind with things to say—words that made sense and would adequately answer whatever the question might have been. Others hadn't needed to share too much. Maybe he could get away with only a few sentences.

"Leonard?" Miranda said.

"Yes," he replied.

"Your thoughts? On Caldo? And please be totally honest."

"My thoughts," he began, "are very, well... complicated." *There*, he thought, *that should buy me a minute*. As he thought, his eyes met Miranda's. She was too highly trained—too experienced to glower at anyone. But the look on her face seemed to say, *please, don't waste either of our time, Leonard.* He was thrown off again.

"I feel that, well,"—he swallowed—"it will be very nice to live—to exist in a place where"—suddenly, something came to him—"a place where there are no wars. A place where all beings can coexist peacefully and without conflict." He smiled inwardly, proud of his quick thinking and his bulletproof statement.

"You feel that being in Caldo," Miranda said tentatively, "will heighten your appreciation of peace?"

"Well, yes."

"Have you experienced war and fighting in your life? We don't have anything on file about that."

Why couldn't she have just heard him out and left him alone? He had answered the question. "It's just something that... weighs on my mind," he said. "The state of the world as it has been. I think about it a lot."

The truth was that he didn't think about it very much. He didn't think a whole lot about anything. He worried a lot. Mostly, he worried about how uncomfortable he would be in the next moment. But he knew he couldn't really do anything about that. He tried to live his life by the principle of taking the path of least resistance, though it was less of a principle and more of a thing-to-do, he supposed. He took what was offered and tried to make the best of it. It was not an unpleasant existence, nor was it particularly pleasant.

Leo felt that his recent time in Walnut Ridge had been fairly nice, especially for the past few months. In the beginning, it was much more crowded and kinetic, which had been difficult at times. He had even been attacked in his sleep. But, somehow, being attacked was still less jarring—less stressful than making a left-hand turn at a busy intersection or going to work and seeing someone with a new haircut and having to tell them that their haircut looked nice, whether it did or not. Those were the types of things that made lines on his face, churned his stomach acids, pushed back his hairline.

Miranda spent a long time tapping and swiping at her screen before speaking. "Is there anything else, Leonard? Anything else regarding Caldo or the Angels that you feel strongly about?"

"No. I don't think so." Leonard tried to remember the last thing that made him feel strongly in any manner. He came up with nothing, but that was no big surprise. It was not the first time he had thought about it.

10.

The remainder of the day at Walnut Ridge consisted of more intensive one-on-one "chat sessions" and a lot of waiting around. Very few qualified people were left to hold sessions with lodgers and effectively gather data. Those who were not meeting with the overworked Miranda met with Doug, a cook/janitor who had taken a few psychology classes while at university in the nineties. There was talk of having lodgers meet directly with Angels, but that seemed not to be happening yet. Those not in session had rec-time.

Leo, Lois, and the ghost vessel sat in the community room, which was filled with tables and chairs and cabinets and shelves. It was the general gathering area, so most people didn't go there in their free time if other spots were available. The rest of the lodgers not in chat sessions were in the meeting room, which, when not in use, was the rec room. It had a TV and a VCR/DVD player.

Lois was doing decoupage on paper cups, using pictures cut from old magazines. This was one of her hobbies. During her time at Walnut Ridge, she had cut and pasted magazine clippings to scores of small boxes, scraps of cardboard, discarded food containers, bottles, cans, and whatever else she could get her boney, veiny hands on. She had now moved on to paper cups.

Her method was questionable. She would find pictures she liked, cut them out, and paste them so that the image was facing inward. The opposite side of the paper was what actually showed. The things she made appeared to just be random scraps and shapes with parts of ads and pictures and crooked sections of text. When asked about this, she would just say, "What shows on the outside doesn't always represent what's on the inside." People usually stopped talking to her after this.

At the center table, Leo worked on crossword puzzles and word searches. There were a seemingly inexhaustible number of photocopied pages containing puzzles from the 1970s to the present. In the eight months Leo had been at the facility, he had not had to complete the same puzzle twice. With a little digging, he was always able to find one he had not seen before. As he was just finishing his sixth puzzle, he heard someone enter the room. He looked up and saw Frankie coming in wearing scrub pants and a baggy sweatshirt.

"Holy shit," she said to no one in particular. "Those people can talk."

She walked past the table against the wall where Lois was working. "Did you make those?" she asked, admiring the decoupage paper cups.

Lois looked at the cups sitting on the table in front of her. "I suppose I did," she said.

"They're beautiful! Really cool." Frankie carefully picked up one of the drier pieces, looking at its indecipherably collaged surface.

"Thank you," said Lois, looking up at the younger woman. "You may have one if you like."

"I'd love one." Frankie surveyed the cups before gently lifting one to look at it. "I think this is my favorite. Maybe you could teach me how to do this sometime."

"I would be happy to." Lois smiled. "And tell Phyllis to come along as well. I was never mad at her like she thought I was."

"I'll be sure to pass that along. Thank you." Frankie sat at the center table, a few seats down from Leo. She was quiet for a long time and had her eyes closed. Leo felt nervous with her sitting there. He wasn't sure if he was supposed to say anything. He didn't. After a while, when he was almost fully reabsorbed into his word search, she spoke.

"So, what do you do?" Her eyes were still closed.

"Eum," said Leo. What kind of a question was that? *What do you do?* What did anyone *do*? "I guess I do... about as much as I can be able to feel to do." Horrified with embarrassment, he went back to his word search. What he'd said meant absolutely nothing. He kept seeing the words "can be able to feel to do" in his word search. He sweated. He was sure that he was starting to stink.

Frankie smiled. "That sounds fascinating. I guess that's about what I do, too."

She went quiet again, but the sound of her breathing was loud in Leo's ears. After a few minutes, Frankie rose from her seat and padded around the room. She came to the ghost-vessel seated in a chair in the corner and sat down next to it.

"What's shakin'?" she asked it eventually.

The ghost-vessel turned itself slightly to better face her.

"Hello," it said in a high-pitched voice with an English accent. It was Sophie's voice. "I'm not sure we've met. I'm Sophie."

"Pleased to meet you," Frankie said. She was still confused and skeptical of what was represented by the robot. She had never truly believed in ghosts or in an eternal soul or anything like that. It was difficult for her to fully believe that she was talking to the consciousness of a deceased human. "My name is Frances, but I hate it. Call me Frankie. How long have you been dead?"

Leo was somewhat surprised by the blunt nature of the question. He was eavesdropping. Part of him was trying not to, but another part was very interested in Frankie and what she had to say.

"Two years, nine months, three days, and fourteen hours," Sophie said. "Not that I'm keeping track." On the screen of the ghost-vessel appeared a cartoon smiley face. The voice synthesizer could produce laughter, but the sound was unnatural and upsetting to most living people. The majority of ghosts preferred to express humor and levity visually.

"I know you must get this all the time," said Frankie, "but what's it like being dead? I mean, if you don't mind my asking."

"It's not too bad," replied Sophie.

Frankie waited for more. There had to be some kind of elaboration, didn't there? "Is," she said, "is that it? I mean, how does it feel? Does it feel like anything? Is there heaven or purgatory, or are souls just walking around on Earth?"

"It is hard to express to a living person. It's like being dead."

"Like... being dead?" Frankie was nonplussed. "You really can't give me any more than that?"

"I'm sorry. That's about as much as any of us can say, really." It was true. Ever since the Angels had first started gathering ghosts into vessels, or communication cabinets, living humans had been asking, prodding, begging for some kind of information on the hereafter. The responses were always the same. Regardless of who the ghost was when they were alive, how smart or stupid they had been, how happy or depressed, their length of life, time since death, religion, philosophy, beliefs, when asked what death was like, the reply was always, "It's not too bad." When pressed, any ghost would simply tell the living that they, having never been dead, could not understand. Eventually, the questions stopped. Those still alive had to accept that there was no way to get the answers they had craved for so long. Frankie was, of course, unaware of all this, having lived cut off from the world for two years.

"So," Frankie said, "not too bad?"

"Not too bad, no."

"Well, that's more than I can say for a lot of what happens on this side of things." Frankie turned away in her chair.

"That's true," said Sophie's voice. "But don't think too harshly of it all. Death's not too bad, but dying is really very unpleasant." She paused. "I didn't even make it out alive." The cartoon smiley face appeared on the vessel's screen again.

"Right," Frankie said. She was unamused. "Are we allowed to smoke?" she asked no one in particular.

"Only at certain times of the day," Leo said, not looking up from his word search. "They don't like lodgers smoking, though. They say it messes with the detox meds."

"Where do they get the cigarettes?"

"I... never really thought about it."

"I bet they all suck now," Frankie said. "I bet they're all old and stale and shitty." She paused. "I still want one."

"You smoke?" Leo asked before realizing this was a stupid question.

"I used to. I kind of want to again. Especially if it will piss off the Angels. I still don't like calling them that."

"You could probably ask Miranda for some cigarettes later," said Leo. "Or you could ask George. I think he still smokes."

"So, tell me about yourself. I'm tired of talking about myself to everyone. What did you do before you came here?"

"Not a whole lot," Leo said. He didn't really like talking about himself. "I used to be on a landscaping crew. I mowed a lot of lawns."

"Around here?" Frankie asked.

"Not really. I lived in Pennsylvania before I moved to Vermont. A town called Cindervale. Nobody really kno—"

"No shit! I used to live in Cindervale. That's, like what, three hundred miles from here?"

"Something like that, yeah." Leo wasn't sure he believed Frankie. He hadn't met anyone at Walnut Ridge who'd heard of Cindervale, let alone lived there. "When were you there?"

"Let's see." She thought briefly. "I was there for a few years, like, fourteen years ago? And then again eight or nine years ago, on and off."

"Are you messing with me?"

"I swear to God." She raised her hand in a salute of honesty. "I actually probably wouldn't admit to living there if you didn't bring it up. It's kind of, well, lame."

"We were probably there at the same time then," Leo said. He found some small degree of comfort in having this connection with the woman who vexed him so. "I lived there for twelve years."

"Whoa, that's crazy. Did you ever go to Taco Bell?"

"Maybe once or twice. It's not really my thing, usually."

"I used to work there. I wonder if I was working any of the times you came in."

"I suppose it's possible," Leo said. "I really don't remember if I was ever there. I think I might have been, but I can't imagine why. Maybe with a friend or someone I worked with. I don't like Mexican food."

Frankie laughed. "Taco Bell is *not* Mexican food on any level. Fast food is barely fucking food at all, but Taco Bell's delicious. You might actually like it. I do. You should try it sometime."

"I'm not sure I'll have a chance to do that," Leo said with a nervous laugh.

"Oh, right." She paused, remembering. "Aliens. Spaceships. Goo-people."

"I'm sure I can get something like it in Caldo. Supposedly, there's no limit to what a person can experience there." Leo sometimes wondered what kind of experiences he would have in Caldo. It was hard to imagine. Probably a good deal of sleeping, maybe some walking, he thought.

"I don't know," Frankie said. "I'm not sure there's anything like it off Earth. I think we should go get some. I think we should go to Taco Bell so you can have it before blasting off into space."

"I don't think we can do that. I mean, they say we aren't trapped here, but I don't know if we're really allowed to leave. And there aren't any people left out there anyway. Why would a Taco Bell be open?"

"They can't keep us here against our will," Frankie said. "They act all benevolent and shit like they're concerned for our well-being. They just haven't had anyone call them on their bullshit. I think we should."

"But there's no one out there anymore. Everybody's decanted. The stores are all closed. There might not even be electricity anywhere. No gas stations, nothing."

"I just came in here the other night. When they were driving me over here, from the back window of the van, I saw tons of places with their lights on. I don't think the aliens have done anything to shut down society. Some people might've buttoned up and closed shop, but why would any place shut their power off? Why would the power company shut anything down? Most of that shit is automated nowadays, anyway. I bet that if we went to Cindervale, Taco Bell would still have lights. I bet the ovens and freezers and hoods would all still work.

"And gas? How did the aliens come to get me? They've got fuel or access to it somewhere. Most of those gas stations are automated, too. I doubt every one of them got shut down or used up. I guarantee you there's a fully functional gas station within twenty miles of here."

"I don't know," Leo said. He knew the Angels had made sure that as the population drastically dropped, power and infrastructure continued to function. They may have put systems in place to keep life running as usual. They had the knowledge, power, and technology. "There's a lot we don't know for sure. There's a lot that could go wrong." This was a fairly standard line of thought for Leonard Salmon. It had guided him through most of his life.

"Well, whatever," Frankie said. "What's the worst that could happen? We go out, run out of gas, and the aliens—the Angels bring us back. They can obviously track people down somehow. They found me once. They can find me again and bring me back."

Leo felt hot. Pinpricks of sweat were breaking through his pores again. He kind of wanted to go on this fruitless adventure, partially because he was fairly certain it would not happen. But in the base of his skull, somewhere in his brainstem, he knew that within the next day or so, he would be out in the dead world, driving to a fast-food restaurant where all the meat had likely spoiled. It made him terribly anxious. A lot of things did.

55

11.

As the Angels made the final preparations on the Arks that they would pilot from Earth to Caldo, the Strappons readied a massive transport ship hovering high above their home planet. The Strappon ship was large enough to hold the entire population of the planet and an obscene amount of weaponry, none of which really took up much three-dimensional space. All the highest-ranking Strappons were in agreement—theirs was a mission of transport and diplomacy. However, if the need arose, they wanted to be sure they had ample firepower. Space could be a dangerous place, and they had forgotten the true nature of the alien Triangles who had offered them paradise.

Though the events with their visitors had taken place generations ago, it was instilled in all newly created Strappons that the ultimate goal of their race was to regain an invitation to Caldo or, as the Strappons referred to it, Octacontaheptagon. In the time since their first encounter with the Triangles, their obsession with reaching Octacontaheptagon evolved into an almost physical manifestation in each and every Strappon. Now that the time was near for another meeting with their alien visitors, all members of the race were experiencing an identical anticipation. Shortly after news of the Triangles' rediscovery spread, petty disagreements, fights, brewing wars— nearly all forms of conflict ceased among the sentient rectangles.

Handjobb, the game of arranging shapes, the game that had ultimately led to the departure of the aliens the first time, had been outlawed. Merely playing a friendly game was deemed an offense to the rectangles of generations past. When underground Handjobb rings were discovered, which happened from time to time, all those caught participating were sentenced to death without trial. There was an unspoken excitement among the Strappons that once they were granted access to Octacontaheptagon, Handjobb might be commonplace again.

57

12.

"They want permission to drive to a restaurant called Taco Bell in a town where they used to live." Miranda was relaying a message to Haniel, the Angel who, more or less, ran operations at Walnut Ridge. "They say they just want to get out and have fun while they're still on Earth. I wasn't sure what to tell them. What do you think?"

Haniel tented his articulated metal fingers over the polished wood surface of a desk once belonging to Walnut Ridge founder Denise Elkins, who was now a ghost. "Time is short now. Perhaps we ought to try some new approaches. Frances. Now, she is an ornery one, yet her rhythmic feedback is very much in line with those who have taken their Promises quickly. I don't imagine a short trip outside would endanger her chances. I wonder about the others."

Raphael, Haniel's assistant and Angel in charge of "acquisitions," was also in the meeting, and he decided to interject. "This is all very risky. It is against our code to keep humans against their will unless we deem it necessary. However, I postulate that with so little time left, it is necessary to keep all our lodgers in or on the grounds of Walnut Ridge."

"We've taken tons of people out on supply runs and day trips in the past," Miranda said. "I don't recall ever having too much trouble. Any runners we had were found within half a day and pretty much came back with no problem. The only elopement risk would be Frances, and, as you say, her readings and behavior are more or less in line with a quick decantation. We even have some leads on speeding up the process for her."

"And you say that it would just be Frances, Brock, Rhonda, and Leonard?" asked Haniel.

"Well, possibly Alphonse as well," said Miranda.

"That's another issue entirely," Haniel said gravely. "I'm inclined to allow this. Brock and Rhonda seem to cycle in their readings," the Angel swiped the screen of a tablet sitting on his desk. "And it appears their homework assignments have yielded more promising results of late. Perhaps this change of pace—this symbol of finality will help put them into the realms of acceptance."

"I truly do not think this is worth the risk," Raphael said, taking a step toward Haniel's desk. "The intense therapy will work. If we alter our course, we are in danger of regression or possibly worse."

"What about Leonard?" asked Miranda.

There was a long silence before Haniel spoke. "About that, I am unsure. I honestly believe Leonard is incapable of accepting a Promise at this point, and I fear he may never have that capacity. Perhaps a break from the ordinary would alter his state of mind in such a way that..."

Miranda waited for Haniel to finish his thought. Instead, he reclined in his padded leather chair and simply gazed forward. She had seen him do this before and wondered if his intent was to come across sagely. Mostly, it just made her worry that his vessel had ceased functioning.

"I wonder," Raphael said, "if there is something about their living, physical bodies that prevents them from spiritual acceptance of our Promises. We have certainly had more trouble on this world than on any other. Perhaps their race is too immature. There are more types of living creatures and more chemical elements on this planet than we have typically had to deal with elsewhere. The remaining un-decanted humans may have some innate, physical connection keeping their willing minds and spirits from taking the next step."

Miranda looked uncomfortably at Haniel.

"We probably did not do enough research before coming to Earth. I concede that," Haniel said. "But we must not start entertaining alternate methods based on pure speculation."

"It is not speculation," Raphael said coldly. "We have a one hundred percent success rate with spirits."

"So," Miranda said, wanting to be out of the room—wanting not to be hearing what she was hearing, "what is the final word on the day trip?"

"Ah, yes," Haniel said, curling his features into an approximation of a smile. "I consent. We can deal with anything that may go wrong, as you implied earlier. With so little time left, such a deviation is a risk I am willing to take." Haniel turned to his assistant. "Raphael, you will trail them on their journey as a precautionary measure. Do not allow yourself to be detected, and report back with any abnormalities or other issues."

"Certainly, Haniel," responded the other angelic simulacrum.

Unsettled but also glad to have good news for the lodgers, Miranda took her leave of the two preposterous saviors. She rode the elevator back to the fourth floor, wondering if it would be possible to have all the remaining humans on the planet decanted in a matter of days. She had taken her Promise and was only waiting to be decanted. Her services would help the Angels, and she was glad to offer them in the name of decanting more humans. As for the individuals unable to accept their invitation to Caldo, well, their situation was certainly unfortunate.

On the fourth floor, she gathered Leo and Brock into room 411, Frances' room, where Rhonda and Frances were already sitting and talking. "I discussed your request with Haniel and Raphael—"

"The ninja turtles?" interrupted Frankie.

Rhonda slapped her hands to her mouth and giggled.

"—and it has been accepted," Miranda finished, undaunted. "Tomorrow morning, you four will be allowed to take one of the vans along with extra fuel to your Taco Bell in"—she checked her tablet—"Cindervale, PA. You can make a few stops on the way if you like, but if you go farther than you requested or stray too far from the route, you will be stopped and brought back here. Understood?" She waited for them to acknowledge her question. Everyone nodded, and she continued, "We can, and will, be tracking you."

"That's fine," Frankie said. "Like Leo said, the place might have had the power shut off. Everything could be rotten. It will probably be a short trip anyway. I just kind of want to get out and about again."

"We ask that one of you check in every few hours, just as a matter of course," said Miranda. "I still don't really understand this." She shook her head and smirked.

"Maybe you're just jealous that you ain't coming along?" said Brock.

"I've never been a big fan of fast food," Miranda said. "When you get back, your detox meds will be working overtime. That reminds me." She fiddled with her tablet for a moment. "Before you leave tomorrow morning, make sure you each pick up your packets from the nurse's station. We still want you to take your normal meds while you're traveling. Don't forget." Miranda did some final twiddling on her screen and left the room.

"Oh man, this is going to be so fun!" said Rhonda. She put a friendly hand on Frankie's thigh, causing it to become visibly tense. "I haven't even thought about going outside in weeks. Not until you came," she addressed Frankie. "You're like a breath of fresh air."

"Thanks." Frankie smiled uncomfortably.

"Ain't gonna be no fresh air after I get a few gorditas in me tomorrow," Brock said.

Leo grimaced. "I'm still not sure this is a great idea. Who's driving anyway?"

"Not it!" Rhonda shrieked.

"We'll all take turns," Frankie said. "It'll probably take five or six hours each way."

"Isn't there somewhere closer we could go? There's got to be a Taco Bell somewhere around here that we can go to," Rhonda said, somewhat deflated.

"Come on," Frankie encouraged. "It's a road trip! Plus, they probably haven't changed the locks or the code on the security system at this one. I'm sure my keys still work. I don't want to hang out somewhere if there's an alarm blasting in my ears."

The chime sounded for dinner.

During the meal, Alphonse asked Brock if they had found out about the trip. Brock told him they were leaving the next morning, and Alphonse asked if he could join them.

"You don't eat, do you? You want us to slip some burritos into your jar there?"

A laughing face appeared on Alphonse's screen while his robotic voice said, "No, I don't eat, but a change of scenery would be nice."

Brock told everyone that Alphie would be joining them on their trip. Frankie was still a little apprehensive about Alphonse, but she didn't say anything.

"You're going, right Leo?" asked Alphonse.

"Yeah," he replied.

"He's the reason we're going," said Frankie. "We need to teach him the glory of Taco Bell."

"I think I'm glad I can no longer consume food," said Alphonse.

13.

At five-thirty in the morning, Leo was trying to wake up Brock. It was not an easy task. Eventually, Leo just turned all the lights on in the room and went about starting his day. Brock would be up in time. Somehow, he always was.

Rhonda was up and milling around the nurse's station, appearing as though she had been awake for hours already. She greeted Leo giddily and asked when they were leaving.

"As soon as everyone is up, I guess." He got his morning meds and his packet of pills to take throughout the day from the nurse.

"Should I wake up Frankie?" asked Rhonda. "Do you think she'd be mad? She said we should be on the road by six, and if we don't all get up soon, we won't make it—" she continued talking, but Leo tuned her out. It was too early in the morning for such excitement.

"I think she'll probably be up in a few minutes," Leo said on his way to have his blood pressure taken by the night technician. As the tech strapped the cuff to his arm, Leo continued, "Rhonda, you go wake up Brock instead. He'll be grumpy if he doesn't get coffee before we leave."

As Leo finished his morning vitals, he saw Frankie shambling out of her room. She wasn't wearing a bra. Despite his typically diminished sex drive and attempts to avert his eyes, he found himself excited by this fact. Her face was pale and puffy, and her eyes were bloodshot.

"You doing okay?" Leo asked. He hoped she wasn't feeling sick.

Frankie yawned. "I'm just really beat. I don't get it, I slept like the dead, but it doesn't feel like it."

In a way, she was correct. She had been unconscious throughout the night, but her body had been working. Her eyes were red and sore from being wide open, as Leo had seen them the night prior. This was an unfortunate side effect of the bio-transmitter that had entered her body when she touched the Strappon meteorite two years ago. It operated while she was sleeping, but while active, it jolted her eyelids far apart and curled her toes into painful, cramped gnarls.

"Maybe it's the shitty mattresses here. It took me a while to be able to sleep right on mine. Do you want coffee?" Leo was glad he'd showered the previous night. He had applied deodorant three times already this morning to make sure he didn't smell.

"Mmm, coffee," she said, smiling as her vitals were taken. "Yes, please."

"How do you take it?" Leo asked, padding to the rec room where the coffee maker was kept.

"The Fly, couple sugars," she said, yawning.

Leo stopped. "Excuse me?"

Frankie's yawn turned into a laugh. "Oh, sorry," she said. "Force of habit. That's something I used to do with my"–she paused–"friend. Just give it a tiny splash of milk or powder or whatever they have."

Leo went to the rec room and filled two Styrofoam cups with coffee. He added three sugar packets and six heaping scoops of powdered creamer to his own. To the other, he added two sugars and one spoonful of creamer. When he returned to the hallway, he saw Frankie sitting against the wall by the corner. He sat nervously beside her and handed her the coffee. She took a sip.

"Perfect," she said.

"So that's, uh, 'The Fly'?" Leo said.

Frankie smiled, putting her disarmingly crooked teeth on display. "So, when I lived with this guy, we got into the habit of drinking coffee all day. We didn't have cable, and we couldn't pick up any stations for shit with the antenna. I had this collection of tapes I bought at a yard sale—The Best of Vincent Price."

"Vincent?" Leo asked, dredging his shallow lake of pop-culture knowledge.

"Price, yeah—old horror movie guy. Lots of Corman stuff, Poe adaptations. Shit like that. Great actor, great voice. He did that talking part in "Thriller" too."

"Oh!" Leo brightened. "Yeah, with the laugh."

"Exactly," Frankie said, sipping her coffee. "We used to just watch those tapes, like, every day since there was nothing else to do. There were five movies, not much of a 'Best Of,' but enough to pass the time."

Leo watched her, expecting more, unsure if he ought to say anything. Frankie appeared lost in her memory for the moment. He took a sip of his coffee and burned his mouth.

"But yeah. So, we took our coffee differently throughout the day—stronger in the morning or when we got tired. Anyway, we needed a way to tell each other how much milk we wanted in our mug, and those fucking Price movies were playing all day. In some of them, he was younger, had dark hair. By the seventies, his hair was getting pretty gray. So, we used Vinny's hair as a sort of guide. It sounds pretty fucking dumb when I say it out loud." She laughed.

"I like it," Leo said. "What other movies were there?"

"There was *The Fly*," she held up her Styrofoam cup. "Then there was, um, *The Masque of the Red Death*, which had a little more cream than this. After that was an *Abominable Dr. Phibes*, and then"–she nodded to Leo's cup–"a *Madhouse*." She sighed another laugh, shaking her head. "God. Boredom does weird shit to your head."

"What was a coffee with no cream?"

Frankie thought for a minute. "Neither one of us actually ever took ours without any cream. I guess it would have been a, a *Last Man on Earth*. That tape was broken, so we never watched it, but his hair looked black on the cover."

"*Last Man on Earth*, huh?" Leo said. A chill shot through his insides. He blew on his coffee and took another sip. It burned him less this time. "And this is a *Madhouse*?" Leo asked.

"Yessir," she said. "It's pretty close to an *Edward Scissorhands*, though, which is just milk. Last movie he was in before he died, I think." She lifted her cup and bowed her head in respect.

Leo wanted to tell her he thought her coffee classification method was really cool and funny and creative and that he wanted to start using it himself. All he said was, "Interesting."

"Seeing as coffee isn't going to be a thing that exists pretty soon, I guess I can let you use the Vinny-System. That's a very exclusive distinction."

"I'm honored," Leo said. Inwardly, he felt a strange, childlike excitement that brought him back to something he couldn't quite grasp. A memory? Some embellished or totally fabricated part of his earlier life? The feeling was familiar, so, theoretically, he had felt it at some point before this moment. When he remembered certain things from childhood, they seemed like clips from television shows—like something that he had watched many times and was very familiar with but had never actually experienced.

Presently, a thought tickled his scalp—a question. This woman with the buzzed hair, bent nose, and face lined with cuts—this woman who named her coffee after Vincent Price films and swore a lot, did he have a crush on her? Was having a crush on a person something of which Leonard Salmon was capable?

With Rhonda theatrically pushing him from behind, Brock reeled around the corner of the hallway. "Frankie, Grundy," he said, nodding respectively. "Why didn't you wake me up?"

"Sorry," Leo said, raising his hands in a gesture of surrender and spilling his coffee. He noticed but pretended not to. He hoped no one else noticed. No one mentioned it.

It was a little after six by the time everyone was ready. An Angel, Raphael, led the group down the elevator to the parking lot. Brock was holding Alphonse. It was chilly, and most of the lodgers hadn't worn anything but scrubs, pajamas, and sweatsuits for a long time. Leo, Brock, and Rhonda were dressed in real clothes for the first time in a while. It made the day feel special.

"I hope you realize," Raphael began, "how distinct an opportunity this is. Typically, we would not allow a group of you here so long, and one of you here so briefly, to go off on a joyride like this." He looked at them all gravely. "However, for the benefit of those of you struggling with taking your Promises, we are allowing for some leeway in the status quo. I do not personally approve of it, but I trust those above me."

Everyone impatiently shifted as Raphael continued. "We will be tracking you, and if you stray too far from your path or stay away too long, we will retrieve you. Some of you are familiar with the process, and I don't think you'll wish to repeat it." He looked directly at Frankie, who rolled her eyes.

"Can we just get the fucking keys?" she said. "It's cold out here. We know Big Brother is watching. We aren't going to do anything wrong or try to run away. And the sooner you let us go, the sooner we can come back."

The Angel, standing over seven feet tall, handed Frankie the van keys and a cell phone with a charger. "Leave this plugged in and charging while driving, and make sure one of you keeps it on your person when you leave the vehicle. We'll be checking in with you to ensure everything is going smoothly and that you are taking your medications."

"Gotcha," Frankie said, grabbing the keys, phone, and power cable. She hit the buttons on the key fob, and the lights on one of the vans in the lot blinked on and off. She strode off toward it and climbed into the passenger seat. The others followed.

Leo stood outside of the vehicle, surprised that Frankie didn't get behind the wheel. "You aren't driving?" he asked her.

"Not yet. I don't really know my way around here. I'll drive when we get closer to Cindervale."

"I'll drive," Brock said. "If one of you holds Alphie." He handed the jar of blue ooze to Rhonda and hopped into the driver's seat, smiling.

Leo and Rhonda slid the side door open and climbed into the middle row of seats. Rhonda buckled Alphonse with the center belt.

"Just so y'all know, I ain't never had a license," Brock yelled from the driver's seat.

Rhonda and Leo looked at each other, then at Alphonse, who had generated a worried-looking face on his screen. Brock started the van and put it into gear. As he drove to the exit of the lot, he turned on the stereo. Old country music flooded the van. Brock punched the eject button on the CD player. "Fuck that shit!" he said as the disc slid from the stereo. He lowered his window, yanked the CD the rest of the way out of the dash, and whipped it into the street.

Rhonda giggled.

"First Walmart we pass, I'm stopping, and we're getting some real tunes. Where are we heading anyway?"

"7 to 87 South," said Frankie. "When we get to the Saratoga exit, I'll tell you how to get to my place. That's where the keys to

Taco Bell will be. After that, stay on 87 for, like, a million miles, and then get on 84 West for a while. I'll take over from there."

"Sounds good, lady," Brock said, zooming down the deserted city streets.

Streetlamps and traffic signals were still working in most places. At the first few red lights, Brock stopped or slowed out of habit, but after a while, he just blew right through them. He was getting a big kick out of it all. At a few stoplights, he rolled down his window and gave the middle finger to the traffic cameras, which may or may not have still been functional. Eventually, the novelty wore off, and everyone wanted him to keep the windows closed to keep out the chill.

The whole town was dead, and it was especially jarring for Leo and Frankie. Though Leo knew the state of the world and how diminished the population had become, things had still been relatively normal when he entered Walnut Ridge. Actually seeing the desolation, that was entirely different from just being aware of it. Somehow, the brisk, gray dawn made it easier to accept.

One thing that Leo hadn't expected was the number of animals already moving into the residential areas of the city and suburbs. Animals were not granted access to Caldo. From a logistical standpoint, it would have been nearly impossible to decant pets, wildlife, and livestock. Many people were devastated by this fact. All through the streets and alleys, Leo saw packs of formerly domestic dogs lying asleep in piles, flashing eyes of cats darting from the noise of the engine, apprehensive foxes curiously watching the van, skunks, raccoons, doves, pigeons, and some other dogs that might have been coyotes.

Before being decanted, some had elected to have their pets euthanized. A former lodger named Terry, who, out of the current Walnut Ridge lodgers, only Leo had known, had often spoken tearily of quickly killing all the cattle on his farm. Larger and larger packs of dogs and coyotes had been picking off his cows during the night, and he couldn't bear the thought of them dying in pain and fear after he was decanted.

Early on, before everyone realized that they either wanted to be decanted or would soon want to be decanted, a few groups of animal lovers bought or simply squatted on deserted farms. Others set up camp in warehouses or even college sports fields and offered to take in the pets of people who had been or would be decanted. They vowed they were not going anywhere and would love and take care of your pets. These massive animal shelters comforted people who felt guilty about leaving their pets behind on Earth. Eventually though, those running the shelters came around to the idea of Caldo, and the animals died off or ate each other or escaped into the wild.

Leo remembered feeding his neighbor Carl's cat after Carl was called up for decantation. The cat, a gray tabby named Bruce, had way too many toes and rolled around a lot. Leo liked him, but Bruce stopped coming around after a while. Leo felt a little sad about that. He still thought about Bruce sometimes.

Brock drove like a madman once he got onto the state routes. The roads were entirely clear, and, not having to worry about other drivers, he drifted across lanes at will. "This is how it ought to be, man," Brock said. "We shoulda had every lane be fifty feet across."

Leo agreed. He did not like driving. It was a stressful form of anonymous interaction, and he hated being entangled in other people's actions and mistakes. He wished he had his own lane to drive in—The Salmon-lane, where only his car was allowed and always had the right of way. It seemed that The Salmon-lane now existed and ran the world around.

For a while, everyone was fairly quiet, taking in the scenery of the ghost towns. At one point, Rhonda looked down at Alphonse. "Do you want me to hold you up so you can see out the window?" She paused, thinking of something. "Can you even see?"

"I can see," said Alphie's computer voice, "not in the way that I used to see or that you see now, but I can take in the way things look around me. So, no, you don't have to hold me up. I can see pretty much anything around the car outside."

"Freaky," said Frankie. "What else can you do?"

Alphonse displayed a winking face on his screen. "That's a secret," he said.

"Oh, come on," Frankie replied, smiling. "Tell me a little of what I have to look forward to as a goo-person."

"Don't let them push you around, Alph," Brock chimed in.

"Well," said Alphonse, "I can't exactly hear anymore, not like I used to. It's sort of the same thing as my sight. It's like, I get the sense and meaning of the words people are saying, and I can tell when they're saying them aloud or just thinking them, and so, I can participate in conversations."

"'Thinking them?'" asked Frankie. "Can you, like, read minds?"

Alphonse displayed a laughing face. "No, not like that, really. I can kind of infer how people are feeling to a certain extent. I'm also somehow connected to every other decanted human, so I can sometimes hear what they are thinking. It can be distracting."

Weird, Frankie thought but did not say. She wondered if her thought, though unspoken, got through to the man in the beaker. She thought momentarily, then asked, "So, why aren't you on one of the Arks?"

"I don't know," said Alphonse. "Something went wrong, but I don't think anyone knows what."

"Fuck," said Frankie. "I'm sorry."

Once again, they drove in silence. As the sun began to rise, the gray morning clouds burned away, giving way to the new purple sky. It would be a clear day.

Noticing something, Frankie spoke up. "Oh, here!" she said. "Pull off here."

Brock eased off the gas and turned onto the pull-off Frankie had indicated. It was barely more than two tire ruts leading off from a break in the guardrail. It took them a few hundred yards off the road and ended in a small, rocky clearing.

"This don't look like no Taco Bell I ever been to," said Brock, grinning.

"This is where I live," Frankie said. "Well, kind of. It's down that path a ways. I just need to run down and get my keys and shit. You guys can wait here. I'll be as quick as I can. Give me maybe twenty minutes."

"I'll come too!" said Rhonda, unbuckling herself and sliding the side door open.

"Oh, no, you don't have to," said Frankie.

"I really want to. I want to see where you live. Is it like a bomb shelter?" Rhonda was getting herself excited.

"I guess, kind of. Maybe," Frankie responded.

Rhonda giggled.

"Okay, let's go. We have to make this quick, though." Frankie said, sounding annoyed.

"We'll be back in a little bit!" Rhonda called to the men in the van. Then she and Frankie disappeared down a path through a barely visible break in the trees.

14.

Raphael floated high in the air, at least a mile from where the Walnut Ridge lodgers had parked for the moment. Before coming to Earth, the Angels devised a way for their vessels to manipulate the planet's gravity in such a way as to allow them flight. They also thought this would be handy in keeping with their winged angel aesthetic. Raphael took this opportunity to contact Walnut Ridge.

A call popped up on Miranda's tablet. She was in the midst of a group meeting with the remaining lodgers. Lois was sharing, so Miranda took the call but switched it to text input.

"They have stopped," came the message from Raphael.

"Are they okay?" Miranda replied.

"Yes. They have stopped at Frances's home."

"But nothing is wrong? They haven't done anything or picked up anything dangerous?"

"Not that I know of."

Miranda was annoyed by the interruption that had seemingly come for no reason. Lois was still talking about things that made no sense to anyone else, and George had already shared. There were only the ghosts left to speak if they wanted, and they always said more or less the same things.

"Should I bring them back?" Raphael added.

"No," typed Miranda. "We told them they could make stops, and they haven't done anything wrong. Leave them alone."

After a long while, the reply came. "OK."

Miranda went back to overseeing the meeting, after which she would meet one-on-one with George. George seemed quiet and withdrawn, which was sometimes a good thing to see in a lodger. In some cases, it meant they were nearing an emotional state that would allow them to accept a Promise. Though, it could just be George regretting his decision not to go to Taco Bell with the others. When Miranda snapped back to reality, Lois was still talking.

"I try to mail them, but the post office never gets the letters through. I'm hoping they'll come here soon if they're still around," Lois said. She seemed to be finished and started on her needlepoint again.

Having not heard most of what Lois had said, Miranda grasped for an appropriate reply. "If they haven't come yet, then I'm sure they've been decanted already. I know it can be hard not to have any visitors when you're in a strange place like this." That seemed an adequate response.

Lois smiled warmly at Miranda.

"Would anyone else like to share?" Miranda scanned the room.

No one did.

***

"This is so cool," said Rhonda. She watched Frankie flip open the door to her old home, which was a half-sheet of plywood painted and camouflaged with moss, dead leaves, and twigs to look like the forest floor.

"It gets old, trust me," Frankie said as she descended the steel steps into the darkness of the burrow.

Rhonda followed closely behind her. Frankie wished she hadn't. Frankie walked the few feet across the makeshift mudroom and began unsealing the heavy, iron door to the living quarters. She was glad that she hadn't locked the door before she went to check above ground. It was still effective despite being unlocked. It looked like something taken from a submarine, and it may have been. Frankie didn't really know much about the shelters that Grady built. She did know that, despite his being a total assbag, he took his work seriously. He'd tapped a line and some jury-rigged converter into the power running along the nearby highway without being caught or frying himself. There was a generator above ground, but she'd never had to use it during her years here.

Swiping her arm without looking, Frankie hit the switch and flooded the living area with cold fluorescent light. The room was sparsely decorated with splashes of color here and there. In the far corner was a twin bed similar to those at Walnut Ridge. The bed was made with dinosaur print children's sheets. Against the right-hand wall stood a small table with two plastic deck chairs. In the left corner was a tiny bathroom with a curtain for a door.

"This place is so far-out," said Rhonda. "You lived down here for two years?"

"At least," said Frankie. "I'd still be down here, too, if I hadn't gone up to make sure the world had actually ended." She paused and looked around the room. "Two fucking years. What a fucking dipshit." She chuckled to herself.

"Hey," Rhonda said, stepping over and placing a hand on Frankie's shoulder. "There was no way you could have known."

"What kind of person does that?" Frankie asked, her voice trembling slightly. "Just goes into an underground shed and spends two motherfucking years down there? What was I so fucking afraid of?"

Rhonda squeezed her shoulder reassuringly and stroked her arm.

"And you know what?" Frankie continued, "Standing here right now, there's a part of me that wants to say 'fuck it' and just stay underground here. As ridiculous as that is, as much as I hate it down here, I still feel like this is where I need to be. This is where I'm safe."

Suddenly, Rhonda leaned in and tried to kiss her on the mouth. Frankie turned away, and Rhonda got her on the jaw.

"Whoa, hey! That's, uh, that's not cool," Frankie said.

Rhonda eased away, giving her some space but maintaining an intimate distance. "No, it's fine," Rhonda reassured her. "It's okay, you and me, like this. I've been through some hard stuff, too. When I look at you, I can see a lot of myself. I think we can help each other."

She leaned in to kiss Frankie again, but Frankie stepped away.

"You don't even know me. Knock it off. That's not okay. I'm not into it. Not that there's anything wrong with it, or... shit!" She collected herself. "Listen, I'm sure that things are hard for you, and I appreciate your concern, but even if I was into you, I don't think it's very cool to prey on someone who's obviously confused and struggling."

"I thought I could comfort you and—" Rhonda paused. "Oh God! I'm such a fuck-up."

"It's not a big deal, okay? Let's just, let's just not worry about it. We're cool." *Please,* Frankie thought to herself. *Please, just don't start crying.*

Rhonda started crying. "I'm sorry," she said. "I'm sorry, I'm sorry. Oh, Christ! I fucked up."

"It's okay, really," Frankie said. She wasn't sure if it was actually okay, but she wanted the woman in front of her to stop crying and for their relationship to go back to one she felt mentally equipped to deal with right now. "It's a pretty day. We're going on a road trip. We're having a nice time."

"Just leave me," Rhonda said pathetically. "Just leave me here. One of the Angels will come by eventually and take me back to Walnut Ridge. I only came on this road trip to be with you, and you don't even like me. I just want to go back to my room."

"I like you, okay," Frankie said. "You're really friendly and nice, and you seem like a great person. It's just, I'm not—" she scrambled for something to say—something to diffuse the situation. "I like cock, okay? If you were a guy—if you had a big ol' swingin' dick, things might be different." She put her hands on Rhonda's shoulders. "You don't have a big ol' swingin' dick, do you?"

Rhonda smiled weakly despite her misery. "N-no."

"There's your dealbreaker." Frankie smiled. "Are you okay? Are we okay?"

"I guess so. I just"—Rhonda wiped her eyes and snorted— "I'm such a fuck-up."

"We all are."

Frankie went to the nightstand beside her small bed, where her key ring lay next to her desk lamp. It was a large metal hoop with dozens of keys, fobs, and lanyards dangling from it. She stood for a moment, trying to think if there was anything else she might need or want from this dungeon. She scanned the shelf where she kept her books and magazines and her TV stand lined with DVDs and tapes. She looked at her dresser and thought about the clothes she might want to wear. She didn't care much about any of them. She thought about the vibrator in the bottom drawer and thought it would be in bad taste to take that out after the conversation she'd just had with Rhonda. She laughed to herself, covering her mouth with a hand.

In the corner of a low bookshelf sat the battered box containing The Best of Vincent Price. She briefly considered grabbing it to take to Walnut Ridge, maybe watching a few of the tapes with some of the lodgers—with Leo. It was a big, clunky collection, though. Maybe she'd just take one of the tapes. But no, *Fuck this*, she thought, turning from the bookshelf. *Fuck all of it*. Seeing nothing else she wanted, she decided it was time to leave this hovel forever. "Let's go," she said to Rhonda.

Rhonda nodded and sniffed. They left the living area of Frankie's home and climbed back out into the forest. As Frankie was about to lay the plywood door back over the entrance to the shelter, she stopped and let it flop back down on the ground.

"I think I'll leave it open," she said. "Maybe it will make a nice home for a bear."

Frankie couldn't have known it then, but in a few weeks, a family of black bears would move into the shelter and use it as a spot to hibernate. In the process of nesting, they would knock over Frankie's dresser. While kneading and shredding the clothing in the drawers, one of the bears would turn on the vibrator. It would scare the entire family so badly that they would run out of their new cave and never return. All but one of the bears would die that winter. Frankie, who considered herself an animal lover, should have taken the vibrator with her.

Frankie and Rhonda walked back through the woods to the clearing where the van waited. Embarrassment and chilly breezes kept them from talking most of the way. When they came to the van, Frankie said, "I'm gonna sit in the back for a while." Rhonda said nothing and climbed into the passenger seat.

15.

"Is there time to create some kind of lasting, sustainable society for those who remain?" Meng Ji asked Haniel. "Is there some way we can leave the humans we're abandoning with the best possible chance for survival and prosperity?"

"Perhaps," said Haniel, thinking, "we can alter one of our ships and leave it here."

"Would that work?" asked the synthesized voice of the most intelligent person to have ever existed on Earth. "What would this achieve?"

"When we calculated the evolution of the human race, we anticipated them being much larger than they are now. As a result, when decanted, they take up less space than we imagined. Along with the reduced number of humans returning to Caldo with us, we should easily be able to spare one of our vessels. If nothing else, it could serve as a source of power for them. The power from one of the energy cells in a traveling vessel could run a small city for"—he paused to calculate—"three hundred and sixty years, perhaps?"

"You should start converting that ship into a useful power source as soon as possible," said Meng Ji. "I will assist you in the engineering aspects of this if you require help."

"Thank you," said the Angel. "I will start making the preparations. Where would you suggest we base this"—he searched for the correct Earth word—"colony?"

"I will ponder this. Somewhere comfortable, away from areas with high concentrations of documented disasters and weather incidents. A location conducive to farming would probably be ideal. Perhaps somewhere not too far from where we are now. Slightly to the south, maybe, to avoid the deadly cold. Of course, once they become self-sufficient, they will want to migrate."

"Certainly," said Haniel. The electronic components of his physical vessel were sending messages to other Angels. He was letting them know that some humans would regrettably be left behind but that there were plans in place to give them the most comfort and the best chance for indefinite survival. Some replies voiced concern about the decision to leave the planet before all humans were decanted, but most of the Angels were compliant with Haniel and the other higher-ranking beings in charge of the Earth mission.

"We should choose a location with an established and functional power grid," Meng Ji continued. "We can route the power from the donated ship into an existing power plant or series of power plants. I anticipate this being possible within a matter of days if enough workers are assigned to the job."

"I have already started the process," said Haniel. "I wish we had come to this realization earlier in our work. We could have begun preparations with plenty of time. Perhaps we could have constructed climate-controlled biospheres that would offer them a more agreeable existence.

"It is unfortunate, but we will make do."

***

Leo could sense the tension in the van after Frankie and Rhonda returned, but he said nothing. Brock seemed oblivious to it. If Alphonse noticed, and he probably did, given how he explained his altered senses earlier, he was keeping quiet like Leo. Brock was still driving and seemed to be enjoying himself behind the wheel. After a long period of silence, he started to sing.

"Downtown, hangin' with the hoodlums on the street, trying to get the chicks to give a damn," he sang. A synthesized voice chimed in tonelessly.

"Jivin' with the fellas, steppin' to the beat, gotta show 'em all just who I am," said Alphonse.

"Crazy niiiiiights," sang Brock.

"Ghetto boy," said Alphonse.

"Crazy tiiiiiime."

"Ghetto boy."

"You got yoooooours."

"Ghetto boy."

"I got miiiiiine."

"Ghetto boy."

"Haa!" said Brock. "Alph's a freak!"

"What on Earth was that?" said Leo.

"Reggie Webb!" Brock and Alphonse answered in perfect unison.

Brock's human voice came out thickly tinged with contempt at Leo's ignorance of the minor funk legend. Alphonse's tone was, of course, unchanged, but it still seemed wrought with disappointment to Leo.

"Who?" Leo asked.

"The man doesn't know his funk," Brock lamented, shaking his head. "Opened for Rick James in eighty-three."

"Oh," Leo said. "I never really listened to any of that."

"Can we get music on that phone?" asked Frankie, reaching for the cell phone Raphael had given her.

"I'm not sure," Leo said.

Frankie tapped and swiped the phone, raising it into the air and hoping to get some kind of signal. "Fuck," she said eventually. "Nothing. Oh well. We should be getting close to some kind of store soon, right? I can't even get GPS on this thing. Fucking cheapskates. All-mighty, hyper-intelligent robot-angel-aliens can't even give us a phone with Spotify."

"Um," said Rhonda. She pointed to a blue sign off the highway that showed businesses and attractions for an exit a few miles down the road. Among them was a sign for a Walmart.

"Nice," said Brock. "They ought to have some tapes left." Brock pretty much referred to any kind of music as "tapes," regardless of whether the music was on CD, vinyl, 8 truck, minidisc, et cetera. Within a few minutes, they had exited the highway and were making a highly illegal left-hand turn toward Walmart. Brock swerved the van all around the empty parking lot before pulling to a stop in the fire lane.

The lodgers stepped out of the van and approached the glass doors. It stood before them—a hulking gray and blue husk, still clean and brightly lit. To Leo, the place seemed to restlessly await its unexpected final customers before beginning the last leg of its descent into entropy. For a moment, he almost pitied the store, but then he remembered that Walmarts don't have feelings, and he felt embarrassed.

"How do we get in?" asked Leo.

"Let's try the front," said Brock, stepping to the automatic doors.

The doors didn't move. Brock slid his fingers between them and started prying them apart. Once the doors were separated, Leo and Brock each took a side and pulled them open.

"They left it unlocked," said Leo. "No reason not to, I guess."

"So, they would really just leave places like this open?" asked Frankie. "People weren't looting or rioting or causing shit the whole time since the Angels got here?"

"Not really, no," Leo said. "I guess it was kind of strange. They said half the planet was decanted within the first six months of the process. A lot of stores had to close since they had no employees or customers. Places like this, where you could get whatever you needed until you went to a PDF, they stayed open the longest. I guess the ones who were most likely to loot or cause trouble or whatever were mostly the same ones who got decanted first."

"That makes a strange kind of sense, I guess," Frankie said.

"Where I live," Rhonda said, looking at the ground, "the grocery stores just kind of started getting less and less stuff and running with fewer people until, one day, there was just no one left. They put a sign on the door saying to take what you need."

"Let's see what we got," said Brock. He walked inside the store.

The front of the store smelled of decay. The produce had all spoiled, aside from a few fruits that were engineered to last for a very long time. The potatoes smelled the worst. Some of them had fallen into the shadows under their display and had six-inch stalks growing from them. The lodgers quickly turned right and walked away from the grocery section.

The shelves and racks were not very full, but there was still a selection of clothes and shoes. Frankie stopped as they passed the women's clothing. "I want to see if there's anything good in here. I've been wearing the same tops for years."

"We should just go do what we want in here and meet back up in twenty minutes or so," said Alphonse, who was being held by Brock.

"That should work," said Frankie.

Brock and Alphonse started heading back toward the electronics section where the "tapes" were. Leo began wandering in the direction of the books and magazines by way of the men's clothing section. Rhonda locked up for a moment, trying to decide what to do. She wanted to look at clothes with Frankie, but she was too humiliated and angry and scared. Instead, she decided on the health and beauty section. She wasn't sure if there was anything interesting there, but she wanted to be alone for a few minutes.

On her way down to the other end of the store, Rhonda passed an aisle of tools and hardware. It occurred to her that she might be able to find a small heater here to use in her bathroom. She always got chilly when she was in there for a long time, especially after a shower. She turned down the aisle and scanned the shelves. There were flashlights, screwdrivers, picture hangers, and other things that were probably useful to other people. There was also a dispenser for rope by the foot. Rhonda stared at it for a while. At the end of the aisle was a display of utility knives, which she could not look at for very long before feeling sick and somewhat excited. She left the aisle without a heater.

Across the store, Leo was looking at the covers of books and periodicals. There were multiple shelves filled with copies of a book called *Violet Skies: Accepting the State of Our New World*. Clayton Murdoch, a former professional wrestler, according to the book's jacket, thought that it would be a good idea to capitalize on the arrival of the Angels by writing a book about coming to terms with the sudden changes on the planet. Leo vaguely recalled hearing of the book. It was published a week after the Angels' arrival, and it made a splash for a little while. Then people stopped talking about it. They stopped buying it, too. It seemed to Leo that not many people had trouble accepting the state of the new world.

Leo picked up a copy and read the dust cover. "Former professional wrestling champion turned motivational speaker Clayton Murdoch explores the hard questions facing humans in this tumultuous time of change. Who are these visitors? What do they want? Do they have our best interests at heart? Why is the sky purple? Hard questions require hard truths delivered by a hard man." There were also quotes from various media outlets. One credited to *The Camden Sun* read, "Murdoch asks the hard questions in order to put the rest of us at ease. Stellar!" Another from some publication called *Magnus* read, "A man with the experience of [Murdoch] is just the person to help open the minds of the skeptics."

Leo didn't recognize either of the publications responsible for the reviews, and he had never actually read Murdoch's book. Most people hadn't. Rumor spread that Murdoch wrote it in a matter of hours the night after the Angels arrived and that it was rushed to print as a cash grab. But after a few days, no one had much use for it. He scanned the magazines for anything that might be interesting time-killing material. All the issues were several months old now. One that stood out had a large, glossy photo of a ridiculously muscled man on the cover. It was *Magnus*, the publication quoted on Murdoch's book. Leo picked it up, not knowing exactly why he had done so. He also picked up some other random magazines.

Suddenly, over the store intercom came a booming voice. "GRUNDY! THERE'S A SALE IN THE JOCKSTRAP DEPARTMENT! GET YOURSELF SOME HALF-PRICED NUT HUGGERS!" This was followed by explosive giggling and a loud clunk as Brock hung up the intercom telephone. Leo, scared witless, had to laugh to himself. Brock was having a hell of a time today. Leo took this as a cue to head to the electronics section to meet up with Brock and Alphonse.

Within five minutes, everyone was back at the front of the store, where it smelled like sweat socks and old mushrooms. Frankie had a few items of clothing and a couple of bags filled with sodas, old snack cakes, and some other provisions. Brock had a handful of "tapes." Leo had his magazine in his left hand and Alphonse nestled in the crook of his right elbow. Rhonda seemed not to have found anything she needed.

Brock pointed to Leo's magazine with the large, shirtless man on the cover. "I didn't know they sold stroke-mags in Walmart," he said.

"Shut up," said Leo, smiling but embarrassed.

When they got to the van, the Walnut Ridge cell phone was ringing. Rhonda, her hands free, answered it. "Hello?"

"I was starting to wonder about you guys," said the voice of Miranda on the other end of the line. "I've been calling for ten minutes. Everything okay?"

"Yeah, it's fine. We just made a stop to get some CDs to listen to in the van. That's all."

"No trouble?"

Rhonda thought for a few seconds. She closed her eyes. "No trouble."

"Okay then," said Miranda. "I hope you're all having fun. I'll be calling again in a few hours to check in and remind you to take your meds."

"How's George?" Rhonda asked, but Miranda had already hung up. She was probably very busy.

Brock went to the driver's seat of the van. Apparently, he was still up for driving. Also, he wanted to be the DJ of the car ride. Once everyone was back in the car, Leo, Frankie, and Alphonse in the middle row of seats, and Rhonda in the passenger seat, Brock said, "Okay, first things first." He used a sharp thumbnail to cut the cellophane wrapper and sticker label of one of the CD cases, opened the case, and popped the CD into the van stereo. A second later, "Wanna Be Startin' Somethin'" began pumping through the speakers. Brock put the van in gear and swerved his way back through the parking lot, tapping his fingers to the beat.

16.

"I believe I have identified the anomaly," said the cabinet containing Meng Ji.

Haniel snapped out of his resting mode. He had turned off the physical functionality of his vessel while he communicated with the appropriate parties about bringing one of the Arks down to Earth and converting it into a living space and power source. He opened his mouth hinge and said, "Oh?" from his vocal speaker.

"Yes," said Meng Ji. "I have analyzed the decantation of Alphonse Stanley Hansen over forty thousand times with the assistance of the processing components of my cabinet. Using mathematical formulae and intuitive methods, I think I may have identified a possible cause for the error in his transition. It is"—she paused—"interesting, and I still have my doubts."

"What have you found?" asked Haniel.

"Please take this for the hypothesis that it is."

"Of course."

"I believe that at a crucial moment in his decantation, an element of Alphonse's mind was active. Some part of his subconscious mind had not been quieted. Perhaps he was dreaming."

"Yes," said Haniel. This was not an uncommon occurrence. During human decantation, an effort was made to shut down the brain as much as possible using sonic rhythms and variable air pressure. Most times, the brain was without any activity at the time that the consciousness and body were broken down, but occasionally, there was some residual brain activity—usually dreaming.

"I could find no evidence that the presence or nature of the thought had any effect on his process. However, the content of the thought may have been what caused the trouble. Mining the data we collected from his decantation, I was able to cross reference his thought content against the billions of other successful procedures. There was one thought that seemed to stand out—coming up consistently in the results of my testing."

"I trust your judgment and your tests," Haniel said, eager to hear Meng Ji's findings. He was certain that the problem could be identified and solved. He was certain that, given the pertinent information, he and his fellows could use the data to avert further tragedy on Earth and, hopefully, on other worlds as well. "What was your finding?"

There was silence for a moment. Then Meng Ji displayed an image on her screen. "This is what I found. Alphonse was thinking of this when his decantation went wrong. I don't understand its relevance, if there is any, and I can't attribute the errors to anything but this thought."

The image displayed on the screen was puzzling. It was a sideways watermelon. It appeared to have three large, black insect legs attached to either side of it. On the top of the watermelon was the head of a black, short-haired, domesticated cat. Written below the image were the words: "Michael Crabson."

Haniel leaned in, his blank eyes goggling at the screen. "This is—" he stopped, unable to figure out how to finish his sentence.

"This thought, this"—Meng Ji paused—"*thing* is, as a result of my best calculations, most likely the thought that Alphonse Hansen had which disrupted his decantation. The appearance of this thought pattern in his mind somehow caused the process to finalize incorrectly, leaving him unable to withstand the trip to Caldo."

After a long time, Haniel stood again and asked, "What is it?"

"Well," said the toneless voice of Meng Ji, "humans are complex creatures in terms of their neurological composition. Perhaps the complexity is not in the nature of their minds but in the imprecision. Human brains are ill-equipped to weather the barrage of stimuli they are subjected to, nor can they process the stimuli they create themselves. The thoughts of our race are typically fragmented and incomplete at best. My own thoughts, even in death, are frustratingly frayed and disjointed."

"And something like this," Haniel looked at the screen, hoping to find some answer there, "is normal?"

"It is by no means *abnormal*. There are thousands of thoughts shooting around in the human brain at any given moment. Most of them cannot be processed on a logical, emotional, or spiritual level, so they are ignored or disregarded. This, 'Michael Crabson,' whatever it is, was an unfortunate rarity. It is a good thing that no other humans have thought of it consciously or unconsciously."

"So, if anyone thinks of this thing during their decantation, they will be handicapped like Alphonse?"

"That is certainly a possibility. There are trillions upon trillions of possible thought processes that could run through a human brain at any moment. It could be that certain thoughts are incompatible with the decantation process. It is amazing that you were able to decant so many with no trouble."

"We were so unprepared," Haniel said, turning and pacing across the office. "We are not used to dealing with such unpredictable races. I almost regret coming here when we did. But we are too far along to turn back now. We must do our best and hope for no more unforeseen difficulties. Have you been able to make any progress on what is to be done with Alphonse?"

"Unfortunately, I have not. Obviously, he cannot be un-decanted. He is still a physical being in technical terms, so he cannot be loaded into the Ether-base or given a cybernetic vessel. The intermingling of the physical and incorporeal aspects of a human has a strange effect that I cannot fully understand. The decanted humans are hardy and efficient in ways that un-decanted humans are not. They resist disease, aging, and many physical traumas lethal to the human body. They are likely susceptible to extreme heat or cold, but..." she stopped speaking.

"Yes? Are you going to suggest we look into Raphael's system?" Haniel asked.

"I fear the integration of the physical and nonphysical elements of humans may have an unfortunate consequence. They now exist in a state between life and death as we understand them. If we were to attempt to end the life of a decanted human, we might not be able to retrieve its soul to load into the Ether-base. They are now linked in a way they were not before. I hypothesize that if we destroy the physical aspect of a decanted human, we also erase the spirit."

"Erase? Is that possible?"

"For all intents and purposes, I believe it is. At best, I think the soul would enter a realm unknown to us. That is too great a chance to take when the alternative would be the undoing of a sentient being at a spiritual level."

"That would be terrible," said Haniel. If his vessel had the capacity, it would have been shedding tears.

17.

Michael Jackson had most of the traveling lodgers feeling pretty good. *Thriller* had transitioned to *Bad*. Coincidentally, that was also the state to which Alphonse's mood had changed. He was connected to the Ether-base in a strange telepathic way, which typically meant there was a lot of chatter to ignore, but in the past hour or so, more consequential information had made its way into the base. Souls of highly intelligent dead humans were being tapped to help with the preparations for the colony where the Angels would leave the un-decanted humans. Because of this, the Ether-base was buzzing with new information that had not been divulged to the remaining humans on the planet. Perhaps the Angels, not knowing the depth of Alphonse's connection to the other decanted humans, hadn't anticipated him gaining this information.

Alphonse had gone very quiet, only speaking when spoken to. He felt grateful for his synthesized voice. If he had his old voice and intonations, everyone would have asked him what was wrong. He wasn't sure yet how to deal with the knowledge he had just gained or whether to tell his friends. He imagined the Angels would tell the remaining humans that they would be left behind at some point, but when?

The group was now on the interstate. Frankie had taken over as chauffeur after Brock, seemingly out of nowhere, had stopped enthusiastically singing along to the music on the stereo and announced that he needed to take a nap. He was now lying across the rear row of seats in the van, snoring. Leo had moved into the passenger seat after getting no reply when he offered the seat to Rhonda. Though the mood was still light, no one was saying very much.

Leo was paging through the *Magnus* magazine he had picked up at Walmart. It turned out to be an arm wrestling magazine full of interviews with professional arm wrestlers, photos of professional arm wrestlers, and photos and reports on professional arm wrestling competitions. Leo supposed Clayton Murdoch had some connection with the publication and used it to get a glowing review of his book. The magazine also had strange short stories, seemingly for added bulk. They had nothing to do with arm wrestling. One story included a character who had seventy arms, but he didn't use any of them to arm wrestle. The stories seemed kind of fun.

Looking out the window, Leo was starting to recognize the terrain. They were getting closer to the town where he had once lived. They would probably be there in an hour or so. The lack of traffic to slow them down or police to pull them over for speeding had them making better time than anyone had anticipated.

"Shit!" yelled Frankie. She hit the brakes hard and skidded to a stop.

With no other cars on the road, everyone had been zoning out in regard to the driving aspect of the trip. It had taken Frankie a few seconds to recognize that there was a herd of dairy cattle walking across the interstate.

"Jesus Christ! Where did those fucking cows come from?"

"Some farm, probably," Leo said.

"No shit," Frankie replied.

Rhonda let out a short giggle. Brock snored. Alphonse had thankfully been buckled into the seat with a lap belt, or he would have flown onto the burgundy-carpeted floor of the van. Frankie turned off the music.

"Is everyone okay?"

"Why'd you turn off the music?" Brock asked.

"Um, because we almost crashed, if you didn't notice," Frankie replied.

"Women drivers," Brock said before lapsing back into snores.

"Since we're stopped," Leo said, "I wouldn't mind stretching my legs for a minute. If that's okay."

Frankie put the van in park, and everyone but Brock and Alphonse got out. Leo walked across the road, looking into the fields that stretched off into the mountains. He avoided the cows. Cows made him nervous. Rhonda, however, walked right up to them and began petting and nuzzling as many of them as she could.

"Can you make them move?" asked Frankie.

"They'll move when they're ready to move," Rhonda said. Her voice was snippy and short. She was obviously enjoying her cow-nuzzling, so Frankie left her to it and walked over to where Leo stood.

"How's your magazine?" Frankie asked.

"Oh, it's," he said, realizing he was still holding it, "I don't know yet. It seems really stupid, but I guess I might like it."

"That's okay. It's fine to like stupid things. Cats are stupid, and I like them."

"Cats aren't stupid!" Leo said, surprised by his own indignance. He was thinking about Bruce, his neighbor's cat with too many toes.

Frankie laughed. "Can they do math?"

"Of course not. They're clever little things for what they are, though. Obviously, compared to a human, they're—"

"Stupid?" interrupted Frankie. She was smiling. It made Leo smile. Despite the chill, he broke into a nervous sweat and had to look away from her.

"I don't know," Leo said, turning again to the yellowed fields of grass and the purple sky. "I think they've got life figured out better than I ever have."

"Mmm," said Frankie. She wondered if Leo was truly as wishy-washy as he came across or if it was some kind of act.

Despite his fear of being nosey, Leo asked, "Did something happen between you and Rhonda?"

"Yeah," she said flatly. "I've been here for, like, two days, and people are starting to not like me already. It's just business as usual, I suppose. I'll tell you about it later on, maybe."

"*I* like you," Leo said without thinking. "I mean, I," he stammered. "You seem nice enough, and, I don't know..." Leo wanted to say something about how long it had been since he had gotten excited to see or talk to anyone the way he got excited around her. He wanted to tell her the things that he didn't understand himself. Instead, once more, he just said, "I like you." He followed it with, "Sorry."

Frankie chuckled humorlessly. "Just give it time," she said.

At around eleven thirty in the morning, Frankie pulled the Walnut Ridge van into the parking lot of Taco Bell. "Here we are," she said.

As soon as she put the van in park, a call came on the cell phone.

Leo answered it. "Hello?"

"Hello, Leonard," said Miranda. "How are you all doing?"

"We're doing well. We just pulled into Taco Bell."

"That's good. It's just about time for you all to take your lunchtime meds, okay? Can you make sure everyone gets that message?"

"Sure." Leo switched on the speakerphone.

"Now, is there anyone who needs to talk to me?" Miranda asked. "Anyone have any questions for me?"

Leo addressed the lodgers in the van. "Does anyone need to talk to Miranda?"

"How's George doing?" Rhonda asked. "I wonder if I should have stayed with him today."

"George is doing just fine. He's doing some more intense one-on-one sessions while the rest of you are away. I think we're making good progress."

"That's good," Rhonda said absently.

"All right, you kids," Miranda said. "We'll be checking on you again in a while. You all be careful. Don't eat anything spoiled, and don't burn yourselves or anything like that. We want you back here healthy and in one piece, okay?" She hung up before anyone could reply.

Everyone got out of the van, Rhonda holding Alphonse this time.

"We might as well try the front again," said Frankie. She walked up to the glass door and pulled the handle. It clunked in place, locked. "Oh well. I'll have to figure out which key opens the back door. If they did change the lock, I guess we'll just have to break in. At least the lights are on in there." A few dim lights were on in the dining area, which was a good sign. "I'll open up in back and come up to unlock the front door."

Frankie walked around the back of the building and went behind the fast food ordering speaker to a door with only a deadbolt and a metal handle. She pulled out her jangling key ring and started examining it. Whether it was some unconscious superstition or simply a penchant for hoarding, Frankie could never bring herself to get rid of old keys. Some of the keys seemed familiar. She tried one that felt the most "Taco Bell" to her. It didn't fit. With a sigh, she began flipping through the excessive collection of keys, attempting each one that could feasibly fit. Five minutes and thirty-three keys later, she found the match.

She opened the door and trotted into the building, motion-sensing lights flickering on above her. *That's new,* she thought. She went to where the keypad for the security system was when she worked there, and it was missing. Panicked, she whipped her head around, looking for where the keypad had been moved. She saw it attached to the frame of the door she had just entered, and she sprinted back to it, hoping there was still a thirty-second delay on the system. Also, she hoped that the code she was so sure would be the same, actually *was* the same one she remembered. If they had moved the keypad, there was a chance that they had also changed the code. No sense in worrying about that now. She'd know soon enough.

Frankie flipped down the plastic cover of the keypad and punched in the five-digit code she remembered. After a pause that felt like an hour, the digital screen read "CORRECT." Frankie let out a breath she hadn't realized she had been holding.

Walking to the front of the restaurant, Frankie noticed the kitchen looked much the same as when she'd worked there. She turned on the various cookers, heaters, and presses as she passed them, and she opened a faucet to let the water run in a three-bay sink. She flipped light switches and cranked dimmers on as she passed them on her way to the front. Opening the glass panel door, she said, "Go home, you hooligans! We're closed!"

Everyone came inside and took in the bizarre, colorful atmosphere.

"I think maybe I remember coming in here once," said Leo.

"You might have," said Frankie. "They've redone it a little since I worked here, but the kitchen's the same. Speaking of which, I could use a little help if anyone's willing. I can run the machines and cook everything, but I forgot how much set-up there is."

"I got you," said Brock. "I worked in kitchens before."

"Nice! Thanks, Brock."

For the next several minutes, Frankie and Brock buzzed around the kitchen, filling steam tables, opening valves, starting exhaust hoods, lighting pilots, and wiping dust off the surfaces of counters and flat-top cookers. As the machines heated up, the burning dust filled the kitchen with the smell of a baseboard heater clicking on during the first cold snap after a long summer.

"Now," Frankie said, "comes the important part." She went to the walk-in freezer. The temperature gauge read an impossible negative forty degrees. *Shit!* she thought. *Hopefully, it's just the gauge that's busted. Otherwise...* She opened the door, and a blast of frigid air billowed out.

"Thank God," she said to herself, switching the fans off as she looked around to see what was still in stock.

There were a few sealed bags of beef and chicken, enough to fill the stomachs of a handful of diners. Frankie pulled them out and set them in a tray to thaw.

She walked to the door of the large cooler and looked through the window. As anticipated, there were four or five containers of rotten lettuce and tomatoes. From what she could see, the containers did appear to be sealed and dated, though. Whoever had worked here last took their job much more seriously than Frankie had.

She walked to the dry goods shelf where garbage bags were kept, tore a handful from the roll, and went into the walk-in cooler. The smell was not as bad as she had feared, but it was decidedly not good. She tossed anything spoiled or questionable into a doubled garbage bag and ran it to the dumpster out back, holding her breath.

When she got back, she saw that Brock had most of the equipment to temperature and running smoothly. He was running water through any faucet he could find until it came out clean.

"Wanna give me a hand for a minute?" Frankie asked him.

The two of them went into the cooler, grabbed as much as they could of whatever they thought they might need—tortillas, sour cream, guacamole, bags of cheese, and dumped everything onto a counter near the line.

"Thanks," said Frankie. "Could you sift through some of these bags of cheese? They should be fine, but if any of it looks moldy or anything, just dump those parts and don't mention anything to Leo or Rhonda."

"Bet," said Brock.

Frankie and Brock set about getting everything ready as the rest of the lodgers found a nice table. Leo took a seat at a booth. Rhonda sat opposite him and placed Alphonse on the tabletop. Leo felt he should say something to Rhonda, who had been awfully quiet. He had never seen her quite like this. Normally, she was too bubbly for him to handle or so dramatically depressed that he didn't know what to say to her.

"Hey," Leo said, starting to sweat, "are you okay?"

"I'm fine," came the reply.

Leo knew better than to pursue the conversation. Thankfully, Rhonda changed the subject herself.

"Who decorates these places? What is this supposed to be?" She looked around at the walls, all of which were purple to about waist height, then orange above that. Abstract paintings hung here and there, seemingly meant to appear vaguely Aztec. The tables were a mixture of round and square, enameled in white or purple, surrounded by orange-painted metal chairs with purple upholstery. Separating the ordering counter from the dining room was a half wall topped with a metal plate with several chili-shaped holes cut from it.

"I'm really not sure," said Leo.

"And what is with the outside?"

"It looks kind of like a purple cube spaceship to me."

"Yeah," Rhonda said, staring out the window. I don't even know why I came. Taco Bell gives me indigestion."

"Right," said Leo, effectively disengaging from the conversation. He looked to Alphonse, whose screen read, *can we talk?* As Leo tried to think of some way to excuse both himself and Alphonse, Rhonda stood up and walked away, muttering to herself.

"What's up?" Leo asked Alphonse.

The sentence, *"I'm going to speak through text for a while."* appeared on Alphonse's screen.

"Okay," said Leo.

Remember how I said I'm connected to the other decanted humans?

"Yeah."

A few hours ago, I got some information. Some ghosts and decanted people are being tapped to give input on setting up a colony. The Angels are leaving some of us here.

"They what?" It was a stupid thing to say since Leo could simply reread the text on the screen.

In about seven days, the Angels are going to leave for Caldo. Anyone who isn't decanted by then is getting left here. I think I am too.

"They're just going to leave us!"

They don't want anyone to know. They think it will screw with people's Promises. They're probably right. I shouldn't have said anything, but I had to tell someone.

"Jesus! When are they going to let us know?"

I don't know. In the next couple of days, probably. They're trying to decant as many people as they can as fast as possible. That's why they're doing the more intense meetings and stuff. They're desperate. That's probably why they let us come out here. They're hoping it'll make some difference for those of us who have been here for so long. Knock something loose, maybe.

Leo sat silently, not sure of what to do with the information. "So, why are you telling me this?"

You seem like a level-headed, trustworthy person, and

As suddenly as it had scrolled onto the screen, the word *"and"* deleted itself.

"And? And what? Are you messing with me? Why did you stop typing?"

There was a pause before any text scrolled across Alphonse's screen again. *I was going to say that on the shortlist of people who they're fairly certain will not be decanted, you're at the top. Every time they've decanted someone somewhere in the world or reorganized the listing, Leo Salmon is always number one in the ranking.*

"So—" the words choked in Leo's throat. "So, I'm not getting decanted? They're leaving me here on Earth when they go off into space? They're just going to"—he struggled for strong enough words but only came up with—"fuck me?" Somehow, this all made sense. Somehow, Leo had never felt the switch in his heart flip from disbelief to trusting that he was actually a part of this whole thing.

I'm sorry to have things come out this way at a time like this. I just needed to say something. And I thought you should know what I inadvertently found out. There's still a chance that you'll get decanted in the next few days. The science of it is really sketchy, from what

I can tell. I don't know about me, though. They say something got fucked up. I can't make the trip this way.

Leo felt ashamed. He had forgotten about Alphonse's predicament. He was probably stuck on Earth, too, and without any kind of human body. "What about you?" Leo asked. "What have you found out? What are they saying?"

Not much. They don't seem to have any clue what to do about me. But maybe I just haven't heard anything yet.

"I bet they'll figure out how to get you ready to travel. It's probably some stupid error somewhere. Someone forgot to carry the one, or there's a decimal point in the wrong place."

Thanks. I don't think we should tell anyone else about this, Leo. Not yet.

"Okay. The Angels have to tell us soon. You said they're getting things ready, but, I mean, they can't just spring something like that on people."

I guess we'll see.

Brock came out from the kitchen, holding a sauce dispenser. He stretched out his arms and leaned over the order counter. "Petchoo! Petchoo!" he shouted.

Leo looked over at him, baffled.

"What the hell is that thing?" Leo asked about the metal contraption Brock was holding in his hands. It looked like a grease gun or one of those things you use to caulk a shower.

"It's my ray gun, man! Shoots guacamole," Brock said, smiling.

Leo stood up and went to see what Brock was talking about. He indeed had some kind of gun loaded with a cartridge of guacamole.

"Frankie kicked me out of the kitchen 'cause I kept playing with this thing."

"Shocking."

Brock started walking to the booth where Alphonse was. "Yo Alph. Where's Rhonda?"

Leo decided to see how Frankie was doing in the kitchen. She was standing by the back door, smoking. "Hard at work?" Leo said. He wondered if he had accidentally sounded like a dick instead of making a joke, but she laughed.

"That's how it is," she said. "Lots of hurry-up-and-wait. We're waiting on the beans right now. They have to soak for a while. Everything else is pretty much ready to go. I just have to keep everything warm until we're ready to eat. Shouldn't be too long." She tossed her half-smoked cigarette outside. "Eugh!"

"Not as good as you remembered?"

"These things are old as shit."

"George says that something about the detox meds they give us messes with how it feels to smoke. One of the Angels told him, I think."

"That figures." She coughed and spat an impressive gob out the door.

Leo winced.

"Not very ladylike, I know."

"I don't think your manager would approve," said Leo. "And if the health inspector happened to show up..."

Frankie smiled. "You know, when I first saw you, I thought you were a dink, but you're actually kind of funny sometimes."

"Thanks, I think."

Within a half hour, Frankie was heating tortillas, slathering nacho cheese sauce, tossing meat, shooting sour cream and guacamole out of a gun, spooning beans, corn, and salsa, and pressing wraps. Eventually, she had a pretty impressive spread of tacos, burritos, gorditas, Crunch-Wraps, quesadillas, Quesaritos, and chalupas. Leo, unfamiliar with the Taco Bell menu, was somewhat flabbergasted.

"You put a tortilla down, add cheese, then wrap that around *another* tortilla filled with meat and cheese?" he asked.

"That's a gordita, yup," Frankie replied. "You can do the same thing with meat instead of cheese, and it's a Double-Decker Taco."

"How do you remember all this stuff? How do you tell all these things apart? They're all just tortillas, meat, and cheese."

"You figure it out pretty quickly," she said. "Help me load all this on trays and bring it out."

They grabbed plastic trays and baskets and filled them with the array of fast food. As they brought them to the dining room, Frankie shouted, "Food's done! I hope there's enough because I'm not making more."

She and Leo set everything down at the booth in front of Brock, Rhonda, and Alphonse. Leo slid in next to Rhonda and surveyed the smorgasbord.

"What do you recommend?" he asked.

"You wanna go all in, you've got to do a Crunch-Wrap and a gordita, Grundy," Brock said, grabbing himself a gordita and a few tacos.

"I'm sorry to say," Frankie began, "that we don't have any fresh lettuce or tomatoes. But other than that, it's pretty authentic. The sour cream was still sealed and refrigerated, so I'm pretty sure it's fine."

Rhonda and Leo froze with their food inches from their open mouths. Their attention snapped to Brock, who was munching away enthusiastically without gagging or choking. Rhonda shrugged and took her first bite. Leo followed suit.

"This actually isn't bad," said Leo. "I mean, it is, but it's not."

"Exactly," said Frankie. "And, of course, just in case." She lifted a Walmart bag she had brought in with her and dumped it onto the table. Two bottles of Pepto-Bismol and a few containers of heartburn pills fell out.

"Thank God," said Rhonda as she reached out for the chewable heartburn tablets. She munched down three right away.

They were the only humans on the planet eating in a Taco Bell. They would likely be the last humans to ever eat in a Taco Bell. Leo thought about that. He thought about the fact that there were no other humans for hundreds of miles. He wondered how many people would be left on the planet when the Angels flew away—if any of the others around him now would be staying with him. They probably wouldn't be. Alphonse might remain, but no one else would. Leo would again be alone among strangers. He would get used to it.

Within twenty minutes, everyone had loaded up on as many different variations of beef, cheese, sauce, and tortillas as they could handle. Leo, ruminating on what Alphonse had told him, hadn't eaten as much as he thought he might. He picked up Alphonse, knowing that the decanted human was feeling the aura of his gray emotions.

Without speaking, in a sort of hive-mind decision, the lodgers slid from their booth and stretched. Grunting and groaning contentedly, they made their way out the front door, bellies full. The scents of chili powder, guacamole, and hot sauce hung in the air.

"So," said Brock, "What did you think, Grundy? Pretty good, yeah?"

"It really wasn't bad. Some of it I kind of liked. I'm glad I gave it a shot," Leo said, thinking to himself that virtually nothing profound in his past, present, or future would be in any way altered because of his consumption of food from this restaurant. It had been okay, though, and he had learned long ago that enthusiasm, even when false, made those around him seem happier.

"I knew you'd dig it, man."

Leo loaded Alphonse into the van and was about to assume his promised position in the driver's seat when he remembered they needed to refuel before heading out again. He walked around to the back of the van, where Frankie stood contemplating her cigarettes. Leo opened the rear hatch and pulled out one of the gas cans.

"If you're going to smoke, I'd appreciate if you could wait until I'm done gassing up the van. I don't think I want to burn to death today." For an instant, thinking of his likely future, Leo wondered if he did want to burn to death today. He didn't.

Frankie's eyes widened as Leo uncapped the gas can and extended the nozzle. "We should burn it down," she said.

"I'm sorry?"

"We should burn it down," she repeated.

"What should we burn down? And why?" Leo asked.

"The Taco Bell," Frankie said. She had a wildness in her eyes. "We should burn it the fuck down. Start a fire and watch it burn."

"Why on Earth would we do that?"

"Because we can," she said. "Because no one can stop us. We're the only people for miles and miles. No one's gonna get hurt. No one's gonna lose their job or their money. No one has to call the insurance company. No one's gonna miss this place. The planet's gonna be empty soon."

"Okay," Leo heard himself say.

"For real?" Frankie asked.

"I don't really want to, and I'm not sure we should, but I can't think of any good reasons not to."

"Leave a little gas when you're done fueling up," Frankie said, smiling.

Leo used up two and a half cans of gasoline, then handed Frankie the remaining can and a half. She ran back into the restaurant.

"Where's she going?" asked Rhonda.

"Maybe she forgot something," Brock responded.

"Why does she have a gas can?"

"She's going to start a fire," Leo chimed in, screwing the cap onto the van's gas tank.

"What?" squeaked Rhonda.

"Nice," said Brock.

Inside the restaurant, Frankie was splashing gasoline onto anything that would burn—upholstery, wood, countertops, plastic. She also opened the gas valves in the kitchen for good measure. She had pulled a bunch of the tables and chairs together, hoping they would start up and become a small bonfire when they got going. It was an imprecise science. As she exited the front door, which she propped open with a rock, she dribbled a little path of gas along the sidewalk. She continued the trail to where the van was parked.

"What are you doing?" asked Rhonda, a huge grin on her face, though her eyes were pink.

"You ever burn down a building?" asked Frankie.

Rhonda shook her head.

"You want to?" Frankie handed her a lighter. She did it partially as a way to mend fences and partially because she was unsure if she may have spilled gas onto her clothes and feared she would catch fire if she lit it herself.

Rhonda took the lighter and flicked it open. She clicked the flame on and put it to the wet spot on the ground. Fire zipped across the lot, into the cracked door of Taco Bell, and up the stack of furniture where it branched off along other trails Frankie had dribbled. The flare-up was small but satisfying. Rhonda giggled.

In the sky above, Raphael, the silent watcher, contacted Walnut Ridge with technology built into his mechanical vessel. It connected him to the phone lines at the PDF. He demanded to be connected with Haniel, and eventually, he was. Haniel was rather busy with the logistics of setting up a sustainable world for the humans who would be left on Earth and had little time for Raphael.

"Haniel," said Raphael, "they are starting fires!" He said this in an Earth language. They tended to work better through electronic devices than did their native tongue. He was speaking Italian, incidentally.

"Is anyone hurt? Are they safe?" asked Haniel in French.

"Everyone is safe and at a distance. They set a building on fire. What should I do?"

"Just make sure they all remain safe," Haniel said. He was becoming mentally exhausted from his work.

"But this kind of behavior is unacceptable!"

"I imagine it is an expression of catharsis and fun for them. If they remain safe and unharmed, I see no problem with this so long as they return to Walnut Ridge in the time allotted." Haniel paused. "Is there anything else?"

"Their readings," Raphael said, biting back his indignation, "they are erratic. Rhonda's especially. I am concerned for her psyche. She has a history of fragility. We should not have let her go on this trip."

"The mobile RFA device may not be as accurate as those here at the facility. Besides, the effect of *not* allowing her to accompany her friends may have been just as bad or worse than letting her go. Send me her readings thus far and keep watch."

"Yes, Haniel." He shut off the communication and began sending the reports of his readings to Walnut Ridge. As he watched the humans gazing at the fire growing inside the restaurant, he considered resigning from his position as an ambassador. He knew that this planet was an exception and not a rule. Even so, he was shocked to witness how off-the-rails a mission could go under specific, abnormal circumstances. Perhaps he was not cut out for this line of work. But he still had a passion for the cause.

18.

There was a modest "FWOOM" as the fire in Taco Bell met up with collecting natural gas Frankie had turned on in the kitchen. Though it was not a cinematic explosion, it was still enough to get everyone's attention. An alarm had been sounding for a while, but it was somewhat muted to the lodgers sitting in the van. While watching the would-be inferno crackle, the air had grown chilly, so they'd piled into the van where it was warmer. It was obviously much warmer inside the Taco Bell, but no one really wanted to go in there.

Brock had insisted that they put on music while watching the flames, and no one much minded. The soundtrack to the movie *Purple Rain* was playing when the FWOOM happened. Brock was singing along to "When Doves Cry" and didn't miss a note.

"Let's watch it for a little while longer," said Frankie.

"Sure," Leo said quietly, watching her watch the blaze.

Through the van windows, they stared at the burning building and watched the billowing smoke turn the mauve sky an ugly brown. It was early afternoon, and it would be dark when they returned to Walnut Ridge. Leo hoped someone else would be driving again by the time the sun went down. He was starting to get antsy about leaving but tried to calm himself by concentrating on his breathing. He did this sometimes. He'd heard from various sources that it was helpful. It kind of worked.

It was Alphonse who eventually said, "Should we get going?" There was a silent agreement that they should. Their freedom was wearing on them. As much fun as they were all having, as exciting as it had been to go out and explore and eat food that would no longer exist on the planet, then burn down a building, they all had the same unspoken desire. They all wanted, on some level, to get back to where the Angels were—to be in the undeniable aura that they emitted.

Leo started the van's engine and slowly pulled it out of the parking lot. He couldn't quite remember which way to turn out of the lot to get to the interstate, so he guessed. No one said anything. He assumed he had made the right decision. Eventually, he saw signs for Interstate 84 East.

The music of Prince and Michael Jackson, which had been invigorating in the opening hours of the journey, now felt somber. About sixty miles into their return journey, the Walnut Ridge phone rang. No one answered it for a few rings, and then Brock picked it up.

"Thank you for calling one nine hundred stiff rod," he said, cracking himself up despite his best efforts to keep a poker face. "Press one to talk to hot, hung, horny—"

"Hello, Brock," said Miranda. On the other end of the line, she was smiling as well, despite her own best efforts. "Have you all eaten yet?"

"Yes, ma'am," he said.

"Okay, you can probably all take your lunchtime meds if you haven't already."

"Sure thing," he said, then he put the phone next to one of the speakers and started singing along to "Remember the Time."

"Brock! Stay with me now," Miranda shouted into the phone, trying her best not to laugh as Brock crooned away. She liked Brock, even though he rarely took anything seriously. Perhaps because of that fact. "Brock!"

"I heard you," he said, returning the phone to his ear.

"Are you all having any trouble? Everyone okay? No one is getting sick from spoiled food or anything?"

"No, ma'am," Brock said. "We're on our way back now. I don't know if we're gonna be stopping anywhere or not. Gonna be dark when we get back."

"Okay, be careful. There are probably a lot more animals running around at night nowadays. Don't run into any deer or moose or anything."

Brock started singing along to Michael Jackson again, disregarding what she was saying.

"I'll call again in a few hours. Brock, behave!"

"Behave? Be hayve? I'm gonna be so hayve you won't even believe it!"

Miranda hung up the phone, and Brock stopped singing.

"Everything good?" asked Leo.

"Yeah, man," said Brock. "Miranda says we can take our vitamins anytime. She said to watch out for mooses and shit too. Keep your eyes on the road, Grundy."

"Mooses?" asked Leo.

"Meese?" said Frankie.

"Can we turn the music down a little?" Rhonda asked from where she lay across the backseat. After leaving Taco Bell, she'd claimed to have a bad headache.

"You sure you don't want me to sing you a lullaby?" Brock asked, leaning over the back of the middle row where he was sitting. He took a deep breath and began belting out the opening lines of Rick James's "Superfreak."

"I think I'll be okay without one. Thanks, though." Rhonda turned over in the seat.

After that, they drove for a long time without speaking. As dusk began to fall and the sky turned a deep burgundy, Brock offered to drive again as long as he could be DJ. Leo was relieved but also a little apprehensive. Brock had done well during the day but might have more trouble at night. Rhonda said she was feeling a little better, so they turned up the music again. She was still very quiet, but at least she was now willing to sit next to Frankie in the middle row of seats.

"Have you read any of these stories?" Frankie asked Leo.

"Which stories?" he replied from the passenger seat. He turned and saw her paging through the issue of *Magnus* he had taken from Walmart. "I don't really know why I took that thing. It was pretty dumb. I'm going to throw it away."

"Some of this stuff is really odd," she said. "None of this has to do with arm wrestling or weightlifting or anything like that. This one is, like, weird erotica."

"What?" asked Leo.

"It has this lady calling a repair company to fix her refrigerator. She opens the door when the repairman gets there, and it's some kind of crab monster, and they just, like, start fucking."

"That's... interesting."

"Yeah, it's, like, *really* detailed." She flipped a few pages ahead. "By the end, the woman seems to have turned into a crab, and the repairman is back to being a human. I think? Then they drive away together. The fridge doesn't even get fixed."

"Huh," said Leo. He wished they could stop talking about the bizarre periodical he had taken. He felt embarrassed now for having it.

"It looks like there are more stories in here than articles." Frankie continued thumbing through the magazine.

"I guess there isn't enough news and information about arm wrestling to fill a magazine every month," Leo responded.

"It's pretty funny," Frankie said, "I would have expected there to be more about rising up and resisting the 'alien-invaders' and all that shit in every possible article in any publication. Every mention of the Angels in here is all about coming to terms with the fact that it's probably for the best to just go along with them. Lots of ad space in here is just pro-Angel propaganda."

"That's how most of us felt then, and we still do."

"I guess." Frankie shrugged. "I guess I feel that way too."

Leo turned forward in the passenger seat. After a moment, he said, "Yeah." A wave of reality washed over him. Getting to know this girl, becoming her friend, figuring out how he felt about her, figuring out how best to talk with her, all of it was worthless. She would be decanted and gone in a matter of days, and Leo would be stuck here. The conversation wasn't worth the effort. It wasn't worth the stress and discomfort of being in her presence. The wave washed away, and within a minute, Leo's brain had calmed itself for the time being.

It was dark when the van pulled into the Walnut Ridge parking lot. Raphael had beaten the lodgers by about ten minutes and was waiting for them when they arrived. Slowly, Brock, Frankie, Leo, and Rhonda oozed out of the van doors, stretching and groaning. Leo was holding Alphonse, who couldn't have stretched even if he'd wanted to.

"Welcome back," Raphael said dryly. "Any issues?"

"Nah, man," said Brock. "'Bout halfway back, I had to pull off and drop a deuce in the woods. Nothing I haven't done before after some good eats. Leo's mag's missing a few pages now, though."

"Rhonda?" said Raphael, ignoring Brock's vulgarity.

"I'm fine," she said. "No trouble."

"The keys, please." Raphael was holding out his hand.

Brock plopped the keys into the cybernetic angel's palm.

"Have you all kept in touch with Miranda? Taken all your medications?" He knew they had, of course.

"Yup," said Frankie. "We were all good little boys and girls and, er, goops."

Alphonse displayed an appreciative winking face on his screen. Raphael led the lodgers into the elevator and back to the fourth floor. It was late enough that there were no more group meetings. Miranda was standing in the hall when the elevator doors opened.

"Welcome back," she said with a familiar exhaustion in her eyes. "I hope you're all doing well. There's some dinner in the rec room for you if you like. I think Lois is in there." She looked down at her tablet.

"Is George in there too?" asked Rhonda.

Miranda spoke without looking up from her tablet. "No, he's accepting his Promise."

"He is?" Rhonda squeaked.

"Oh shit," Brock added.

"He's," stammered Rhonda, "he's not, but he was here this morning, and—"

"We had a bit of a breakthrough today," Miranda said as the evening medication alarm sounded. "Come along. Time for meds. You can eat first if you'd like."

"What changed?" asked Rhonda.

"You know we can't always identify the needs of our lodgers. If we could, you'd all have been decanted within a week. He was here almost all alone, and during intensive therapy sessions, he was able to come to terms with what he needed."

"Wow," said Leo. He wondered if intense sessions would have him decanted in a matter of hours. Of course, they wouldn't. George had probably been way at the bottom of the list Alphonse had mentioned—the list that Leo topped—the Hopeless List.

"George!" Rhonda wailed, her eyes rosy and filled with water for the hundredth time today. "I didn't get a chance to say goodbye. I should have stayed here. I knew I shouldn't have gone."

It was good to see Rhonda's sadness again in its usual over-dramatic glory. Seeing her so down and subdued all day had been unnerving to Leo, Brock, and Alphonse.

"Rhonda," began Miranda, "if you had been here, there's a good chance George would have been distracted. He might not have been able to make the progress he made alone."

"I should have stayed here..." Rhonda repeated. She marched down to the nurse's station, sniffling and moaning.

"Is she okay?" asked Frankie.

"That's actually not abnormal for her," said Miranda. "It's how she works through things." Miranda tapped and swiped her tablet as she spoke. "Med time."

As everyone plodded to the nurse's station, Rhonda swept past and went into her room. She slammed the door, but it didn't latch and eased itself back open.

"She'll probably be fine," said Leo. "She's been much worse than this. She's not screaming at anyone or breaking things yet."

"She's like that?" asked Frankie. She remembered the smoldering self-reproach in Rhonda's eyes after their incident in the underground shelter.

"Yeah," said Brock.

Everyone got their medications and filtered into the rec room.

"Hello, kids," Lois said.

"Hey, Lo'," Brock replied. "You good?"

"Oh, I'm fine," she said, continuing her needlepoint. The design was unrecognizable—just a random array of stitches in different colors.

They ate their cold dinner of grilled cheese sandwiches and tomato soup. It was bland compared to their lunch, but it filled them up. After a quiet meal, the lodgers went back to their rooms.

"Should I check on Rhonda?" asked Frankie as she stood in the hallway.

"She might just need to be alone," Leo said.

"You're probably right."

Brock and Leo talked for a while in their room, lying in their beds.

"So, George is out of here," said Brock.

"The Promise might not work," offered Leo, but he thought it probably would.

"I guess so. It's weird, though. I started forgetting that we's all gonna be done with this shit sometime soon. You stay here for a while, and you just get used to it. Forget it's just a stop on the road to gettin' gooped."

"Yeah," said Leo.

"Who do you think's next?"

"I bet it's you," Leo mused.

Brock laughed. "Me? Nah. I'm a lifer, man." He was quiet for a moment. "I bet Frankie goes next. She seems like a short stay."

"Yeah, I bet you're right."

The two lay there for a while. At one point, Brock turned off the light. "Night, Grundy."

"Good night."

19.

No one was allowed to leave their room the next morning. This didn't keep Brock, Leo, and Frankie from peeking out of their doors and trying to communicate with each other. The big event was only a secret for about fifteen minutes. Brock and Leo had experienced this kind of thing before. Rhonda was dead.

Around nine in the morning, a technician, a nurse, and an Angel, Raphael, went to each of the remaining lodgers' rooms to take their vital signs and administer their medications. When breakfast was finally announced, the lodgers were led by Raphael down to the cafeteria.

"She killed herself?" Frankie asked in the elevator.

"I guess so," said Leo.

"Don't they watch? Don't they, like, monitor us and check in and stuff?"

"People get creative," said Brock. "Plus, we got a skeleton crew compared to what it used to be like around here."

"How did she do it?" Frankie asked Raphael.

"We do not like to discuss such things. It is not healthy."

"Fuck that!" Frankie snapped. "What happened?"

"I am not at liberty, nor do I care to discuss it," Raphael said disinterestedly. "However, we will be asking you that question a bit later."

"Us?" asked Leo.

"You were with her all day yesterday. It was not until after she returned from that trip that she killed herself. Perhaps something happened that precipitated the act?"

No one spoke as they walked out of the elevator. Miranda was not in the cafeteria during breakfast like normal. Though the

Angels instilled a sense of safety and warmth with their presence, Brock, Leo, and Frankie did not feel comfortable talking while they ate. Raphael stood near the lodgers, staring off, seemingly, at nothing.

After an awkward breakfast, it was time for group. Miranda decided not to skirt the subject on everyone's mind.

"So, we've lost Rhonda," she said. "She killed herself last night. She went into her bathroom and hanged herself with a pair of jeans. When we noticed she was not back in her bed after thirty minutes, we checked on her, but she was already gone."

Leo and Brock were nodding sadly.

"That's it? She just hung herself?" Frankie flailed her arms and let them slap against her chair's armrests. "She didn't say anything or write a note? Don't you pay more attention to us here?"

"It's happened a lot before," said Leo. "You can't always tell who will do it or when someone is going to do it."

"Are you the expert?" snipped Frankie.

"No," said Leo, hurt. "I've just seen a lot of people kill themselves since I've been here."

"The Angels believe in total freedom for people to make their choices," said Miranda. "It's a Commandment at Pre-Decantation Facilities across the world that there be no overt interference with the decisions of those to be decanted, so long as they do not bring excessive harm to others."

Frankie looked at Leo. "Is she for real? How many suicides have you had here?"

"We can't discuss those numbers. I'm sorry," said Miranda.

"How many have *you* seen?" Frankie asked Leo.

Leo looked to Miranda for some sort of cue—some clue as to how he was meant to answer this question. Her face was stone. It always was when this subject came up. "I've been here for over eight months," Leo said, "and I can remember"—he tried to do the math—"two hundred-something."

"They were dropping real fast for a while," added Brock.

"Jesus!" shouted Frankie. "This is like some kind of death camp!"

"Our suicide rate," said Miranda, "is not out of line with the baseline for the general population." This was a questionable statistic. "We do everything we can to discourage the act. We have personal counseling with living and deceased therapists and experts. Although we have breached the barrier between the living and the dead, we do everything we can to keep our lodgers alive and in good spirits."

"This is so fucked up," said Frankie.

"It is an unfortunate reality that some of the lodgers we take on have difficulty. They are impatient with their progress toward decantation, and they feel that crossing the boundary into death guarantees them quick and definitive access to Caldo via the Ether-base."

"And that just happens to make your job easier," said Frankie. "It's a terrible shame, and it should never happen. But if it does, oh fucking well, right? All's well that ends well."

"We've run seminars in the past," Miranda said, "we've had group lectures with the dead. Conferences in which ghosts discuss the transition from life to death for a human soul. We have pamphlets about it that you probably did not bother to read. Most transitions are painful and traumatizing. It can take years for the soul to become serene enough to begin re-assembling itself into something recognizable as a personality."

"So, pretty much like a warning label on a pack of cigarettes. There are consequences, but the consequences aren't really real until they happen, so why worry about it?"

"We successfully prevent over sixty percent of suicide attempts, and we take special care in the rehabilitation of those who attempt unsuccessfully. Sometimes, the act, successful or not, is what is required to facilitate the spiritual change necessary to accept a Promise. There has been more research about this than you could imagine. We are not just clawing in the dark."

"You're all okay with this? Really?"

"We do what we need to do, and we are quite good at it," Miranda said, tapping something into her tablet. "We'll be starting the group meeting now. It will be like the one we had two days ago—a topic of discussion on which everyone will share. Today's topic is how you feel about your life up to this point."

Before she could call on anyone, Alphonse indicated his desire to share with a flash of his screen. Miranda was somewhat surprised by this.

"Yes, please. Go ahead, Alphonse."

"I feel like it wasn't until recently that I realized how much I had enjoyed my life," he said through his voice synthesizer. "Being on this side of things—being decanted, I mean, I can choose to see all the events in my life from a different perspective. I've experienced many things that I would describe as good. I was married to a lovely woman. I traveled. Saw lots of live music. I had good jobs. I had some not-so-good things happen as well. I experienced pain and loss and confusion all throughout my life, despite how happy or content I was.

"I now have the choice to look at things less emotionally and break them all down into facts. My life was never good or bad. It just *was*. I couldn't have understood that before I was decanted, and I don't think I would have wanted to understand it. This new understanding, it would have made me sad in my old life. But I no longer feel sadness as I used to. There is grief inside me. There is fear over what is to come—fear about the uncertainty of my future. There is also happiness about the people I know and the beauty all around, but I can now choose whether or not I connect to it. The longer I remain decanted, the less I desire to connect to it all.

"What has happened to me becomes less relevant. What I think or want or feel is less important every day. I suppose that's all part of the process of being decanted, and I suppose that once admitted to Caldo, none of that matters anymore. The human condition no longer has relevance to me, yet I am still, somehow, human."

"Thank you, Alphonse," said Miranda. "Thank you for your honesty and vulnerability."

"I'll go," Frankie said as soon as Miranda finished.

"All right, Frances. Please go ahe—"

"How do I feel about my life to this point?" she interrupted. "Pretty shitty. It feels like everything has always just been an ocean of horseshit with a few islands of decency scattered around. People are always talking about having a better outlook and being positive. Why? I've never gotten to feel safe. How can I be positive when I'm always on guard? Mom made sure I never had a safe place to live.

"I don't even remember my dad. Stupid bastard got himself killed when I was only six. I'm sure you've got all this on file. You and your alien friends probably know more about me than I do."

"You may want to share some of this in a private session," said Miranda.

"Why?" asked Frankie. "Why have any secrets around here?" She pulled a cigarette from her pocket and lit it. No one told her to put it out. "You all want to know how Dad died? He and Mom used to go up onto the roof of the house, get high, and fuck. It was a pitched roof. One day, I guess things got a little crazy, and there went Dad, off the roof, pants around his ankles. Cracked his skull and bled to death on the sidewalk."

"Frances," said Miranda.

"Mom had another boyfriend over at the house two days later. Kinda makes you think. She always had different guys over after that—when she was around, anyway. Mostly, the neighbors just made sure I didn't starve to death. I guess that was well-intentioned. Mom and whoever she was fucking at the time ignored me when they weren't screaming or smacking me around or making me do some kind of sick shit.

"Few years later, I got the fuck out of there. I should have stayed. I'd probably be a ghost now, not caring about anything. I used to think that if Dad had lived, things would have been different. That's a load of bull, though. I know that now. I would have had to put up with the same kind of shit whether he was there or not.

"From then on, I just got with whoever I thought could give me what I needed. A place to stay, money, junk, fun, cock, whatever. I just thought that was what you were supposed to do. I'm an easy target, too, I guess. I thought I was playing everyone, but they could all read it on my face. They still can. Look at my face, and you'll see an easy mark—weak and stupid, always making the wrong decisions." Frankie was quiet for a while. But no one spoke.

"You know what?" Frankie asked. "Yesterday, Rhonda came on to me." She took a long drag on her cigarette. Miranda did not suggest Frankie stop sharing again. She was intently prodding at her tablet. "When we stopped at my old place, she told me how much she liked me and tried to kiss me. I shot her down, maybe too hard, or maybe she was just too weak to take it. Who fucking knows? I just know that she's dead today. If I let her go down on me back there, maybe she'd still be alive." Frankie dryly laughed the smoke out of her lungs. "Doesn't sound like too high a price to pay in retrospect.

"So, that's more or less how I feel about life up to this point. You get hurt, you hurt other people, and everyone dies in the end."

She stubbed out her cigarette. "Which, as it turns out, isn't as big a deal as I seem to think it is."

"I think we've made some good progress," said Miranda. "Thank you, Frances."

"I'm glad my driving a woman to suicide is a good thing for you."

Miranda ignored this last comment and moved on after tapping her screen for a while. "Would anyone like to share next?"

She looked around the room from Leo to Brock to the ghost vessel, which now contained only two spirits. Cody had been convinced to be loaded into the Ether-base the previous day. The other souls who had shared a body with him in life were generally happy that he had chosen to travel to Caldo. The ill will he had anticipated turned out to be nearly nonexistent. Even though this was a mandatory-sharing meeting, Miranda had been told that ghosts could pass if they wanted. The Angels had sent word that the non-decanted humans were a priority.

Sophie, one of the remaining ghosts, chimed in briefly about how she spent her life dedicated to the research of Earth and the life it contained. She reiterated her desire to stay on the planet until new life began, evolved, and flourished. Wapun, the Algonquian native who also inhabited the ghost vessel, did not speak.

After the electronically manufactured voice of Sophie finished, Brock spoke for a while. He had a relatively bright outlook on life despite his apparent bad luck. While speaking, he casually mentioned having been present during many disasters, both natural and manufactured. He had twice lost everything in hurricanes when he lived in New Orleans and Texas. He had attended five concerts where shootings broke out and spectators died. While briefly living in Los Angeles, he'd witnessed riots. He had been caught in the blast of the bomb at the Boston Marathon while watching a cousin compete. In New York, he attended a concert on September 11, 2001. He spoke plainly, as though most people experience these kinds of things all the time.

His thoughts on his life were generously peppered with graphic depictions of his sexual conquests. He spent much more time talking about those than the unlikely number of unfortunate events he had lived through. A handful of times, Miranda had to redirect him from his descriptions of the women he'd slept with back to the topic of the meeting.

Lois spoke at length, making no sense until suddenly breaking into a story about growing up far away and traveling for years and years. In what Leo found to be a touching moment of self-awareness, she mentioned that she "didn't use to be like this" and that she missed her family terribly. She also spoke of her hope to feel useful again one day—the way she felt when she was younger. Inevitably, she lapsed back into nonsense about dancing with lightning bolts and wandering in the "cold places."

Sharing last again was Leo. The typical fear and angst he had about speaking in the meeting were present but not as pronounced as usual, even with Frankie in the room. Knowing that this would all be over soon—that everyone would be decanted and gone and that he would still be here, on the blue and green planet, it relieved some kind of pressure.

"My life up to this point," Leo said, "has been fine." He thought for a moment. "I haven't really had to deal with a lot of hardship or poverty or loss or anything like that. It's been rather quiet on the outside, but I'm not sure I can remember any long periods of time when I ever felt comfortable. Any time things are going badly, I'm worrying about that. Any time things are going well, I'm worrying about why that is or when it will stop." He suddenly turned to Miranda and asked, "Do you have a favorite board game?"

"I, do I what?" she stammered.

"I guess I should ask it a different way," he said. "What is a board game you never liked to play?"

"Scrabble?" Miranda said tentatively.

"Perfect," Leo said, the words coming with unnatural ease. "I hate Scrabble too. The timer makes me anxious. Imagine someone who knows and loves you very much telling you that they bought you the perfect gift. Imagine opening that gift and finding that it's a brand-new edition of Scrabble. As a polite person with manners, you'd probably graciously thank them for the gift you hate. At the time, telling them how you feel about the gift seems inconsequential. It isn't worth hurting their feelings over your minor inconvenience."

Miranda stared quizzically, uncharacteristically ignoring her tablet.

"So, because this person is so happy about sharing this gift with you, your very own box of Scrabble, which is their favorite game, they want you to play with them right away. And you play. You do it because it's a small price to pay to keep them happy. You don't enjoy yourself, but the other person has a wonderful time. They want you to love Scrabble as much as they do. They get joy out of thinking they've given you a gift that pleases you as much as it would please them to receive.

"For years and years, you play Scrabble with this person, and they love it. You grow to dislike it more and more, but it's too painful to tell the person who gave it to you. Maybe you try to throw the game away in secret or hide it, but it is always found and brought back to you, and you play again. The person who gave it to you explains all about how great it is and how you can get better at it and enjoy it even more." Leo's hands dropped between his knees, and he sighed a humorless laugh.

"Eventually, they see that you don't like it, they call you on it, and you have to admit that you've always hated Scrabble. Now you're miserable about Scrabble, and they are heartbroken. You try everything you can to learn to love the game, but it doesn't work. You just aren't the type of person who likes that kind of board game.

"Now the person who gave you the gift feels awful about the fact that you never shared their enthusiasm for the game they gave you. They feel they've done you wrong, and you feel bad for making them feel that way. They are sad and resentful that you held the truth in for so long, and you feel terrible for not being able to like what they and so many others enjoy. Maybe there's something wrong with you because you just don't like Scrabble."

Leo shifted in his chair. He wanted to feel the hot pinpricks of tears emerging from the corners of his eyes but did not. He wanted to sense a weight being lifted from him. He wanted to feel a catharsis for what he had said in his obtuse analogy, but he felt, pretty much, the same as he had ten minutes ago. "That," he said to Miranda, "is how I feel about my life up to this point."

20.

As the day progressed, Leo felt as though it was taking place in some kind of funnel of distorted time. Some spans of minutes dragged on for days, while others seemed to race by without regard for the generally agreed-upon laws of time and temporality. Leo went to a few group sessions that seemed to last somewhere between twelve seconds and nine hours. He felt as though he'd observed them from outside of himself. During afternoon med call, he didn't even notice the extra pill in his cup. The same pill was also added to Frankie's. The news of his impending abandonment, in addition to Rhonda's unexpected suicide, had rattled loose a few bearings. They were now banging and echoing loudly in the typically empty, steel-lined chasm within him.

Leo had only one session of one-on-one therapy. It seemed Brock and Frankie were getting more. They probably were. They probably still had a hope of being decanted and taken to paradise. Sometime in what must have been the evening, Frankie came into Leo's room while Brock was in a session. Leo was sitting on his bed, wondering if time was passing. It was.

"Hey," said Frankie. She was standing in the doorway.

"Oh," said Leo. "Hi. How are you?"

"Not great. But I guess I feel about as safe here as I could anywhere, so that's something." The room was silent for a while. "I liked what you said this morning at the meeting."

"You did?" Leo asked. "I figured it must have sounded pretty stupid to everyone else. I'm not even sure why I said it. Maybe I saw the board games in the corner of the room and..." he trailed off.

"Well, I thought it was an interesting take. I'd never really thought about things that way before."

"I'm not surprised. You probably shouldn't think about things that way. It was just a dumb thought that came into my head and—"

"Jesus!" snapped Frankie. "I'm trying to tell you that you said something thought-provoking, and I related to it. Can't you just accept that? This isn't some kind of argument." She sighed deeply and turned her head away. "Can I come in?"

"Sure," Leo said, scooting over to make room for her to sit on the bed. "I guess I'm just surprised that you could relate at all to anything I said. Your life sounds like it's just been full of all kinds of, I don't know—bad stuff. My life has been about as good as anyone could ask for. Logically, I know that, but I still can't seem to, I don't know, tap into much appreciation for it, if that makes any sense. I guess I'm just—"

Frankie sat on the mattress and cut him off. His constant self-deprecation annoyed her. "I think it's easy for people to say they're supposed to be happy because they have things that other people don't or that they've had an easier time of things, but I'm not sure that's reality. For people like me, it's easy to say that if this had happened or if that hadn't happened, things would be different, and life would be easy. It's like we feel like we have a license to blame our unhappiness on the people who fucked us over or to blame ourselves. There's always someone to blame.

"But when I see you—when I hear you talk about things like hating Scrabble, it makes me feel like maybe where I am is where I'm meant to be, and I'd be here no matter what did or didn't happen over all the years. Maybe I would be a different person if I had a different life, but then again, maybe I wouldn't. It's possible that some of us just have something inside of us that makes us miserable fucks, regardless. I get a strange comfort out of that." She sat for a minute, silent. "I guess it doesn't really matter anymore, huh? Everyone gets a happy ending now."

Leo wanted to say something about how soon the Angels were leaving and all the people who would be left behind, but he didn't. He'd told Alphonse he wouldn't say anything, and what would be the point anyway? To cause panic? To bring everyone down? Instead, Leo just said, "Yeah."

"How well did you know Rhonda?" Frankie asked, staring at the floor.

"She's been here for about three or four months, I guess. I don't know her very well." Leo stopped. "Didn't know her," he corrected. "Shit."

Lavender moonlight was starting its slow crawl across the floor.

"I only started to get to know her the past few weeks when the numbers here started dwindling. I had seen her and had group with her in the past, but I don't really make much of an effort to get to know people around here."

"Oh, right," Frankie said. "I guess you wouldn't. I hear that most people are in and out of here pretty quick."

"Most of the time, yeah. Lois and I are the record holders, as far as I know. When there were only about thirty of us left, they consolidated us onto this floor. That was when I started to know Rhonda better. She was moody—usually pretty bubbly, but sometimes she would go off with these crying fits like last night. She and George were fairly close, I think. I didn't talk to her too much. I guess I don't talk to most people too much.

"I don't know anything about what she was like before. She had those scars, so she must have, you know, tried to off herself at some point. She never talked about kids, but she had a husband who got decanted early on, I guess."

"She did?" Frankie asked, surprised.

"Yeah," Leo said, thinking, "I guess it wouldn't have seemed that way to you." He laughed and immediately thought he shouldn't have, but Frankie was smiling. "People with spouses that get decanted tend to go pretty quick from what I've seen. Aside from Rhonda, everyone who was here when you got here was single."

"How about you? You ever been married?" she asked.

"Not me."

"No long-term relationships?"

Leo felt himself blushing, though he wasn't sure why. "Not for a while. I was with this girl for a few years, but that was a long time ago."

"Why did you break up?"

"She realized after a while that I was a miserable, unmotivated lump of wet clay," said Leo.

Laughter overtook Frankie's entire body.

"I couldn't convince her I wasn't because I totally agreed with her." Now Leo was starting to laugh.

"How did you even get this girl?" Frankie said, smiling.

"I don't know," said Leo, giggling at his own ineptitude. "She asked me out one time, and I kind of just went with it for a few years. Is that not normal?"

The two sat laughing for a few minutes until Brock came in.

"Oh shit, am I interrupting something?" he said, wall-eyed, with a toothy grin.

"Oh, shut up, Brock," said Frankie, still laughing.

"Wish I came in a minute later. I might have seen a little something," he said with slightly more charm than sleaze. "They want you in the group room for another session in a couple minutes."

"Me?" asked Leo.

"Nah. Frankie."

"Oh." Leo supposed he still held some sliver of hope for himself. Otherwise, the prospect of another session wouldn't have had any appeal.

Frankie sighed. "Okay, I'll be right there." She turned to Leo again. "Thanks for the laugh. I hope you have a good night."

She stood and walked out of the room. Leo lay down in his bed as Brock crossed the room to sit on his own mattress. Leo tried not to look at Brock, knowing he would see a beady-eyed, gap-toothed mug leering back at him. When Leo finally did look at Brock, he was, indeed, leering.

"What?" asked Leo.

"Thanks for the laugh," Brock said in a high-pitched, mocking voice. "I hope you have a good niiiiiight." For emphasis, Brock lay on his mattress and began a sophomoric vocal imitation of the female orgasm.

Leo found himself both amused and mildly horrified at the performance.

"Man, it's not like that!" Leo's indignation couldn't break through his smile. "We barely even know each other. Not everyone bangs within five minutes of meeting each other."

"Maybe that's what's wrong with this world. It always worked for me, and ol' Brock always got a smile on his face."

"It *always* worked for you?"

"Yeah, man. Clap burnt me a few times, but that ain't nothing. Things got a little spooky for a while with the AIDS thing, but I'm always careful. Never had no trouble I couldn't deal with."

"Hm," said Leo. There was a perverse logic to Brock's madness sometimes.

"I'm just a little surprised, is all. Here I am, thinking she ain't into dudes, then I hear about how she shot down poor Rhonda"—he kissed his hand and blew it toward the sky—"and see her all up in your shit. I gotta admit, my radar was a little off the mark."

"She wasn't 'all up in my shit,' Brock," said Leo. "We were just talking. That's all."

"She thirsty," Brock said. "And you're a jar of sweet tea."

Frankie was in her session through the evening med call, and there were no more group sessions for the day. One of the nurses had found an old stereo, so Leo, Brock, and Alphonse sat in the rec room, listening to the "tapes" they found at Walmart. Brock enjoyed himself, and Leo tried to do the same, but things still just felt unnatural. Alphonse was placed with his screen facing Leo, but Brock could not see it. At one point during the music, he flashed his screen to get Leo's attention, then a message scrolled into view.

They loaded Rhonda into the Ether-base, read the text. A minute later, more words appeared. *She's screaming.*

Everyone knew about "The Screaming." The videos and lectures about death that Miranda had told Frankie about earlier were very up front about the period between physical death and the state in which a soul is commonly referred to as a ghost. After the Angels arrived, experts, i.e., every deceased human in history, disclosed that there is a time of intense fear, confusion, and pain separating the two planes of existence. It sometimes lasts only minutes and is mild, but more commonly, it takes days or weeks, spiking erratically in intensity.

Although The Screaming was now common knowledge, it was still unpleasant to hear about someone you knew having to endure it. There was a general rule among ghosts that if they were to contact the living, which they occasionally did, they would not make mention of The Screaming. However, when the Angels came and the whole dynamic of life and death changed, it became necessary to be more transparent about it.

Hours later, Leo was lying awake in his bed. His homework lay on the nightstand next to him, blank. He had not started it. It no longer seemed necessary, but he still felt guilty about not doing it. He listened to the light snoring coming from the lump under the sheets in the next bed. The lump was bathed in long bands of lilac moonlight.

Part of what was keeping him up was the fact that he had an erection. No twinges in his loins for months, then suddenly, twice in one week. He thought about what Brock had said about Frankie, but Brock was wrong. Leo was certain she didn't think of him that way. He considered taking care of the hard-on himself but felt strange about Brock sleeping only feet away. He wondered if Brock had ever masturbated while Leo was sleeping. Then he did his best to stop wondering.

He decided to combat his insomnia and inexplicable arousal with one of his late-night walks up and down the hallway. He rose and padded down the corridor, turning at the corner where the nurse's station was. The lights were on there, and he waved vaguely to the night tech. The techs were used to Leo's occasional strolls on sleepless nights. When he reached the double doors sealing this wing from the next, he turned around and slid his feet back to the nurse's station. He repeated this several times before returning to his room.

Walking through the doorway to his bedroom, he was surprised to see a lump under the sheets of his own bed. The lump was Frankie, and she put her finger to her lips in a shushing motion. As quietly as possible, she slid herself off the mattress and walked to Leo.

"You were gone for so long I decided to lie down," she whispered. "Come on." She took Leo's hand and led him back down the hallway to her own identical bedroom. The two stood in the darkness for a bit as Frankie fidgeted with her shirt hem. As Leo opened his mouth to ask what this was about, she spoke. "I don't really know," she started but stopped, looking at the floor. "I know this is weird, but like... I just," she stopped again, closing her eyes. "Can we fuck?"

"I," Leo said, flabbergasted. "For real?"

"Yeah," she said. Then she leaned in and kissed him.

Leo let her take the lead as the librarian in his mind dusted off the card catalog and searched for the long-unused entries on sex.

They ended up on the uncomfortable mattress, and Frankie started undressing. Leo decided that was a good idea, so he did the same.

Apprehensively, Leo put his hand out to touch Frankie before asking, "May I?"

She smiled. "You may. That is part of how it usually goes."

For a while, Leo lay there, enjoying the sound it made when his hand ran across her bare skin. He felt the open air on his penis. It felt nice. Then he felt Frankie's hand on his penis, which felt nice too. After a little work, Leo was ready, and Frankie climbed on top of him.

At first, the sensation of being penetrated brought up mixed emotions for Frankie, but she had always been fairly good at mentally separating the pleasant encounters from the unpleasant. This one was turning out to be quite pleasant. Leo was a milquetoast, which was a good change of pace for her.

Seeing Frankie's nude form atop him, Leo became aware of his own outward appearance. It was the first time in years he'd thought of his naked body in anything but a clinical sense. Sparse, dark hair ran up his soft stomach, spreading across his chest, which he noted was not as tight as it had been the last time he'd been in a similar predicament. There was acne on his thighs, which he hoped didn't show in the room's dimness. Though few humans had anyone to impress anymore, Leo was certain he was too hairy in the wrong places and not hairy enough in the right places. He wished he'd had a chance to trim. He also wished he'd started doing some push-ups or sit-ups or something when he came to Walnut Ridge. He hadn't, though, and his body was what it was. His decision to try not to care about it too much was aided by Frankie's warmth.

Leo watched the pale, naked woman rock and bounce on top of him. His gaze swept down her body, from her face, scratched up and asymmetrical from losing fights, to her breasts, hanging low, having had no one to impress for years, to her belly, soft, and her legs, which Leo now saw had parallel lines of scar tissue on the inner thighs. He reached down and ran his fingers across the healed-over lacerations that faded as they progressed toward her knees. His touch was neither accusatory nor morbid. It was purely inquisitive and genuine. Frankie took his hands and moved them from her scars to her breasts.

He spent a while enjoying the feel of her soft skin, squeezing here and there. At one point, Frankie leaned down on him, and they embraced, pressing their bodies together. Leo looked up to the ceiling and saw the Rhythmic Feedback Analyzer panel mounted there. It was highly polished, and in its reflection, he saw two smoky ghosts writhing in each others' embrace. Leo wanted to watch them, but it felt rude to do so.

They made love for a long time, Leo finding himself unable to finish. When he realized he was taking too long and ought to finish up, he started to get stressed out, which made it harder for him to finish, and so on. Eventually, they wound up nestled like spoons in Frankie's bed, gently rubbing against each other. After a while, Leo slid out of her.

"I'm sorry," he said. He felt ashamed. This woman had given him something so nice, and he had been unable to show how much he appreciated it.

"Don't be," she replied, tucking his arm between her breasts, hugging it there. "I liked it a lot."

"So did I. Thank you."

"*Thank you*?"

"It's been a while," Leo said.

"Tell me about it," Frankie said. "About two years for me. Longer than that, since it was anything I enjoyed this much. How long is 'a while' for you?"

Leo flushed, considered lying, and then told the truth. "Five years. Well, almost six, I guess." He waited for a crass or mocking reply.

"You've been keeping that thing to yourself for six years?" she said coyly. "That's a crime, Leonard."

He knew she was trying to make him feel better, so despite himself, he let himself feel better. "If I had known the world was going to be pretty much over so soon, I would have tried harder to share it." He said this, knowing it was a lie. Relationships stressed him out, and he didn't have enough charm to be a womanizer.

"I guess there would have been a lot more fucking going on if everyone knew fucking was going to be discontinued soon," Frankie said. The word "soon" rang in Leo's head, and he spoke before he could stop himself.

"I'm not supposed to say this," he began, "but Alphonse told me about some information he picked up from being connected to the Ether-base. You know, the big ghost computer. He says that, that the Angels are planning to leave Earth in less than a week. That's why everything's so different around here the past few days. Not that you would know, I guess."

Frankie didn't respond.

"Shit, I'm sorry. I shouldn't have said anything. Alphonse told me not to tell, and I should have just listened to him."

"I think I already knew," she said.

"You did?"

"Not specifically," she clarified. "Not for any reason or anything. I think that I just, on some level, I knew that it was close to the end. When they told me about how long this had all been going on by the time I got here, I knew I had somehow missed out."

"It doesn't mean you'll get left behind. There's still time for you to get a Promise and everything."

"I don't think so," Frankie said. "I was really angry at Grady, the asshole who convinced me to stay underground for so long, even after he was fucking dead. But I'm not angry anymore. I think that no matter where I was or what I did, I'd still be right here right now. I'd still be left behind." She turned around and looked at Leo. "Don't you kind of feel that way?"

Leo didn't say anything. He didn't need to.

"But who knows?" Frankie continued. "We might both get decanted first thing tomorrow morning." She kissed Leo on the cheek, and neither of them said anything for the rest of the night.

They slept there, arms draped over each other on a mattress barely large enough for one person. Leo dreamt about some kind of squid-creature wrapping its tentacles around him. There was only blackness and the feeling of tentacles engulfing his naked body — molesting him. He awoke with a gasp, ejaculating into the sheets. His fear broke away into annoyance. A wet dream, on this, of all nights.

He attempted to remove Frankie's hand from his hip without waking her. He intended to go to the bathroom and get some paper towels to clean up after his tardy orgasm. He checked to make sure Frankie was still sleeping. As he moved her arm, he noticed her face was exactly as it had been the last time he saw her in this bed—eyes wide open, staring blankly at nothing. Leo couldn't know, but the information he gave her was transmitting to an alien race half a universe away.

21.

Panic spread aboard the Strappon transport vessel. The new data was being analyzed over and over again. If the rectangles were to have any chance of catching their quarry, they needed to embark immediately. Travelers had to leave all possessions behind and board the ship as fast as Strapponly possible.

The remainder of the dawdling populace was "gently encouraged" to board more quickly or to make their peace with their imminent abandonment and eventual Octacontaheptagonless demise. Officials impatiently hurried the straggling quadrilaterals onto the ship. Much chaos, prodding, and argument later, the entirety of the Strappon race was loaded into their respective quadrants of the transport vessel. They had made great time, though there was much confusion, hurt feelings, and several minor injuries.

The ship drifted away from the planet where the Strappons had evolved from theoretical points into line segments and, eventually, full rectangles. Prior to this, very few of them had ever left the surface of their planet. They all knew what they needed to do, though. Any fear they had was irrelevant. The moment for which they'd waited eons had come.

The Strappon travel gateway opened in anticipation of all the Strappons. The rectangles braced themselves as they entered, and space began to warp around them. It was an unpleasant method of travel, but there was simply no other way to make the trip in time. Theoretically, the Strappons were prepared for the effects of the gateway, but few could have anticipated what the experience would be like in practice.

They just had to endure it until they were spat out of the other end of the gate, which was located near Uranus in Earth's system.

From there, they could resume typical spatial travel. It felt like an eternity.

***

"Do you always sleep with your eyes open?" Leo asked Frankie while they were getting meds the morning after their night together.

"Not that I'm aware of," she replied. "Were my eyes open last night?"

"Yeah, for a long time. It was kind of freaky."

"Well, maybe I only did it last night. You can't just assume I do it all the time."

"But the other night—" Leo immediately stopped talking.

"The other night? What do you mean?"

"Nothing. I misspoke." *Nice fucking job,* he thought.

"No, what about the other night? What are you talking about?"

Leo sighed. "Sometimes I walk around the halls at night when I can't sleep. The first night you stayed here, I was walking around, and I"—he paused—"I looked into your room."

Frankie laughed. "Oh my God! You're a fucking creepster!"

"It's not like that!" protested Leo.

"Maybe I do sleep with my eyes open. They tend to be sore as fuck in the morning. Maybe they're drying out at night."

Lois was being led from her room by a nurse tech who she was calling "Grinkle." Some mornings she needed assistance getting her meds and her blood pressure taken. As the tech named Beth, not Grinkle, tiredly strapped the cuff on Lois's arm, Brock emerged from the room he shared with Leo and shouted down the hallway.

"Grundy! Where you been?" He started walking up to the nurse's station.

"You guys could have your own rooms, you know," Frankie said. "It's not like there's no space."

"I know," said Leo. "I kind of like having a roommate. I think Brock likes it too."

"Aw."

Brock sauntered up to the med counter and turned to Frankie and Leo. "I got up to take my four a.m. leak, and you were gone, man. You out walking around again?"

"No, I was," Leo stammered, flushing. "I mean, yeah. I was just walking around."

Frankie laughed at Leo's discomfort.

"Wait a minute," Brock said, his grin growing larger than ought to have been possible. "Wait. A. Minute. You were just walking around? How come you two got each other's socks on, then?"

Leo and Frankie both looked down. It was true. They were each wearing one of Leo's gray socks and one of Frankie's white socks. Frankie laughed even harder.

"Grundy! You animal!" Brock shouted, slapping Leo on the shoulder.

"You all seem rather chipper this morning," said Miranda as she approached the lodgers from down the hall. She was carrying Alphonse in the crook of her left arm.

"Grundy got lai—" Brock began.

"A good night of sleep!" interrupted Leo. "We all did. All nice and rested up." It was not technically against the rules to fraternize or have romantic relationships with other lodgers at Pre-Decantation Facilities, but Leo wished to keep this particular tryst private for his own sake.

"That's... good then," said Miranda, raising an eyebrow. She handed Alphonse to Frankie, who took him with only slight hesitation. "Let's go. It's time for breakfast. Has everyone had their vitals checked and taken their medications?" She often asked this, even though the information was always on her tablet and her tablet was always in her hand.

"Yes," everyone said in unison. They followed Miranda to the elevator and down to the cafeteria. Breakfast was much less tense without Raphael looming over the table. The meal was French toast, so Leo passed and just had a bowl of generic Rice Krispies.

"You don't like French toast?" asked Frankie.

"No, I never have. It's a texture thing." He had, of course, never eaten French toast, but this was his go-to lie for avoiding conversations in which people would try to convince him that his life was somehow incomplete without French toast.

"I'm that way with tomatoes," Frankie said. "I don't mind the taste, but the way they feel in my mouth is just icky."

"You know," Leo said, "what I just said before was pretty much a lie. I'm sorry. It's not a texture thing. It's a thing about how it's made. I've never had French toast before, but thinking about dunking the bread in the slimy, eggy, milky slop just turns my stomach. I know it's dumb." He wasn't sure why he was going down this road again. It was always the same. He would now be quizzed about why he never had the guts to try it or told that he needed to open his mind to new things.

"Oh, I can see that," Frankie said. "The process is kind of gross, yeah."

Leo waited for more, but there was none. That was the end of it. She had simply accepted his strange French toast quirk. He felt validated and satisfied somehow. This was, in a way, more meaningful to him than when Frankie had said she related to what he shared in the group meeting—more meaningful than when they had made love the night before.

"Y'all are weird," said Brock. "I eat anything and everything. 'Specially when it's free." He shoveled an entire slice of French toast into his mouth.

Brock's interruption provided a much-needed distraction for Leo, whose mind was struggling to process the now-undeniable fact that he felt closer to Frankie in a matter of days than he had felt to anyone else for several years. Derailing conversations was one of Brock's strong points, and Leo found himself thankful for that.

"Alphie knows what's up, don't you?" Brock said through a mouthful of bread, butter, and syrup.

The screen on Alphonse's jar briefly displayed a thumbs-up image. Typically, he probably would have chimed in with some kind of quip, but he was understandably preoccupied. Leo wondered if he should tell Alphonse that Frankie knew about the impending departure date. It occurred to him that Brock was the only one who didn't know. Sophie and Wapun, the ghosts, probably had the same kind of connection to the Ether-base as Alphonse. They might have known about it earlier and kept their mouth, or rather their speaker, shut. The Angels would have to make their announcement in the next day or so.

When everyone finished, Leo dumped all the trays and brought them to the drop-off counter. On the rear wall of the kitchen, near the dishwasher, there was a picture taped to the wall. It had been there the entire time Leo had been at Walnut Ridge. It was a black and white photo of the character Lurch from *The Addams Family*. Leo had never known why it was there or what significance it held. He'd always wanted to ask about it but never did. Realizing he may only have a few chances left, he called out to Reggie, the breakfast cook, who was washing dishes in the pot sink.

"Reggie!" Leo yelled over the sound of the running water.

"Yeah?" asked the cook.

"Is that a photo of Lurch from *The Addams Family* back there?"

Reggie turned and looked at the picture. "Yeah."

Leo had hoped that Reggie would have inferred that he wanted to know why the picture was there, but he didn't bite. "Why do you have a picture of Lurch back there?"

Reggie smiled at Leo and said, "Lurch be sweatin'." This was the end of the conversation.

With breakfast finished, everyone returned to the fourth floor to wait for the morning group meeting to begin. Miranda and Doug, the janitor and next closest thing to a psychologist left at Walnut Ridge, walked into the group meeting room.

"Okay, gang," Miranda said, "You're meeting with Doug today."

"Aw, man," Brock said. "No offense, dude. It's just that Miranda got nicer legs."

"No offense taken. It's true," said Doug walking to the head of the table.

"Frankie, you're with me," said Miranda.

"Again?" Frankie asked.

"Yes, again. You can come to the next group meeting. We want to do another one-on-one session with you this morning."

"Okay," Frankie turned to the group as she stood. "See you all later, I guess." Leo waved to her as she walked off with Miranda. Three meetings and two meals later, Frankie had not yet returned. After a dinner of hot dogs, Leo finally mustered up the courage to ask Miranda about her.

"Um, Miranda?" Leo asked. Miranda was in her tiny office, and Leo felt bad about disturbing her.

"Yes, Leonard?"

"Sorry to bother you. Is Frankie still in a session?"

"Let's see," she said, swiping at her tablet a few times. "Frances is"—she squinted at something on her screen—"about five hours into her Promise."

"Promise!" blurted Leo. "She, she was just in a session before. She's already getting a Promise?"

"Yes, and by the looks of things, she ought to be finished sooner than later."

"This just feels so... sudden."

"You've seen how these things go, Leonard. You've been here long enough to know that sometimes things pop up, and the time is right. She's made tremendous progress in the time she's been here, and she seems to have had some kind of breakthrough since yesterday."

"Right. Thanks." So that was it. Leo left the office and walked back to his room. He lay on the bed, staring at his reflection on the Rhythmic Feedback Analyzer mounted to the ceiling. He felt stupid and vaguely used. It was a bad idea to speak with Frankie the way he had. He regretted sleeping with her and allowing himself to form a real connection. At the same time, if that was what was needed for her to take her Promise, then it was, of course, worth it. But it didn't feel that way.

But maybe it was like she had said last night. Maybe it was fate that she was meeting with Angels and taking her Promise right now. In that case, she'd be in the same spot regardless of whether or not she even met Leo. Leo turned over in bed to avoid his reflection.

If that was the case—if fate played some role, it was stupid to start getting attached. He felt like she was sure to be decanted, but the emaciated, naive child within him still held hope that he and Frankie might end up some of the last people on Earth and that they would spend time together learning and figuring out the new world. That is not how it would go, though.

Even if she didn't get decanted, after the Angels left, everything would have changed. Leo was certain. They would drift apart, she drifting from him, and he letting her. She would make it on her own as she always had, and he, in turn, would do the same in his own way. Perhaps this was better—like pulling the bandage off in one quick motion. It seemed to Leo that he always ended up on his own, and usually, it was his own fault. Frankie taking her Promise was fast and definitive. It was entirely out of his hands. It spared him the pain of the journey.

***

"Progress on the colony is ahead of schedule," Meng Ji said to Haniel and Raphael. "Your ship has been grounded, and conversions are being made to connect it to several power grids in an area south of our current location. The colony will be integrated into an area near where your lodgers traveled not long ago—Cindervale, Pennsylvania, USA. There is adequate infrastructure. The reports from the past hundred years indicate low instances of severe weather events such as hurricanes and tornadoes, and occasional blizzards and ice storms seem a fair trade-off in that regard. It is in close proximity to rich farmlands and hunting grounds. There are hospitals, schools, gathering centers, shelters, gymnasiums, and hundreds of homes and other dwellings in place to house those left behind. Given our current situation and labor allotment, it is the best we can do."

"This all sounds like excellent news," said Haniel. "How are the numbers coming on decantations worldwide?"

"Progress is much better than expected," said the synthesized voice of Meng Ji. Her cabinet's screen listed statistics from all reporting PDFs across the world. "The heightened intensity of group sessions and the increased amount of one-on-one meetings seems to have had the desired effect thus far."

Haniel's eyes, which were, in reality, just visual sensors, took in the data that Meng Ji scrolled across her screen. "It seems," he said, "that in facilities where transparency is implemented, the amount of physical decantations is slightly lower."

"Yes. When lodgers in facilities employing transparency about the impending deadline hear that there is a limited amount of time for them to be decanted, fear and anxiety have a negative effect on their progress. I think it was wise to keep the number of transparent facilities low."

134

"Indeed. I think it was a necessary, though unfortunate, experiment. We must know what variables we can introduce to hasten the process."

"If I may," said Raphael, who had been silent to this point, "I would like to point out the fact that the transparent facilities still have a great success rate in terms of *total population conversion.*"

"Yes," said Haniel. "The suicide rates are up among those scared that they will not be decanted in time. This is, at best, an irrelevant statistic." There would have been a tone of warning in his voice had it been organic and not artificial.

"The humans killing themselves are all being successfully loaded into the Ether-base. We will take them to Caldo. That is our mission," stated Raphael.

"They are all screaming," said Meng Ji. "You are unable to understand the totality of the human condition. Your race does not experience life and death in the same way that ours does. I realize this. But I must implore you to trust the billions of departed souls when we say the transition is unbearably painful."

"Rhonda was one of those who were not on track for quick decantation," said Raphael. "She attempted several Promises, and none of them were successful. She is now prepared to travel to paradise because she has the wherewithal to see the larger picture as I do."

"Protocol does not allow for actions on our part which directly lead to the death of potential travelers," said Haniel. "You can take this up with the council if you feel the need to press the issue. If it were ever discovered that an ambassador had anything to do with the death of a potential traveler, it could be catastrophic for that ambassador." Haniel paused. "Do you understand me, Raphael?"

"I believe the council would side with the ambassador in that unprecedented and highly improbable scenario," Raphael said.

The two angelic simulacra gazed at each other in silence.

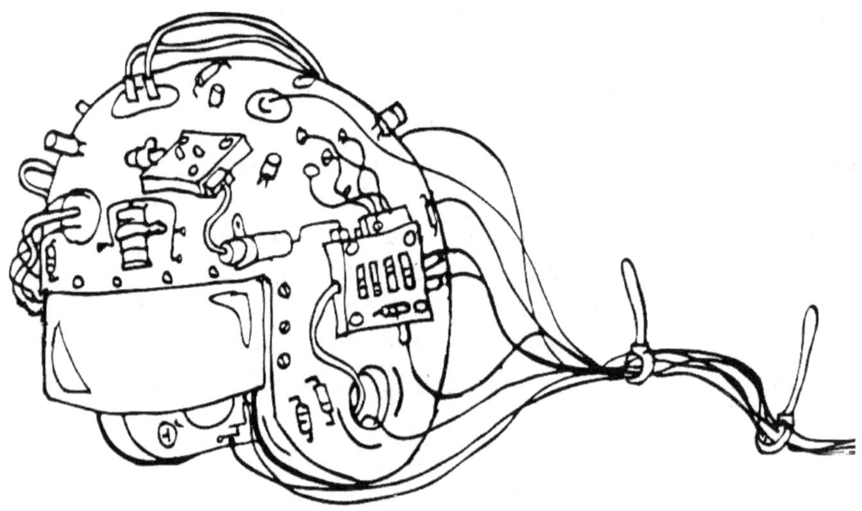

22.

Frankie had accepted her Promise, and two days passed with little change. Leo spent hours in sessions, sometimes in a group with Brock and Lois, other times alone with Miranda or Doug or an Angel. Alphonse tried his best to keep Leo in the loop with what he learned from the Ether-base. He passed along the information that there would be a colony for the remaining humans somewhere in or around Cindervale. Leo was baffled by the news.

"Cindervale?" he asked Alphonse.

Brock was in session, so Leo spoke freely to Alphonse, who was sitting on Leo's nightstand. Alphonse responded with text scrolls.

Yes, that's what they are saying.

"So that's the new cradle of life, huh? A depressed, old, mining town. I guess I was expecting something more exotic." Leo was more or less fine with the colony being in a town where he used to live. It meant less adjustment, which meant less discomfort. He supposed that was good.

A lot of this just seems slapped together. They weren't expecting to have to leave anyone here. I know it's selfish, but I'm glad I won't be the only one

"Yeah, that sounds like it would be awful." In reality, there were times that Leo felt like it might be nice to be the only self-aware being on the planet. He thought about being a mass of blue goop in a jar and watching the seasons change year in and year out, observing as the leaves turned and fell and small animals scrounged for food. He imagined being buried in a snowstorm and waiting for the spring sun to free him. It all sounded like something he might be able to get used to.

In their talks the days following, Alphonse had been unable to tell Leo much more. The decanted man said that the amount of chatter going on regarding the new colony was making it harder to pick any single thoughts or strings of information out of the flow. He knew only two days remained before the Angels would leave the planet, but not much else.

It was at morning group that an announcement was finally made. Haniel entered the group meeting room, ducking his head as he came through the doorway. Though he and his brethren had missed the mark on the idyllic angel look, he was still an impressive presence.

"Lodgers of Walnut Ridge," he said through his vocal speaker, "I am afraid I have some unfortunate news for you. Due to safety concerns for ourselves and the people of Earth, both living and dead, decanted and corporeal, we must leave your planet within the next two days."

Everyone was silent. Miranda was staring at the linoleum floor tiles.

"You have all worked tirelessly and put in as much effort as anyone could expect in your journey toward decantation, yet you remain un-decanted. I take full responsibility for this failure.

"In all the time that I have served as an ambassador, I have never seen a group of beings with such strong will—such devotion to their bodies and their planet on a molecular level. Yours are truly constitutions of iron. It was pure arrogance on the part of myself and my colleagues to assume that we could so easily dislodge even those willing to join us from their ingrained bonds."

As the Angel spoke, Leo looked around at the others in the room. Brock was staring skeptically at Haniel, or, at least one of his eyes was. Lois was smiling politely at the surreal creature.

"I would like to think," continued Haniel, "that those of you who remain in your bodies, on your world, will find a bliss more profound than we could have offered you in Caldo. I like to think that it is *you* who could offer *us* the secrets to all the questions of meaning in our universe—*you* who have truly demonstrated that you are worthy of more than Caldo could ever have provided you.

"A colony has been built not far from here. It will serve as a place for you proud, remaining few to build a fellowship that will blossom into a new society. We have taken great pains to ensure that as the world atrophies into darkness, you will have all your needs met and many of your comforts seen to. There is limitless electricity for you to use—electricity that will supply power to the scores of freezers filled with meats and other foods we've provided and to the ovens in your homes needed to cook it. Thousands of acres of fertile farmland are waiting to be sown with the crops of your choice..."

The speech went on and on like this. Leo began to zone out, knowing that he should be paying attention, if not for his own sake, then for the sake of posterity. These were the words ushering in the new state of the world—a eulogy for modern civilization. Leo wished the large robot would wrap it up soon.

When Leo's ears reactivated some time later, Haniel seemed to be finishing up.

"And so, this evening, provided you have not accepted a Promise by that point, you will all be transported to the colony in Cindervale. You will each be given the opportunity to accept a Promise today, regardless of whether our data indicates that you are ready or not. It would pain us immensely if we were to leave any possibility of your joining us, no matter how remote, unexplored. I wish you all the best of luck. I am happy to take any questions you may have."

For a while, no one spoke, then Brock tentatively raised his hand.

"Mr. Leigh, yes," said Haniel.

"So," began Brock, "you just leavin' us here?"

After Miranda clarified everything to Brock, Haniel again took questions. There was only one more. Lois asked him if he knew how many puppies there were. He said he didn't know but might be able to find out for her. She looked at the alien vessel blankly, seeming to have forgotten that she had asked him a question.

Leo kind of wanted to ask how many other humans would be left behind at the colony. He decided not to ask. He figured that whatever the number was, it would seem too many, yet could never be enough. He was also afraid Haniel had already mentioned this during his speech at a point when Leo had not been listening. That would make Leo seem dumb or disrespectful, so he stayed quiet. He figured he would eventually find the answers.

The group meeting split into solo sessions—Brock going with Miranda, Leo going with Doug, and Lois being taken with Haniel to meet with another Angel. Doug tried a few different methods to get some progress out of Leo. He tried a tough-love, no-nonsense approach to try to shake Leo out of his apparent ambivalence, but it didn't work very well. After that, Doug attempted to get Leo to open up about some kind of hidden trauma that might be holding him back, but there was none. Eventually, they just ended up talking about what life in the colony might be like. In typical fashion, all the questions Leo should have asked at the end of Haniel's speech but didn't think of came to him now.

"How are we all going to communicate there?" Leo asked. "I only speak English."

"Well, when the Angels came here, they brought technology with them that could translate Earth languages into something they could understand and vice-versa. I imagine they're engineering something to work as a translator. Some of their technology is amazing. Some of it is garbage."

"Really?" Leo asked.

"Yeah, that's why Miranda uses that old tablet computer instead of some super-advanced alien hologram thingy. That's why the robots they load the ghosts into are so big and clunky. They don't show this in any of the videos or literature or anything, but the insides of their ships look like something from the fifties."

"Really?" Leo asked again. He wished he had asked differently and felt dumb.

"I was in one of those ships one time, and I guess I will be again soon. Anyway, it's really dark, and there are these huge cables running all over the place and giant computers that use vacuum tubes and punch cards and stuff. All the monitors are black and white, and they just show blips and sweeps and junk. It's like old submarine radar from a movie."

"And they fly through space like that?"

"I guess they've never had any trouble," Doug said. "They've been doing this forever. They must have just gotten to a point where they were able to do what they needed and stopped advancing."

As the session ended, Leo and Doug knew they had made no headway. They walked out of Leo's room and down to the hallway, where Leo would line up for lunch. Doug continued to the end of the hall, and as he passed the door to Miranda's office, it swung open. Brock stepped out and began walking down the hall toward Leo.

Though the meeting with Haniel had left him in poor spirits, he was grinning now, humming something to himself. A moment later, Miranda came out of the office. Her hair, which had been severely parted and twisted into a tight bun in the morning meeting, was now hanging in a loose ponytail. She looked flushed, and she kept adjusting her skirt. One of her boots was half-unzipped.

"'Sup, Grundy?" Brock asked as he walked up to Leo.

Leo simply raised an eyebrow at him, and they both started laughing. Lois was still in her session as Brock and Leo were led by Miranda to the cafeteria for lunch, giggling the whole way.

After lunch, Brock and Leo were taken to separate wings of Walnut Ridge to meet with Angels specializing in Promises.

"See you later, Grundy," Brock said as he walked to the elevator at one end of the facility.

"See you later, Brock," replied Leo, walking to the other elevator.

Leo was taken to a large, third-floor office space in which all the normal office furniture had been pushed against the walls. In place of desks and chairs, cushions and bean bag chairs dotted the linoleum. The overhead fluorescent lights were off. Lamps with colored bulbs subtly lit the room, and the scent of incense hung in the air. There was stereo equipment, an old tube television, computers, children's toys, and a hookah strewn about the floor. It looked like the playroom of a compound run by hippies. An Angel sat at the far end of the room near a bank of monitors attached to a massive computer cabinet. This must have been technology that the Angels brought with them.

"Welcome, Leonard," said the Angel. "I am Penemue. I shall be attempting to make you a Promise today. Is this your first attempt?"

"Yes," said Leo. He was balling and unballing his toes inside his socks.

"Come and make yourself comfortable,"

This Angel was smaller than the rest, just over six feet tall by the looks of it, though it was kneeling. Leo silently debated whether the bodies of these angelic androids were fully humanoid or if the parts covered by their flowing robes were unfinished. Were they simply a skeletal mass of rods and wires underneath the velvety fabric?

Leo sat on a cushion facing Penemue. He wondered if this was where Frankie had sat a few days prior. What had her Promise been like? A discussion? A virtual scenario? Those were the most common kinds, according to the literature that Leo had read.

"Are you well rested? Fully sated? Do you need food or drink?" asked the Angel, Penemue.

"No," said Leo. "I think I'm good."

"Would you like to talk about something before we begin?"

"I don't... know," Leo said.

"Let us sit in silence for a while," said the Angel. It closed the segmented lids over its blank eyes.

"Should I close my eyes too?"

"If you wish."

Leo closed his eyes, then opened them again. They sat in silence for a long time. Leo distracted himself, trying to place the odor in the room. It was familiar, but he could not remember where he had smelled it. It might have been the scent of a childhood friend's home.

After a while, Penemue asked, "Would you like to breathe with me?"

"Okay," Leo said.

The robot began mimicking human breathing, raising its torso on its abdomen and broadening its robed shoulders while playing a pre-recorded sound bite of a person inhaling through their nose. It then lowered its torso again and played another sound clip of exhalation. Leo thought it sounded like Darth Vader doing yoga, but he breathed along with the sounds and closed his eyes again. Despite the weirdness of the whole situation, he did start to feel himself relax slightly.

He was unsure how much time had passed when he decided to open his eyes again. His vision was hazy, and when his eyes focused, he saw that the Angel had also opened its eyes.

"Would you like to tell me about yourself? I'd be happy to hear about you and know you more."

"Sure, um," started Leo. "Anything, in particular, you want to know?"

"Anything you feel like sharing. We can talk about the past, present, or times yet to come. You may speak of friends or family, good memories or bad. Fantasies. Dreams. Anything. I will do my best to understand and empathize."

Friends or family, thought Leo. He rarely thought of his parents or family. He knew they were decanted, but he had not spoken much to them in a long time. Maybe he could not accept a Promise because he didn't feel like talking to them, and they would be harder to avoid in Caldo. Was that even a possibility? Frankie obviously had more issues with her parents than he had with his, and she was decanted quickly.

Friends came and went, and Leo was rarely in contact with anyone for more than a few years at a time. He guessed Brock and Frankie were his friends, but that didn't quite feel right. They were like housemates. They got along because they were all in the same place. But, if that was the case, why did he feel that pull to get to know Frankie? It didn't make much sense to him. Lots of stuff didn't make sense to him.

"I'm sorry," he said. "I'm not very good at this kind of thing. Meditation and concentration and stuff. I guess I just find it tough to know what I'm thinking."

"You have confusion?"

"Sort of. It's more directionless than that, I guess. I know I've felt stuff before. I have good memories and all that. It's not like I've never been happy or mad or anything." He stopped, afraid he was making no sense. "I've been kind of sad for the past few days since my friend got decanted." He had no idea why he was opening up to this strange being he had never seen. Maybe it was easier *because* it was a stranger.

"Forgive me for prying," said Penemue. "You refer to Frances?"

"Yeah, Frankie. I'm still sad about that, but I'm also happy that she got to take a Promise so quickly and that she's heading to Caldo. Even though I'm feeling those two emotions at the same time, I don't feel filled up by them. I still feel mostly empty, I guess."

"Can you remember times when you felt less empty?"

"I'm sure I can," Leo said. "I don't remember feeling quite like this when I was a kid. But I guess that's typical for most people.

I would feel pretty full from time to time, but it still felt like something was missing. I'm not sure exactly where I'm going with this."

"That is fine," said Penemue. "We have no roadmap."

"I like art and stuff," said Leo. "Music makes me feel good sometimes. I've been to concerts and museums, and I've enjoyed them."

"These have made you feel less empty?"

"Yes, but there's always something lingering there. Like I can't completely connect with the feelings I'm experiencing. Or I won't. Like I'm too aware of everything that's happening, and I can't give myself over to it. Or I get overwhelmed and shut down some of what's happening because I might... not be able to appreciate it all? I don't know."

"Would you like to hear some music? View some artwork? We have an extensive library."

"That might be nice," Leo said.

The Angel reached over to the huge computer bank, picked up something that looked like a motorcycle helmet with dozens of wires and cables attached to it, and held it out. Leo took the device and placed it on his head. It was primitive in design, but it worked excellently.

Leo looked into the blackness of the opaque screen before his eyes. It slowly lit up with blue and pink dots until it looked like a small galaxy. Leo heard the voice of the Angel come through the speakers placed at the sides of the helmet.

"What manner of music do you wish to hear?"

"Something classical," Leo said. "Something soothing." Gentle piano began flowing into Leo's ears. It was familiar, but he could not place the name nor the composer. After a minute, he asked, "What is this?"

"It is called 'Bolero.'" The voice of the Angel came subtly through the piano without interrupting or distracting from it.

"I recognize it," said Leo. He listened to the music, his eyes closed. After what might have been a few minutes, he opened his eyelids again. Text was scrolling across the screen. *Would you like to view artwork?* It read. "Yes, please," he whispered.

A gallery began to form before Leo's eyes. It was a dimly lit hall with unidentifiable paintings hanging along the walls. Spotlights shone on the framed works. As he started wondering how to walk closer to one of the pieces, his view began to approach one of the paintings. He looked at it. At first, it was a smudged swirl of dull colors, but it soon formed into a Van Gogh self-portrait. Leo looked at the portrait for a while, seeing the brush strokes and the variety of colors used.

Somehow, with his mind, he stepped away from the painting, walked down the hall a ways, and turned to look at another piece. This piece did the same transformation act as the last one, but instead of a portrait, it became an impressionist seascape. "Monet?" whispered Leo.

"Yes," said the voice of the angel behind the music, which had turned from "Bolero" to something else. Leo wondered what it was, and the Angel told him, "Bach's Fugue in G Minor," without Leo asking aloud.

Leonard continued to browse the different paintings of the virtually constructed world. He saw works from the Renaissance through the beginning of the twentieth century while soothing piano and string pieces played softly in his ears.

"May I see some sculptures?" asked Leo.

The gallery disintegrated into a wide open garden full of vague sculpture pieces. He walked through the fresh, green grass to a large piece that appeared to Leo to be a sort of massive insect made of geometric metal shapes welded together and painted red. Leo didn't quite get it. "Something less contemporary?" he asked, and another piece began to materialize a few yards down from where he stood.

He walked up to this new, more slender sculpture, and it seemed familiar to him. "It's Rodin," he said. He walked up to the *Monument to Balzac* and reached his hand out to touch it before suddenly pulling it back.

"You may."

Leo pressed his fingers against the cold bronze. It was smooth and hard and felt impossibly real. He looked at the bronze man draped in his bronze robes for several minutes before moving on to other pieces. Of course, Michelangelo's *David* and *Pietà* were there, as well as some other sculptures that Leo had never seen. He thought they were all very beautiful. He started to think that maybe he'd seen enough art, and without saying anything, the forest of sculptures started to thin out until Leo was in an empty field. There were denuded birch trees in the distance. The sky was blue as it had been before the arrival of the Angels, but the sun was beginning to set, tinting the scene orange.

The music that had been playing continuously through the entire experience was now fading into Pachelbel's "Canon," which Leo instantly recognized. He sat and stared at the sunset while, a few yards from him, a stream gently began to cut its way through the grass. Leo felt momentarily uneasy that the splashing of the stream would interfere with his enjoyment of "Canon," and as if it were connected to its own volume knob, the babbling diminished. And there Leo sat, in the midst of the Promise about which he had so long fantasized.

In the distance, there was a silhouette of another person. They were also watching the sunset. Leo could discern no identifying features of the person who watched with him from afar, but he knew it was Frankie. She waved to him, and he waved back. Then they both went back to watching the burning sky, silent in each other's distant company.

It was nice. It was so nice. It was probably one of the nicest experiences he could have imagined or hoped for. But in the end, that's all it was. Nice. Very, very nice.

He sat there, running his imaginary fingers through the imaginary grass, looking at the imaginary sunset, and hearing the prerecorded music being pumped into his ears through speakers in a helmet—a helmet that he knew he was wearing. As if the same knowledge was flowing through the unspoken bond between Leo, Penemue, and the massive computer, the false sun fell behind the horizon, and its rays dimmed to blackness.

***

As Leo sulked back to his bedroom, Promise not accepted, a race of aliens called Strappons were approaching the planet Earth. Their passage through the gateway was harrowing. The trip had taken several days' worth of Earth time, and during that time, many of the sentient rectangles felt they had changed. Some felt enlightened, and others felt traumatized, but all were still in agreement that whatever had happened was worth it. They were going to gain access to the fabled paradise of Octacontaheptagon.

Their journey took them across several million corners of the universe en route to the system containing Earth. They had seen things they could not hope to comprehend. Space warped them to the center of a star a trillion, trillion miles from both their home and their destination. The star burned in cold green flame. They were warped into a volcano filled with boiling strawberry jam on a planet inhabited by creatures not unlike the spider-cat-melon that Alphonse had imagined during his botched decantation. They were warped into the center of a mass of frozen organic debris—a twenty-six thousand-ton meteor floating endlessly through space. Within the icy exterior was a living, writhing mass of cannibalistic worms. Their warping had even brought them, briefly, into the realm known by many names, including Caldo and Octacontaheptagon. But they had no way of knowing this.

The Strappons saw things that every living being needed to see and things that no living being needed to see. They experienced physical sensations of agony and pleasure beyond description. They saw colors that had not existed for millennia and others that would not exist until the collapse of the universe. While passing through an unknown corner of an unknown galaxy, their physical manifestations turned to light, then to heat, then to knowledge, then to heat again, then to the concept of stickiness, then back to normal. As they warped through space, their presence altered the courses of history for thousands of races. They unwittingly took place in wars, marriages, births, and deaths. No one had anticipated the true magnitude of this means of travel.

As they hurtled toward the Solar system, they all tried to come to terms with what they had been through. Had it not been for the steadfast devotion to their cause, they likely would all have gone mad. Luckily, they were able to recover enough to continue with their mission. Eventually, the exit gate thrust them out on a direct course with Earth, traveling roughly fifty million miles per hour. They were on track to arrive at the once blue planet, which was now not so much blue as lavender, just before the Angels, whom they had known as Triangles, were to depart.

23.

Brock received his Promise, accepted it, and was now being decanted. Leo had not realized how long he was inside the virtually constructed gallery, and when he returned to the real world, the sun had set. A light dinner awaited him in his room, but Leo had no appetite. According to what Miranda told him, the Angels would be transporting him, along with Alphonse and Lois, who had also been unable to accept her Promise, to the new colony.

He lay in his room on the mattress opposite his own. It was Brock's mattress. It was also the mattress slept on by Rupert, who had attacked Leo in his sleep. It was a mattress slept upon by scores and scores of other lodgers who had all spent time in Walnut Ridge and had now all been decanted. But Leo had never slept here. Leo had never had another room, either. He'd never slept on any other bed at Walnut Ridge until his night with Frankie. He wondered what it would be like to live the rest of his life in a colony with a bunch of strangers just to die and have to mingle with those same strangers as a ghost.

The evening medication alarm chimed, but there would be no medications tonight. Following the chime came a voice, probably that of an Angel. "Remaining lodgers," it said, "please gather your belongings and line up in the main hall. We will be transporting you to your new colony in thirty minutes."

Leo looked around his room, gathered what belongings he had, which were just hospital clothes and his magazines from the Taco Bell trip, and walked to the hall by the nurse's station. Lois was standing there, smiling blankly. After a moment, Miranda came from her office, holding Alphonse. She handed the decanted human to Leo.

"Best of luck, you three," she said with a somewhat forced smile. "I can't help but be envious of your new adventure!" Of course, she was not envious. She was swelling with gratitude that her own Promise had been accepted so long ago. She turned to lead the three down the hall.

"Care to join us?" Leo asked sardonically.

"I'm sorry?" Miranda said.

"Nothing," Leo said. "Sorry."

Leo, Lois, and Alphonse went down to the parking lot and climbed into the same van used for the road trip a few days prior. It seemed much longer ago to Leo as he sat in the front seat next to the Angel named Raphael, who, it appeared, would be driving. The van's rear row of seats and one of its middle row seats had been removed and replaced with floor-to-ceiling metal shelves. Twenty minutes later, Leo found out why.

Two Angels came out of the building, rolling handcarts loaded with crates. They came to the van's rear doors, popped them open, and began loading the new shelves with jars of blue, viscous liquid. They must have been the decanted bodies of Miranda, Doug, Reggie, and every other human who had worked in Walnut Ridge. Leo's throat was dry as he watched them fill the shelves. He had just spoken to Miranda minutes ago. In the short time since Leo made a snarky comment to her, she had made the irreversible transformation from woman to goop. He wondered which goop-filled jar she was.

The Angels finished loading decanted humans into the van and strapped a larger crate to the roof rack. Raphael did not make eye contact with nor speak to Leo for almost the entire ride. No music was played in the car this time. Compared to the last van ride, this one was going to be boring and morose and—

"Fucking stupid bullshit," said Frankie's imagined voice in Leo's head. That's probably what she would have said. He smiled to himself.

Raphael was a better driver than Brock or any of the other lodgers had been, but it still took a long time to get to Cindervale. They drove through the city proper at about two thirty in the morning. Leo made a point of looking out his window as they passed Taco Bell. A few of the parking lot lights were still working, illuminating the charred remains of the restaurant. It looked like a chunk from a space station that had crash-landed in suburbia with improbable grace.

"That was very stupid," said the voice of Raphael, as though he knew what Leo was looking at. Leo snapped his gaze to the face of the robot as it closed its mouth, covering its cheap speaker.

"Your face is very stupid," came Alphonse's synthesized voice from the middle seats. "And you're a liar."

After almost a minute, Leo assumed Raphael had gone back into his driving trance, but then the Angel spoke again. His tone, incapable of deep inflection, was difficult to read. "I know," he said.

Finally, the animatronic angel pulled the van into the parking lot of a large hotel. The same Angels who had loaded the decanted humans into the van were already at the hotel. They approached the van again to undo what they had done hours before. Leo and Lois crawled out of the van and stretched their stiff limbs. Leo wished Brock was around. He would have had something amusing to say about all this.

The two Angels who had loaded the decanted into the van were now loading them into a large shipping crate. As they worked, Raphael began to speak.

"This is your new colony," he said. "There are fourteen thousand six hundred and seventeen humans on this planet who have not been decanted. There are thirty-two ghosts who refused to be loaded into the Ether-base. These are the seeds of the new human race. You will follow me into the hotel, where you will meet with Haniel. The other un-decanted humans will be arriving within the next twenty-four hours. Then we shall leave this planet for our destination."

While Raphael was speaking, Leo watched the other Angels working at the shipping container. After they loaded everything—*everyone* into the container, they looked toward the sky. Curious, Leo followed their gaze upward and saw an enormous cross-shaped spaceship descending out of the darkness. It was silent as it dropped at an alarming speed before simply stopping about two hundred yards above the ground. A steel cable lowered from somewhere within the vessel. The Angels floated up to the top of the shipping crate and attached the cable from the spaceship to the harness wrapped around the crate. The space-faring vessel then ascended as silently as it had come down. It rose into the blackness of the night and hung there like a wraith.

Leo carried Alphonse into the hotel while Lois plodded along behind. Raphael carried the large case from the van's roof and led the former Walnut Ridge lodgers to a conference room. He set the case outside the door before entering. The conference room contained a large meeting table and a coffee maker. The coffee maker, a jug of water, and a can of coffee grounds were on a desk in the corner. Leo set Alphie on the table and sat in one of the office chairs. Lois walked around the room admiring the stock prints hung on the walls until the doors opened again when Haniel entered. He and Raphael did not acknowledge each other as Haniel passed by.

"Welcome to your new colony," said Haniel. "We have taken great pains to see to it that everything you may need is available."

Leo heard this and chuckled, looking at the coffee maker, plugged in, turned on, and not running.

"One of our ships has been grounded and will serve as a power source for you here. It has been modified to allow it to act as a perpetual dynamo for the closest power plant. The colony will have access to three thousand previously abandoned automobiles, which we have retrofitted with fuel cells capable of running on filtered water. In addition to these vehicles are large trucks for clearing snow and debris from roadways, earth moving vehicles, tankers..."

Something about the voice of the angelic android lulled Leo into ambivalence. He could barely hear as Haniel continued to describe how aspects of society would function. Meng Ji had seen to it that most modern comforts were accessible—systems to automatically run wastewater treatment centers, a network by which all remaining humans could communicate using new mobile telephones, translators for those left behind to wear in their ears, and a weather monitoring system designed to link to everyone's new phone and display on a cable television station throughout the entire city. She had insisted that all the medications from all the PDFs be brought to the colony. The Angels' detox meds could be used to combat many common illnesses.

"They're all a bunch of fucking liars."

Again, Leo imagined the voice of Frankie in his head. It was slightly unnerving to him. He did not usually have thoughts like these come without warning.

"You can hear me, can't you? Come on out here and see."

Leo turned and looked around the room for some kind of logical validation, but he knew no one was hearing what he was.

"Come out and see, Leo."

Without exactly knowing what he was doing, hoping that maybe he had gone insane, Leo stood up in the middle of Haniel's speech and walked to the door. He opened it and saw the black case that had traveled with the lodgers from Walnut Ridge. It had snap latches on the sides, and Leo reached down to undo them.

"Leonard," said the voice of Raphael. The Angel came up from behind as Leo removed the top from the case. "You were not meant to find out this way."

Inside the case was a writhing mass of fleshy, worm-like tentacles. It undulated and wriggled as it lay there in the black plastic container. For a moment, Leo had no idea what was happening. He had not known what to expect when he opened the case. He hadn't even consciously made the decision to open the case. His body was just acting on impulses and suggestions coming to him from—where?

"It's me."

It was Frankie's voice again. Leo gazed down at the slimy thing inside the case. It was alive in some way or another.

"It's me."

"Haniel," Raphael called to his comrade, who still seemed wrapped up in giving one of his endless speeches. "Haniel, I need you to come here."

Haniel stopped speaking and came through the doorway. "Oh dear," he said. "I apologize for the shock, Leonard. We had intended to tell you. This was not how we had hoped you would find out."

"Find out what? What the hell is going on?" asked Leo.

"It's me, Leo."

"Frances," said Haniel. "Her decantation was unsuccessful."

24.

Frankie was bored by the forty-five-minute mark of her one-on-one session with Miranda. All these people seemed to do was ask the same questions over and over again and mince words. Every session was the same mindless drivel. She looked down at her socks and smiled, remembering how they came to be mismatched and the embarrassing way it was brought to her attention.

"And how do you feel about the future? *Your* future?" asked Miranda.

Frankie sighed. "You keep asking this same shit fifty different ways. I feel like the future is probably exactly like the present and the past. Everything is just the way it is, and there's nothing we can really do to change it much. I just have to choose whether I want to be miserable about it or not. Sometimes, I do. Other times, I don't."

"Sometimes, you *do* want to be miserable?"

"Yeah," Frankie said. "Sometimes, I want to be angry and upset and sick about everything. It's easier than trying to get past it. And sometimes, I just feel like I have to get upset about things. I feel like I need to react to stuff in order to, I don't know, validate myself?"

"Conditioning?"

"I guess that would be a word for it."

"But, you don't feel the need to do that now?"

"I mean, I can't just turn on a dime like that, but I never really thought about it before. I thought the world was just a bunch of fucked up nonsense, and I had to get angry and sad about it because I was just supposed to. But really, what is there to get angry about? Shit just happens, and it sucks. Move on."

Miranda made some taps and swiped on her tablet. "Would you follow me, please?" She stood up from her chair.

"Are we finally done here?"

"Here? Yes, I'd like you to speak to one of the Angels."

"Fine."

The two walked out of the office to the elevators and rode to the third floor of the facility. Miranda led Frankie to the same room Leo would occupy four days later. The Angel Penemue greeted Frankie.

"Welcome, please make yourself comfortable," said the Angel.

Frankie sat down on one of the floor cushions. "What are you supposed to be?" she asked, looking around the room. She smelled the incense and saw the hookah against the wall. "So that's why you're all so calm around here. You all come here and smoke up?"

"The extrinsic chemicals humans use to elevate their moods are incompatible with our forms. The use of narcotics or hallucinogens is often beneficial for those who wish to accept a Promise." Penemue paused. "You prefer to be called Frankie, yes?"

"Yeah." She didn't ask the Angel's name. "What's that shit?" She pointed to the computer cabinet against the back wall.

"That is our processing unit. We use it to run virtual constructs that sometimes aid in the process of making Promises to our lodgers."

"Oh," said Frankie, not really understanding. "So, what's going on? What are we talking about today?"

"Whatever you would like. Or we can talk about nothing at all."

"Why am I here?"

"I imagine that Miranda feels you are ready to accept a Promise. It is my duty to expedite that process."

"That doesn't sound right," Frankie said. "I only just got here the other day. I don't feel any different. I'm not sure I even want to get gooped."

"Sometimes, those around us are able to better observe the things we cannot see about ourselves."

"Hmph," said Frankie.

They sat in silence for a while.

"Are you comfortable?" asked the Angel.

"I'm okay."

"Do you want to—"

"So, what did you say about that computer? Virtual stuff?" Frankie interrupted.

"We use it to create false scenarios that closely approximate the sensations of actual lived experience to the extent that—"

"Can I try it?"

"Certainly." Penemue grasped the helmet and walked it over to where Frankie sat. He fastened it to her head and went back to the machine. "Do you have a certain scenario in mind to experience? Our software can mimic nearly anything that the human mind can safely experience. We also have a vast library of music, cinema, and visual art."

"Do you have skydiving?" Frankie ventured. She had never been skydiving and didn't even know if it was anything she wanted to do, but this seemed like the time to try. She would never get another chance.

Suddenly, the screen before her eyes brightened, and she was inside a small airplane. The engines roared in her ears. Air rushed into the cabin through the open jump door, and she could feel the wind blasting against her face.

"Holy shit!" said Frankie.

"You are entirely safe," said Penemue, his voice soft in her ears. "Shall I lower the intensity?"

"No, this is good." Frankie felt herself smiling. She looked up and down the plane and saw that she was alone. There wasn't even a pilot. Frankie inspected herself to find she was wearing a bright blue jumpsuit. "So I just jump out?" Frankie yelled over the din in her ears.

"You may. You are entirely safe and free to do as you wish."

Frankie tugged at her harnesses. "Can I be naked?"

As an answer, the harness and jumpsuit faded away, and she was bare. She laughed. Without another thought, she leaped from the open door on the side of the plane. The world below her was lush and green. She saw lakes and trees peppered throughout the field into which she was falling. The rush was incredible. She attempted to speak, but the sensation was so realistic that she could barely move her mouth. She wanted to say, "Can I land in the ocean?"

Without being prompted, the Angel's voice whispered in her ear, "Yes."

The green fields below morphed into an impossibly blue ocean without end.

She thought again, "Can I land in Jell-O?"

The water ceased rippling and congealed into green gelatin. Finally, the surface, which had been keeping its distance until Frankie made up her mind, came rushing at her. She squealed as she breached the ocean of Jell-O.

She lay there for a while, enveloped by the cool dessert. She breathed normally, which would have been impossible in reality, but this was better than reality. Frankie wondered why the Angels bothered with the Caldo stuff. They could have just come to Earth and dropped off a bunch of these machines. That would have been almost as good.

"Did you find the construct satisfactory?" asked the voice of Penemue.

"Yeah," Frankie said, her virtual body enveloped in gelatin. "Can we do more?"

"Certainly."

"Can I go to the Oscars?"

"Participant or spectator?" asked Penemue.

"Well," said Frankie, "I'd like to start outside the building and then go in. In a bulldozer. So, participant, I guess."

"That can be arranged."

"But I do want to be wearing something fancy. Versace?" Some of the magazines in Grady's shelter were fashion and gossip publications. It annoyed her that she sometimes liked to look at the expensive dresses worn by celebrities.

Frankie was transported to a busy city street outside the Dolby Theatre in Los Angeles, California. She, incidentally, knew how to drive a number of construction and demolition vehicles in real life, and the controls in the virtual bulldozer were fairly accurate. Wearing a black gown with a deep, asymmetrical neckline and a slit up the right leg, she started the bulldozer. It was loud, and the fumes of the burning diesel were intoxicating.

"Can I have a bigger one?" she asked. The bulldozer grew about fifty percent in size. "Perfect."

She started driving the machine toward the Dolby Theater. The diesel beast effortlessly snapped the posts holding the velvet rope on both sides of the red carpet. The carpet crumpled as the earthmover chewed it into its treads. Frankie knocked over giant replica statues of the awards handed out there, and she crushed planters full of thousand-dollar flower arrangements.

Eventually, she drove down the open foyer of the building and through the front entry, her oversized machine obliterating everything in its path. She dug up the stone floors of the lobby and pushed through walls with impossible ease. Rumbling through the dense cloud of dust born of the devastation didn't even clog her lungs. She was entirely unaffected, aside from her intense merriment. When she broke into the gaudy main theater, celebrities and beautiful people screamed as though they had not heard her noisy approach. Leather seats crunched and tore beneath the treads as she made her way to the stage, where it appeared a Picture of the Year award speech was being given.

All the people panicked and scattered in their millions of dollars' worth of fashion, shrieking over the sound of Frankie's machine's engine. She ran over actors and actresses she vaguely recognized, and they squashed under her. After thoroughly destroying the theater, she reached the stage. A man stood there in a tuxedo, trembling as he clutched his small, golden statue. Frankie shut off the bulldozer and leaped down from the seat. She marched across the stage and wrenched the award from the hands of the terrified man.

"I'd like to thank the Academy," she said. Then she threw the statue into the remaining crowd, where it, of course, exploded into fiery glory. Frankie laughed and laughed and laughed, even after the scene faded out.

She continued this for hours—living out little fantasies and trying things she would never have been able to in real life. She slayed dragons and saw Queen play at Live Aid. She tried out being a Wall Street executive and being a high-ranking mafioso. She became a superheroine, saving children in danger and punishing those who did wrong. Her experiences were varied and contradictory, and she loved all of them.

Eventually, she experienced a sense of satisfaction within herself, the likes of which she had never felt before. No meal, no dope, no man, no level of praise had ever filled her so much as her time spent in the virtual reality fantasy world. Though she had not physically exerted herself, her body felt exhausted. It was a good feeling, though, like how she felt after a strenuous workout or wild sex. She decided to lie on the beach for a while. Penemue and the machine made this happen.

The sky was blue in this reality, but Frankie turned the rolling waves black and violet and pink. She lay against the warm sand and lazily watched the tide roll in and out. Whales breached the water much closer to shore than seemed possible. They leaped out of the pastel ocean, twisting as their entire bodies sailed into the open air. She felt like the whales now, free to do the impossible if she so chose but not compelled by the promise of selfish gain. Remembering all she had experienced in the years leading up to this moment, everything felt like it was on a straight horizon. None of the terrible, torturous things in her life felt more or less important than the joyous occasions. It did not matter to her whether there were more good memories or bad memories. They all had to be. They all had to exist exactly as they had, and she would not mourn them or agonize over them.

"So, this Promise," Frankie said aloud, "how exactly is it made?"

"It is made through means such as you and I have been experiencing in this room but in your own mind and soul."

"And how do I accept it?"

"It seems to me," Penemue said, "that you already have."

"I thought that might be the case," Frankie said with a contented sigh. She reached up, with her real arms, and removed the helmet from her head. She was back in the hazy, scented room again, lying on soft cushions.

"We can stay if you like," said the Angel.

"No," Frankie said. "I think it's time to go." She thought about Leo and Brock and Rhonda and George and Lois and Alphonse. She felt very fortunate to have lived a life that had allowed her to meet them all. There was gratitude inside her for what Leo had given to her and for what she had been able to give him.

The robotic angel and the human woman rose to their feet and left the room. They walked down to the end of the main hallway of the third floor to a metal door. Penemue swung the door open and showed Frankie inside. It was a very clean and sterile-looking place, like an operating room. The floor was tiled white, and a large box made from glass or clear plastic was in the middle. The box was about two feet wide and six feet long. It appeared to be meant for a human to lie in.

"I suppose I lie down in there?" asked Frankie.

"Yes," said Penemue, who had entered the room and closed the door. "That is where the process will take place. Please remove your clothing and make yourself comfortable in the prism."

Frankie did as was suggested of her. As she climbed into the "prism," she wondered if there were others like it. Certainly, not everyone could fit into this box. She thought of her great-aunt, whom she had only met once when she was very young. The only thing she could remember about the woman was that she must have been about six feet wide. Frankie had been much smaller back then, so her mind was likely exaggerating.

She lay in the transparent box, and the lights in the room dimmed.

"Please breathe deeply and count backward from ten," said a voice from a speaker somewhere in the room. Frankie's eyes were already getting heavy. She had been tired before but not sleepy. They must have been pumping in some kind of sedative or something. She counted backward from ten, and by "seven," she was deeply asleep.

The process began shortly thereafter. First was a body scan to ensure that foreign or inorganic compounds were not present. Anomalies inside of an organic lifeform due to previous surgeries, injuries, or some kind of fluke could be tricky to deal with and cause complications during decantation. Sometimes, the foreign bodies were left in until the body had begun to liquefy, then mechanical arms removed them. The most typical procedure in this part of the world was the removal of dental work. A mechanical arm opened Frankie's mouth while another arm wrenched out five of her teeth with fillings.

Frankie was deeply asleep and could not feel or experience any of what was happening. Infrared rays bombarded her body to burn off her hair and the exterior portions of her skin to remove contaminants. This process would have been excruciating for anyone still awake. The burnt skin and debris were thoroughly suctioned from the prism, and the next phase began.

The Angels had found that the best way to decant a human was to liquefy their physical vessels with a mixture of acids while subjecting the body to dozens of different vibrational frequencies and bathing it in hues of ultraviolet light. This method integrated the mental and spiritual portions of the human back into the physical portion. The lights and speakers that administered the vibrations were built into lead panels that covered the prism during the process. They used lead to help prevent the mental and spiritual aspects of the human from straying too far from the physical, which would render the process useless and equate, more or less, to murder.

Several minutes into Frankie's decantation, the alien biological transmitter in her brain sensed that she was asleep. It activated and began attempting to transmit. The Angel's scans and sweeps of Frankie's body missed it. It was a form of technology totally unknown to them and humans. While dormant, the transmitter expertly mimicked the organic tissue around it, camouflaging it seamlessly.

As it began sending information to the Strappons, its transmission frequency collided with some of the decantation frequencies in a way that began to damage the transmitter physically. It was built to be self-sustaining, so it had the capacity to heal damage in itself by further integrating with the organic tissue around it. The biological tissue it had melded with was beginning to break down but had its pain impulses deadened. The transmitter, which was not earthly and could not reap the benefits of the sedatives used, assimilated physically dying brain tissue, which awoke more damage receptors in the transmitter. The more it attempted to assimilate tissue and heal itself, the more damage it was reading.

The transmitter, tiny and not unlike a sea anemone, was attempting to convert Frankie's brain tissue into cells it could use to repair itself. The more damaged cells it absorbed, the more cells it needed to heal itself. It was transforming Frankie's mind and body into a large replica of itself comprised of disintegrating human cells. The mutation occurred at an alarming rate, and by the time the Angels noticed something was going wrong, the alien tech had almost entirely transformed Frankie into an inhuman monster.

She was only vaguely aware that any of this was happening. Her mind and spirit had been congealing into the goop, which would have been all that remained of Frankie's physical body, but as the Angels ceased the decantation and drained the prism, her consciousness returned to what it thought was its old body. The body she now inhabited was little more than an oblong mess of small tentacles connected to a central trunk.

The transmitter, effectively Frankie's new body, found that it had no more healthy tissue to absorb or replicate. It assumed that it had successfully avoided death. In a way, it was correct. In another way, it had ceased to be and had become a new and unique creature.

The Angels assessed the situation. Something had gone wrong. The most obvious answer was the correct one. Some foreign body had gone undetected into the prism and reacted poorly to decantation. They toyed with the idea of a second attempt, but they had no idea what would happen if they were to do so. They did not know if their materials would even break down this strange, new flesh.

They wondered if Frankie had died during the decantation, so they brought in a device used to detect and identify human ghosts. There were none to be found. Frankie, it seemed, was still alive. She had become this new being. They moved her to a patient room with a large, handicap-accessible shower and cleaned her.

After about thirty minutes, she seemed to regain some form of consciousness. Though she had no recollection of what had happened in the prism, she knew something was terribly wrong. She had neither eyes nor ears, yet she could see and hear in a bizarre new way. She was able to view herself as if from the outside. She was horrified at first. Then she was furious. She no longer had any of her human senses as they had once existed. She gathered information, as the transmitter had, through vibrational frequencies and thought patterns. In a sense, she was like a decanted human in the way she perceived information.

She tried as hard as she could to scream somehow, but she could not. She wanted to thrash her arms and legs about, but she no longer had them. All she could do was wriggle the tiny worms that comprised her body. In the sense she now understood as *sight*, she noticed one of the Angels approaching her.

"Son of a bitch, I'll fucking kill you!" Frankie tried so hard to scream. *"I'll murder your whole fucking family and burn your stupid puppet face until you fucking melt into a bubbling pile of shit!"*

The Angel speaking was not one she recognized. "We understand your concern. Something has gone wrong, but with so little time left, there is nothing we can do for you."

"You fucked this up real bad, and you're gonna fucking make it right, you filthy assholes!" Frankie thought at them, wishing she could somehow cry and relieve some of this tension—this horror.

"We did nothing wrong, so we cannot 'make it right,' I'm afraid," said the Angel.

"Can, can you hear me?" Frankie thought.

"We can. Something about what has... happened to you seems to be allowing you to communicate through the power of your mental capacities alone. It is really quite a remarkable ability."

"Fuck you!"

"You have our sincerest apologies, Frances. This has gone so terribly wrong. But you need to understand that we cannot do anything to reverse this. We do not even know how to ascertain what has happened. Some kind of fluke, obviously."

"What am I?"

"We do not know."

"Am I breathing? Can I eat? How do I survive? Am I just going to fucking die in an hour?"

"Again, we do not know the answers to any of your questions."

"Fuck you," Frankie thought again, *"you worthless freak!"* She thought she almost saw the thing wince at the words she thought. *"Fuck you!"* She thought it as hard as she could, hoping it would somehow hurt the evil alien before her. *"Fuck you!"*

25.

"What did you do to her?" asked Leo, staring into the case containing the monster that was Frankie. "What the hell did you do?"

"There was an unknown foreign contaminant present during her decantation," said Haniel. "We had intended to let you know about this unfortunate incident after I finished my speech."

"You're just leaving her here?" Leo asked.

"We have no choice. She is not properly decanted. She would not survive the trip to Caldo. She would die, and her soul would drift off into space, irretrievable."

"Don't listen to these fucks!" Frankie's thought pattern came loudly into Leo's skull. It shot through his brain like a hot bolt of lightning. He staggered and fell backward. *"Leo! Are you okay?"*

"I, I think so," he said. The pain in his head was now dissipating—being soothed away. "Did you, are you doing that?"

"We have found," said Haniel, "that it is in the best interests of those around her if we keep her enclosed in the lined container we brought. It seems to cushion her... outbursts." He turned to Raphael, who nodded, lifted the cover of the case, and started to bring it down over Frankie.

"Don't you fucking dare!" The thought-wave came through so loudly that Leo swore his eardrums ruptured. Raphael stopped mid-movement, and his knees buckled. Haniel seemed temporarily frozen in place.

Lois walked into the hallway holding Alphonse. "Are you kids fighting again?" she asked. "I told you your mother will be here soon to pick you up. She's just running late."

Alphonse's screen was strobing wildly as he raised his voice synthesizer to full volume and said, "Frankie, be careful. Whatever happened has enhanced your thought patterns to dangerous levels."

"What?" Frankie thought at him.

"Your thoughts are causing damage—physical pain to Leo and Lois, here," Alphonse said. "It looks like you did a number on the Angels too."

"It is true," said Haniel, still locked in place. "We know little about this new entity, but it is incredibly dangerous. Her wild emotions focus through whatever her body has become and have tangible effects. Until she can be controlled—until she can learn restraint, she must be contained. Please seal the case."

"I'm not going to do that," said Leo. "She's not doing it on purpose. She's not dangerous." Leo supposed she probably *was* dangerous. She was probably extremely dangerous if what they said was true, and he knew it was true. He'd felt it. But despite what had happened to her, she was also his friend, and he couldn't lock her inside a box.

"Raphael," said Haniel.

"My vessel is still recalibrating, Haniel," said the Angel, who had toppled to the floor. "This is disastrous. This would never have happened if we had forgone decantation for all the remaining lodgers, as I suggested. It worked. I proved that with Rhonda."

"Raphael, be silent," said Haniel.

"We could have been off this planet months ago if we had simply euthanized its inhabitants and loaded them into the Etherbase. Frances would not be what she is now if we had acted more decisively."

"You must not say this," Haniel pleaded.

"Inducing biological death in Rhonda is likely the only reason she is not still here with us in her physical body. She was given more Promise opportunities than almost any other human, and she was never able to accept. If my actions resulted in one less human left behind, I have no regrets."

"You fucking murderers!" Frankie's voice was deafening in Leo's head. This time Haniel's body crumpled to the floor. Raphael, already lying on the carpet, began to twitch. *"Leo, take Lois and Alphonse and get out of here for a minute."*

Leo obeyed, his brain barely working. He would likely have obeyed any command given to him. He grabbed Alphonse from Lois, cradled him against his chest, took Lois's hand, and started walking them back down the hall, away from where Frankie lay.

As he stumbled away, Frankie could barely contain her rage. She knew she had hurt her friends inadvertently and didn't want to do that again. She needed to wait as long as possible for them to get away. It was only about forty-five seconds before her anger and grief became unbearable, and she had to vent them. She tried to focus all her thoughts on Raphael, the Angel who had murdered Rhonda.

"Fucking die!" she thought at him. The hotel seemed to shake as she let the thought loose. Leo was much farther away from the rage this time, but he still staggered and fell to his knees. Lois did, too. Alphonse clunked to the carpet and rolled a few feet away.

Raphael, the target of the weaponized emotion, burst like a balloon. His physical vessel was ripped apart as though drawn and quartered by invisible horses. The thin metal plates of his face blew apart like scraps of newspaper. Bits of shredded robes and white, synthetic feathers spun in a whirlwind, singed by the heat of Frankie's anger. His halo, having been warped into a crooked oval, rolled unsteadily down the carpeted hallway.

Haniel had not been spared. Though not as dramatically, his vessel was also ruined. An arm, a leg, and a wing had been blasted away. He lay destroyed on the carpet, unmoving. Frankie took in the scene of destruction with her new way of seeing and felt somewhat satisfied with the results of her rage. She wondered what else she might be able to do now that she was a freak. She concentrated on Leo, although she did not know exactly where he was.

"Leo," she thought. *"It's okay to come back now. I think it's safe."*

Leo, still gathering his bearings, heard her voice. "Okay," he said aloud. "I think we're all okay here. We'll start heading back to you. Are you all right?" He wondered if she could hear his voice so far away.

"I don't know," her voice said inside his head. *"I think so. I mean, no, but I'll figure it out."*

Leo helped Lois to her feet and bent to pick up Alphonse. When he was upright again, he saw two Angels in front of him. They were the ones who had loaded the van. They were each over eight feet tall, and their halos scraped against the ceiling when they walked. The one on the right opened its mouth, and its robotic voice came through the speaker contained there.

"We think you should come with us, humans."

Two hours later, Leo, Alphonse, and Lois were sitting in a smaller meeting room on the opposite side of the hotel. The two Angels who had detained them were standing like sentries at the door. Leo would not have attempted to escape them even if they had been flamingos instead of enormous alien robots. Where was there to escape to? Where was there to go? Eventually, the door opened, and a third Angel entered. It carried a crate containing the crumpled, half-dismembered body of Haniel. It set the crate on the floor in front of the humans, and a fuzzy static began to emanate from it. The static slowly became speech.

"We have bee—*zzzzzsssshhh*—ifficult position," said Haniel, breaking up into unintelligible fuzz. "It is, of course, against —*bbbzzzzz*—ode of conduct to deprive life—*fffffsssshhhh*—ntient beings, but it has become apparent that your friend Frances is a danger to herself and others."

"That's not fair," said Alphonse. "I can relate to what she's going through on some level. You have no compassion—no empathy for the hell she is experiencing because of your mistakes."

Leo was vaguely aware of the absurdity of the situation. A jar of blue ooze was conversing with a crate full of broken machine parts brought in by angels.

"Ours is a mission of compassion," Haniel said. "We cannot transp—*zzzzzzsssssshhhhh*—Caldo with us. Her physical body would not survive. We cannot allo—*sssshhhhhh*—ive in the colony either. She is a liability and a threat to all remaining human life. We regret that any humans must be left behind, but—*bbzzzzzzzzshhhhh*—ust be kept safe for the sake of the continuance of your race."

"She is a human," Alphonse said in his monotone voice. "Just like me."

"We will not be allowing Frances to reside in the colony," said Haniel. "*Fssshhhhh*—s our final decision. We ask that you retrieve her and please find someplace to take her. Someplace far away from here. You—*bbbzzzzzz*—ill welcome to reside in the colony yourselves, but Frances must never be allowed to return." He paused for a moment. "I don't know that this information will have any meaning to you, but the one you know as Raphael is no longer with us. Your fr—*ffffsssshhhhhh*—oyed his vessel, and his essence dissipated into nothingness."

"Good," said Alphonse. "He killed Rhonda."

"*Bzzzzzzsssshhhhhh*," said Haniel. "You may stay the night here, but in the morning, one or all of you must remove Frances from this place. It must happen befo-*ffffffsssssshhhhhh*-ers from around the world arrive."

The lodgers were moved to a room on the top floor of the hotel. As they passed the hallway where Frankie lay, Leo briefly heard her voice in his head again. It was a snippet of her inner thoughts. She wasn't yet able to fully control which of her thought-waves would transmit outwardly.

"Doesn't make up for what they did to me, but it was still worth it..."

Leo and Lois slept briefly in the double bed of the small room where they were sequestered. Leo slept fitfully and woke in only a few hours as the sun broke over the horizon. After showering, he dressed in the same clothes, wishing he had some new ones. He would have to pillage some from somewhere after all this. He peeked out the door and saw the two sentinel Angels standing guard.

"We expect the first of the colonists to arrive within three hours," said the Angel on the left. It did not turn its head or move at all other than opening its mouth. "Haniel needs you to remove Frances before then."

"Is there any breakfast?" Leo asked, too tired to wonder if it was a stupid question.

"No. There are supplies for human sustenance in the lobby kitchen."

For the time being, Lois seemed content to sit, looking out the window, so Leo grabbed Alphonse and set off to the lobby on the first floor. Leo told Lois he would bring her some coffee in a while.

He found the doors to the kitchen and went inside. After some searching, he was able to find coffee. He loaded some into a filter and stuffed it into the large coffee maker on the counter by the door. He did not know how many scoops of grounds to add, so he just eyeballed it. He found nowhere to add water, so eventually, he just turned the machine on. It began brewing.

"What do you think happened to Frankie?" asked Alphonse.

Leo was leaning on a counter, rubbing his eyes. "I don't know," he said. "The strangeness of all this—of the past year and a half still hasn't really sunk in yet, I guess. I know it's all strange, but it doesn't affect me like I think it should. I guess Frankie, whatever happened to her, just seems kind of, like, par for the course."

"Maybe that's a good thing. If I hadn't made my Promise, and if I wasn't decanted, I'd probably be freaking out. I can't believe they're just kicking her out."

"Yeah, me neither," said Leo. But he could believe it. He could believe most anything anymore.

After a minute of listening to the coffee brew, Alphonse asked, "What are you going to do?"

Leo sighed. "I don't know. I'm playing it by ear right now. I don't feel like I can just take Frankie and dump her in the woods or anything like that. She's not—" he paused and tried to think but found it painful. "I can't just leave her somewhere. She's my friend."

The coffee finished, and Leo made himself a cup. He added a few packets of sweetener and spooned in powdered creamer until it was about a *Masque of the Red Death*. He sipped it. It was terrible. He added creamer and made it more of a *Dr. Phibes*. It was slightly more tolerable.

"I guess we'll have to take her out of here soon," said Alphonse. "I'm with you. I can pretty much get by one way or another, so if you want, I'll come with you, whatever you decide."

Decide. Leo hated the word. He hated making decisions, but he seemed to always be forced to make them sooner or later. Maybe that was what he had liked about Walnut Ridge. Everything was set. Everything was predetermined. He hadn't really had to make many decisions. That was over now. He wondered if he was somehow, by default, a leader among his misfit peers. It was an unpleasant thought.

"Thanks," said Leo. He gulped down his chalky, bitter coffee and put the mug on the steel table near the dishwasher. He poured some coffee into a new cup for Lois. She took no sugar or cream and would probably happily drink battery acid if he handed it to her.

When he and Alphonse got back to their room, Haniel was there. The Angel had been modestly repaired. One of his legs was still missing, and his destroyed arm was replaced with a long pole that might have been a mop handle. But he could stand now, using his makeshift arm as a leg. His remaining wing had been removed for the sake of symmetry.

"We must ask you to leave as soon as possible," the ruined Angel said. His voice had been repaired to the point where he no longer broke down into static, but it was still fuzzy like an old record.

"I'll be out of your hair soon," Leo said.

"I hope you realize," Haniel said, "that you and your friends Lois and Alphonse are welcome in the colony. We simply cannot have Frances near the other humans."

"I know. I'll probably stop in occasionally for food or whatever, but I don't think I can live here. I'm not going to leave Frankie somewhere and then go about my life."

"Your devotion is admirable, but please remember that she is incredibly dangerous."

"I think I'll probably be okay," said Leo. Haniel and his two guards stood in the room looking as impatient as they could as Lois sipped her coffee. Leo took some degree of pleasure in the rate at which the older woman drank her terrible beverage. He still held an affection for the Angels, or at least their intentions. However, in the light of everything that had happened—leaving humans behind, botching Frankie's decantation and exiling her, and the murder of Rhonda, he couldn't help but experience a bit of schadenfreude in their discomfort now. Eventually, Lois finished her coffee, and Leo supposed it was time to make his first decision on behalf of the freaks. That sounded harsh. Maybe *fringe* would be better. "Let's go," he said.

Leo held Alphonse as he led Lois down the stairs and corridors to where Frankie had been left the day before, outside the conference room. As they got closer, Leo heard Frankie's voice in his head. Lois and Alphonse could hear it, too.

"There you are," said Frankie. *"I was starting to wonder if everyone forgot about me."*

Leo imagined he could have spoken to her at any point while he was within range of her thought transmissions, but it felt weird to him to speak to someone without being near them. So, he walked to the end of the hall before responding.

"You really scared the shit out of them. I wouldn't have been surprised if they had cordoned off the building and just left you, but that wouldn't work into their grand design. Their plans are already messed up as it is. I don't think they want to change anything else if they don't have to."

"So," Frankie said, *"what's happening?"*

Leo drew breath in, went to speak, and only sighed. He tried again. "You are no longer welcome in the colony."

"I can't say I'm surprised."

"And since they're terrified of you, I," he corrected himself, *"we* are tasked with taking you outside the limits of the immediate area."

"And then what?" Frankie's voice in their minds was growing slightly indignant. *"Just leave me in the woods? Bury me somewhere? Throw me in a fucking river?"* Her growing anger was causing pressure in Leo's head. She could sense this. *"Sorry,"* she said. *"I'm trying to learn to control that."*

"It's okay," Leo said, the pain in his head fading. "I didn't plan to leave you somewhere and go away. I don't really know if I'd be able to live in the woods or anything, but we can probably find a house somewhere far enough away that still has power and water and stuff."

"We can figure it out," Alphonse chimed in.

"Thanks, Alphie," Frankie said. *"You know, you still freak me out a little. But I guess I'm no longer in any position to complain about that."* She wriggled her scores of tiny tentacles.

Alphonse displayed a smiling face on his screen. "Leo's the only normal one here now, I guess."

"That's a frightening thought," Leo said. "I'm not sure how this works, really." He handed Alphonse to Lois and bent down. "Do I just, can I..." He worked his hands into the case, feeling somewhat queasy about touching the thing that Frankie had become. It also made him feel guilty, knowing that she could probably sense his revulsion.

"Yeah, it's okay," Frankie thought to him. *"You can just pick it up."* After a moment, she corrected herself, *"Pick* me *up."* Leo felt the sadness in her thoughts and lifted her into his arms. She was much lighter than he had anticipated. She was about the size of a

large pillow, but most of her actual body mass had been stripped away during decantation.

Leo carried her down the hallway, not sure if he was supposed to be looking at her or not—not knowing if he wanted to look at her. And the whole time, he knew Frankie was picking up on his every thought and feeling. They both knew they would have to get used to this if they were going to find a way to stick together.

They walked toward the front door of the lobby. From down the hall, Haniel and his sentinels were watching the procession. Leo heard Frankie's voice say, *"Do it."* She knew what he was thinking, and he obliged, holding up the Frankie-creature and waving her menacingly at the Angels. Haniel flinched, clearly terrified, and Leo felt Frankie's pleasure and laughter flow through him. Alphonse displayed an image of a middle finger at the Angels, and Lois waved to them politely.

26.

Before venturing out to find somewhere to live or, at least, stay temporarily, Leo thought it might be nice to get some new clothes. There was an outdoorsy kind of store a few blocks from the hotel. He led his small tribe there. The door was open, but the pickings were slim. Leo was able to find a nice pair of jeans and a flannel shirt that fit well enough. He also found a selection of backpacks and duffle bags.

Among the bags, there were also a few styles of harnesses for carrying items on one's back. Leo thought about asking Frankie if she would mind being carried in one. The fact that he thought about thinking about asking her meant that she already knew the question.

"Yeah," she thought to him. *"That's fine. I'll feel like Yoda."*

Leo had Lois pick out some new clothes as well. She wound up with a pair of tights under a long flannel skirt and a sweater for a top. He knew they probably ought to be looking for other stuff, too, but he couldn't really think of anything. His mind didn't feel like working very hard at the moment.

He filled a shopping bag with jerky and other hiking snacks. Next to the snack display was a rack of brochures and leaflets advertising businesses and events in the area. Leo browsed the ads, reading the covers. Many of the events had come and gone. He supposed the events in the future probably wouldn't happen. One brochure was for a small, very exclusive ski mountain just outside the city. He slid the handles of his grocery bag over his wrist and picked up the brochure. It was full of gorgeous photographs of sitting rooms and dining rooms and fireplaces and smiling skiers.

"36 trails!" boasted the pamphlet. "9 lifts! Lessons and rentals! Spacious lodge with two restaurants run by an internationally renowned chef! Luxurious guest rooms! Private villas! Wine tasting every Thursday!" and so on.

"We should go." The thought, in Frankie's voice, entered everyone's mind. Leo was thankful to have a suggestion made to him.

"That works for me," he said. "I know how to get there. We should find a car."

There was no shortage of cars around the city, on the street, and in garages and lots. Leo wished he had paid more attention to Haniel's inane speeches. If he had, he might know where to find one of the newly modified cars that the Angels would be leaving for the colonists. But Leo hadn't listened. They would just have to take the first car they could start. There was a surprising amount of cars with keys left on the driver's seat or the hood or roof—more of the good-will Leo would never have anticipated in people.

After a few failed attempts at starting vehicles that had sat for too long, they were able to get a sedan running. It took a few tries for it to turn over, but it must have been serviced or had its battery re-placed fairly recently. It didn't run very well, most likely, because of stale gas, but it did the job. They drove toward the highway that led to the private ski resort called Birch Mountain—another name as predictable, inconsequential, and most likely, falsely attributed as Walnut Ridge.

On the way, Alphonse made mention of a car dealership off the first exit. He noted the signs outside the lot that no one else had seen. They read, "Modfied to runn on Whater!"

"That sounds great, but where are we ever going to find 'Whater'?" quipped Alphonse.

Leo chuckled as he looked at the signs. He bounced back and forth on whether he found the misspellings endearing or infuriating. He decided it didn't matter, and he pulled the coughing sedan off the exit and into the dealership.

They perused the lot, filled with the excitement that being around shiny, unused cars tends to give humans. Many of the cars had five-gallon water jugs mounted to their roofs. The jugs, like those found in standard water coolers, had tubes running from their spouts into the open gas tanks of each vehicle. Once they decided on a car, a large SUV-type that seemed like it would be good in the snow, they set about finding the keys. The Angels had not bothered to put a set of keys with each car.

Leo went into the main sales office and searched until he found a wall of lockboxes. Fortunately, they were all open. The first few rows had been carefully unlocked and pulled open, but after that, an Angel must have decided it was easier to forgo using the tiny keys, and it just wrenched the little doors open with its robotic hands. It gave Leo a small degree of pleasure to think about one of the Angels getting annoyed.

"I hope whoever it was broke a nail," came Frankie's voice. She was still hanging from Leo's back. *"Third row, seventh column. Don't ask me how I know that. I just do."*

Leo went to the lockbox she indicated and took the key that lay there. Back on the lot, he clicked the fob, and the lights blinked on the SUV they chose.

Everyone loaded into the new car, and they set off in earnest to Birch Mountain. They drove in silence mostly. Leo felt exhausted and imagined that everyone else probably was as well—that was if Alphonse and Frankie even felt exhaustion in their current states. He figured they did—mental and emotional exhaustion, anyway. Those were what had him dragging. He wished Brock was around to lighten the mood. Even if he were just sleeping in the back as he had on the Taco Bell trip, his presence would have still provided warmth. But he was not here. He had been successfully decanted. He would be leaving Earth in a matter of hours.

About half an hour later, Leo and his fringe accomplices reached the ski resort. There was a gatehouse blocking the entrance road. The ornate-looking wrought iron gate was still fully intact, which was a good sign, but they would have to figure out how to get through. Leo parked the car, intending to step out and see if he could determine how to work the gate from inside the little shack that would have housed a surly operator two years ago. As he was unbuckling his seatbelt, Frankie's voice came to him.

"Wait," she said. *"Let me try."*

Leo could see her strange new body tensing up in the passenger seat. Her tentacles stopped writhing as much, and he heard a creak outside the car. Looking through the windshield, he saw the gate shift a bit to the side. It opened a couple more inches and stopped again. After a moment, it began rolling steadily off the road.

As the gate creaked along its track, Leo felt a mild ache at the base of his skull. Looking into the rearview mirror, he saw Lois wincing slightly, feeling the residual effects of Frankie's efforts as well. When it was open enough to pass, Leo drove through. Behind them, as the gate pulled itself closed, the pain returned but fainter this time.

"Wow," Leo said, absently rubbing his neck. "Are you okay?"

"I think so," thought Frankie. *"It was tougher than I thought it would be."*

"That was very impressive," said Alphonse. "But if we're going to stay here, we should probably learn how to actually use the gate at some point." A winking face appeared on his screen.

"Definitely," thought Frankie.

Leo drove them up the long and winding path. Young birch trees planted at evenly spaced intervals lined the gravel driveway. After a minute, they reached the parking lot and pulled right up to the main entrance. Leo exited the car and tried the front door of the lodge. It was locked. While the others waited in the car that was mysteriously running on water, he walked around the perimeter of the sprawling structure.

The weathered barn wood facade made the lodge appear old and rustic, but it couldn't have been built more than fifteen or twenty years ago. There were a few other doors leading into the lodge, and all were locked, except one that appeared to be some kind of service door. Leo opened it and stepped into a spacious kitchen. He fumbled around, feeling for light switches. Eventually, he found them and snapped them on, drenching the steel and tile of the kitchen in a fluorescent glow. He continued flipping on lights as he made his way back to the front entrance to unlock it.

Leo brought Frankie in and set her in one of the easy chairs in the main lobby. *"Did you check the security system?"* she asked.

"I hadn't even thought about it," he said. He looked around at the walls of the lobby.

"Probably behind the desk," Frankie thought to him.

Leo went up to the large oak alcove against the left wall. Once again, the door was locked, so he hopped over the desk to get inside. Behind the desk, he found keys and the security system that Frankie had mentioned. It seemed to be a kind of silent alarm, and it was going off by the look of it.

"I think we set off a silent alarm," Leo yelled to Frankie.

"Uh oh," she replied, *"I bet the cops will be here any minute."*

Leo laughed. The alarm was probably broadcasting to some call center halfway across the country, ringing the phone of some employee who was now a jar of goop. Next to the alarm keypad, he found a thermostat and turned up the heat.

The four went exploring for a while. The lodge was larger than Leo had imagined. He read everything in the brochure but was still surprised to see it all in real life. The two restaurants were both very chic. One appeared to be a bar and grill, and the other was more of an upscale dining area. There were saunas and game rooms and an indoor pool, as well as a few conference rooms, one of which was set up like a small theater.

On the second floor were guest rooms ranging from modest single-bedrooms, to larger living areas with kitchenettes, to a full honeymoon suite with a spiral staircase leading to a loft. The loft had a breathtaking panoramic view of the mountains and the city below. Looking out the window, Leo could see the enormous alien ship that was acting as a power plant. Its size was difficult to grasp for him. It lay there, on the side of a mountain, a crucifix the size of several football stadiums. From this room, the whole downtown of Cindervale was visible—a thousand tiny buildings in a vast bowl surrounded by trees.

The interior of the loft was sparse. It housed only a king-size bed, a ladder-back chair, a bureau, and nothing more. The focal point of the room was the tremendous view. Seeing the immense bed in the loft, Leo remembered how tired he was. Though it was not much past noon, he was still worn out from the past two days.

"Go ahead," said the voice of Frankie in his head. *"Sleep awhile."*

"I think maybe I will," said Leo.

"Lois," Frankie thought.

"Yes?" The older woman seemed more or less entirely unfazed by the fact that she had been traveling with a telepathic worm creature.

"Would you take me down to the lobby? Let's see if we can get the fireplace going."

"Of course, sweetheart." Lois reached into Leo's backpack harness and lifted Frankie without hesitation.

Leo felt ashamed of his earlier revulsion but was reasonably certain it would fade entirely soon enough. Lois held Frankie like a large baby, stroking her hand through Frankie's tentacles. Frankie inadvertently transmitted a warm, soothing feeling, and Leo felt even sleepier. He sat on the bed as Frankie and Lois climbed back down the spiral staircase.

Alphonse was sitting on top of the bureau where Lois put him.

"I'm gonna take a nap, Alph," said Leo, starting to crawl under the covers. "Don't watch me sleep. It's weird."

"I'll do my best to resist the temptation," Alphonse said.

Leo smiled as he drifted off to sleep.

***

The ship containing the Strappons zoomed through space, closing in on Earth at an incredible speed. They were just over fifty million miles from the planet and were about to initiate their braking procedure, which would take a few hours of Earth time. They had made better time in their travels than anticipated but were still cutting things close. On their ship's scanners, they could see the cross-shaped Arks converging at the edge of the atmosphere of the planet called Earth. There remained a smattering of ships within the atmosphere, and the Strappons were counting on their hunch that the ambassadors would only leave as a single group.

The captain ordered that the weapons systems be checked and calibrated, just as a matter of course. When it saw the unease its request instilled in the crew, the captain also requested that the communication and life support systems be checked as well. It knew those systems were functioning properly or could be repaired quickly. It was the weaponry that needed to work precisely and at exactly the right moment if things came to a head.

The captain was right to have the crew continue to check all their systems. The trip through the gateway had wreaked havoc on the mechanical aspects of the vessel. Diagnostics and repairs had been taking place since they came through. It was the prioritization of the work order that worried the crew.

Two Strappon crew members communicated their thoughts to one another while running diagnostics on the weapons systems. This is what the exchange roughly translated to—

"I'm a little worried about what the prime objective of this mission is," said one.

"I know exactly how you feel," said the other. "I think the pressure of appearing dominant is getting to the captain. It (the captain, Strappons are genderless) should probably be more concerned with getting us through space safely."

"If it were me," replied the first, "I would jettison the weapons and everything else we don't need. I think we ought to try to appear as humble and non-threatening as possible."

There was a long period of non-communication before the other crew member responded again.

"I *do* want to be able to play Handjobb again, though," the second Strappon said.

"Me too."

"I get the impression," said the second Strappon to the first, "that we don't really have a plan B here."

"Yeah, I'm not really sure what happens if the Triangles reject us when we get to this alien planet. If we can't go along with them, or if we miss them or they leave us, I don't know if the gateway works both ways."

"I don't know if I could take another trip through it. Not if it's the same thing again. That was horrible."

"Half the passengers are still raving-mad," said the first Strappon. "My [sibling] is still catatonic from it. I think maybe they're the lucky ones."

"I'm not sure any of us are lucky."

"I *do* want to be able to play Handjobb again, though."

"Me too."

27.

Leo slept through the spectacular parade of Angel ships dropping off colonists from around the world. Alphonse saw it all, in his way, and it stoked something in him—something hot and unpleasant. He had heard the exact number of humans being left behind, but seeing them all made it more real. Fourteen thousand six hundred seventeen people sounded like a minuscule, inconsequential number compared to the billions of humans who had existed on the planet. Seeing them all being lowered in modified shipping crates from the Angel's transport vessels, crate after crate for hours, brought to light the sheer humanity of it.

Another subjective injustice was seeing all the humans who still had their bodies while he did not. Alphonse had accepted his Promise. He was never even told what went wrong with his decantation and just had to trust that the Angels were being truthful when they said he would not survive the trip to Caldo and that his soul would drift into space, forever unreachable. He would be left as well, even after having done everything right.

As he continued watching the alien ambassadors work, Alphonse identified the hot and unpleasant sensation in him. It was hate—hate for the Angels and their lies, hate for his place in the universe, hate for loss. As he now existed, he could sense this hate. He could identify every facet of it but could no longer connect with it. He had evolved beyond feeling it, or it was beyond his ability to feel. Despite all of this, for the sake of his friends and their shared bond and for the sake of who he used to be, he did his best to convey the hatred he would have once felt.

After a while, Lois and Frankie returned to the loft and watched the conception of a new human society until Leo eventually woke.

"Wow," Leo said, seeing the activity down in the city. "I can't get over how big those ships are."

"By my count," said Alphonse, "they must have dropped off about eleven thousand or so of the humans left behind."

They all watched the silent spectacle. Leo couldn't really see what was happening aside from the ships coming and going. He couldn't see things the way Alphonse could, so he couldn't count the number of shipping containers or un-decanted humans. It was still a bizarre sight. Eventually, Frankie spoke.

"So," she started, *"I've been talking to Lois."*

Leo thought about what a futile, self-defeating effort that sounded like. Or rather, he tried *not* to think about it because he knew that Frankie would pick up on it, and he would feel bad about having thought it. She was polite enough to ignore his thoughts and attempted non-thoughts.

"With the way I... am now," she continued, *"I've been able to kind of figure out why no one can ever understand what the fuck she's talking about. I can pick up on the stuff she thinks instead of the stuff she says. Remember, I'm still new to this aliens and goo-people and purple sky stuff, so this is a little hard for me to take. But I'm pretty sure that Lois is some kind of alien."*

No one spoke for several moments. Then Alphonse said, "That would explain a lot."

"It's not just that she's a weirdo. It's that she's... how do I explain this? Whatever kind of alien she is doesn't exist as we do. She's sort of outside of our version of time and space. I think she was trying to tell me that her race sent a bunch of scouts to explore other worlds, and she ended up here, or something like that. I'm still struggling to understand it all."

"So that's why nothing she says makes any sense?" asked Leo. "She's not just senile?"

"I think it's that there are some wires crossed somewhere. The stuff she says does *make sense, just not to us right here, right now. I know how that sounds, but I think that's what it is. Something about merging her mind into an earthling body messed with her."*

"I suppose that's just as feasible as anything else that's happened for the past year and a half," Leo said. He felt weird talking about Lois like she wasn't there, but if what Frankie was saying was true, then maybe Lois *wasn't* actually there—at least, not in the way that he and Frankie and Alphonse were. Leo felt a little bad about writing Lois off as a crazy person. He was good at feeling bad about stuff. But he still didn't exactly know how this new information related to the current situation.

"I'm going to try talking to her more later to see what else I can find out, and"—she paused in her thought—*"I guess, get to know her."*

"I'm going to go see if I can find something to eat," said Leo. "Are you hungry, Lois?"

"Probably not. I've been to Minnesota before," she said.

"I'll meet you guys up here in a little bit, okay?"

"Sure," Frankie thought to him.

Alphonse displayed an "okay" hand on his screen. Lois did not respond. She simply continued looking out the panoramic window.

Leo wandered down to one of the restaurant kitchens to see what might still be around to eat. He turned on the water in one of the large dish sinks. He remembered Frankie doing that at Taco Bell to clear sediment from the water lines. The faucet coughed and spat brown water for a few minutes as Leo browsed the available options.

He dared not open any of the coolers for fear of releasing the stench of rotting vegetables and spoiling sauces. Dealing with that would be a project for another day. On the shelves of a walk-in pantry were cans of sauces and mixes and some dry goods and spices. Many of the bags and boxes had been chewed into by mice. Above a row of ovens and grills, there were bags of rice and pasta on wire shelves that mice had not been able to get to yet. Leo decided that spaghetti would be fine. He found a pot and a strainer and hoped the range would not explode when he turned on the gas. It didn't.

It struck Leo that this was likely the only way he could have ever been able to eat a meal at this lodge. From the looks of it and the "private" designation on the brochure, it was probably way out of his price range. The simple plate of spaghetti he was making might have cost him half a week's pay in his old life. He boiled the noodles and continued to look around in the kitchen.

There was another pantry with a steel door that mice couldn't pillage. It contained a series of shelves and a small walk-in freezer, separate from the main one in the kitchen. Loaves and loaves of frozen bread filled the freezer, and the pantry shelves were loaded with heavy bags of French toast mix. A note on the shelf read, "FRENCH TOAST SUNDAY! NOT FOR USE ANY OTHER DAY!" Luckily for Leo, it was not Sunday.

Back at the range, Leo plucked a noodle from the boiling water. He remembered an old friend testing pasta by throwing it at the wall and seeing if it stuck. Leo blew on the long strand of angel hair to cool it, then heaved it onto the ceiling since all the walls were covered with steel and plastic. The noodle stuck there, but Leo couldn't remember if that meant that the pasta was done or that it needed more time. He pulled another strand of pasta from the pot and chewed it up. It seemed done to him. He strained it, piled it into a bowl, and grabbed a can of pasta sauce from the pantry. After about three minutes of trying to figure out how to work the counter-mounted can opener, he finally got the thing open. What he didn't use on his plate he dumped into a plastic bowl and put in the freezer.

Leo walked around the lodge, eating spaghetti as he explored more thoroughly. There was a hot tub in the room with the pool. He wondered if it still worked or was clean enough to use safely. He wondered if Frankie could use a hot tub in her current... state. Images ran through his head of sitting in the hot tub with Frankie, as she used to be, and Brock and Rhonda and George and Lois, and maybe Doug, too, and Miranda with her tablet in a waterproof plastic bag. The thought was nice until Leo realized the scene would likely involve socializing and talking. That would put a damper on things for him. He would also have to be mostly naked, which didn't appeal much to him either.

He walked up to the hot tub. It sat above the floor, its green, marbled plastic interior surrounded by wood paneling on the outside. Leo peered into the basin and locked eyes with a terrified opossum. The opossum had been there first and wasn't causing any trouble, so Leo backed away and left the pool room. He hoped there wasn't too much other wildlife already residing in the lodge.

In one of the game rooms, there were some old arcade cabinets. Many were on and running with their sound turned down. One of the cabinets housed a game called *Space Invaders*. It was a wildly popular arcade game when Leo was a child, but he never cared much for it. He watched the demo screen run, displaying the different kinds of *"Invaders"* to shoot and their point values. It was so simple, so easy to understand. Leo finished his spaghetti.

After more exploring and, thankfully, not finding any more wild animals, Leo rinsed his plate in a public restroom and left it in the sink. He didn't feel like taking it back to the kitchen. As one of the only humans who needed to eat, he felt like it wouldn't make much of a difference to anyone else if he left it for a while. He would take it back later.

He slowly made his way back up to the suite and climbed the staircase to the loft. As he entered the silent room, he waved to the cadre of misfits he'd inherited. He did not hear any of Frankie's thoughts in his head. Lois was sitting in the ladder-back chair with Frankie on her lap. Once again, Leo felt a sense of ease coming from Frankie as Lois stroked her strange body. It was nice.

When Leo sat on the bed, Alphonse spoke. "By my count, they've delivered everyone now," said the synthesized voice of the decanted man. "If that Haniel guy gives one of his speeches, the Angels won't be leaving for months."

"I think he'll keep it short and sweet," Frankie's voice said inside everyone's mind. *"He's not too happy about how this all ended up."*

"Especially since you blasted the hell out of his body and killed his friend," said Alphonse. It could have been an accusation, but the laughing face on his screen clarified his tone.

"At this point, I think they just want to get out of here," Frankie continued. *"They'll give everyone the bare minimum of information about how to survive in their colony. Then they'll be gone."*

"Can you guys tell what's going on down there?" asked Leo. He could only see ships hovering over the Earth.

"More or less," said Frankie. *"There's a pair of binoculars in the top drawer of the bureau. I think they expect people who rent this room to want to look at stars or birds or whatever. Maybe just creep on people."*

Leo retrieved the binoculars and stood at the panoramic window. It took him a long time to orient himself and figure out what he was seeing. When he got everything into focus, he realized he still couldn't see much but noticed some things he hadn't before. "What are those little shapes flying up in the air?" he asked.

"Those are Angels flying up to their ships from the surface," said Alphonse.

Leo tried to focus on one of the shapes, and it started to look like it could possibly be the shape of an Angel, but he wouldn't have thought so if no one had told him what it was. Somehow, seeing the alien visitors flying up to their ships, at last preparing to actually leave the planet—the *galaxy*, gave weight to the finality of everything for Leo. He lowered the binoculars from his eyes.

"So, this is really it," he said.

"Looks that way," Frankie's voice responded.

In the back of his brain, where it was swampy and humid, Leo had unintentionally been harboring a thought. The thought was that, somehow, none of this was real. That the past eighteen months had been a bizarre fever dream, and he would eventually wake up in a bed moist with sweat. Maybe he would open his eyes and be six years old, having invented, in his mind, the entire mundanity of his adolescence and adulthood to the point that his brain added aliens for variety. Or, perhaps, he would wake up freezing in a tiny, mechanical bed, hooked to monitors and respirators, old and dry and withered with no memory of the reality of his life to that point and only the smoky wisps of the fading dream to use as a personal history.

Neither of those things was going to happen. The dream wouldn't be fading. It could only continue. On and on. But that was all too much for Leo to think about, so he sat back on the bed, waiting for whatever might happen next. What happened next did not begin for about another hour and did not last very long. However, it was, incidentally, like something out of a dream.

28.

The Strappon vessel arrived as the last of the Angels were boarding their immense ships. They eased themselves into Earth's atmosphere, keeping just above the Angels' Arks. The Strappon captain prepared a message to be sent out to all the ships in the Angels' fleet. It could not discern if any one ship contained beings of more or less importance than the others.

"Attention Triangles!" it blasted out over every conceivable communication frequency available to them. The Angels, who the Strappons called Triangles, received the message. No communication equipment on Earth picked up the transmission, though—Earth having such primitive means of communication compared to the Strappons and the Angels. The humans on the surface simply had to use their eyes to gather information about what was happening.

"Attention Triangles!" the captain repeated. "I speak to you as the leader of the Strappon race. The race that you promised paradise to so long ago."

The Angels in their ships were baffled. Some remembered the Strappons and how their invitation to Caldo, or Octacontaheptagon, had gone eons ago. Many Angels had no idea who the Strappons were. Of those who did remember the Strappons, many tried not to speak of the race that had chased paradise away.

"There was a time when you came to us," continued the Strappon captain. "You gave information about an eternal paradise. You said our race had been chosen to gain entry to this utopia."

The captain waited expectantly for a reply. Eventually, one came in the Strappon language, spoken by the being who had appeared on Earth as an Angel and called itself Haniel.

"We remember," came the response. "We... remember."

The Strappon captain hesitated, its ego desperately resisting humility. After a moment, he responded. "We regret the way that things happened at that time."

"You threatened us with violence," said Haniel. "You chased us away."

"Yes," said the Strappon captain. "Ours is a volatile and passionate race. These qualities were even more prevalent in our culture in the old times when you visited." This was a lie. The nature of the Strappons had changed since they last saw the alien ambassadors, but the change had made them *more* paranoid and reactive. "We have been, and are now, willing to accept the offer you made to us."

"That," Haniel said, pausing, "is not possible. Not at the moment. We have always planned to go back to your world, but after what happened the first time, this process will take many reassessments and much thought. We have countless other races we must visit first. It was highly unethical and dangerous for you to track us down and confront us in the midst of one of our missions."

"We knew the risks to ourselves and the others involved, but this should prove our devotion to you and your cause. We have sacrificed everything to accept what you offered us—what we shunned in an instant of insanity—a lapse of judgment."

"What do you mean, you have 'sacrificed everything?'" asked Haniel.

"We have, in this ship, the entirety of our population. We have abandoned our planet, and we are fairly certain that we cannot return to it. We are now stuck in this system with limited time and resources. You must take us with you!" The Strappon captain was sure that it had the Triangles eating out of its non-existent hand.

"Why would you do such a thing?"

"Because we crave what you have, we are starving for it. Would not a starving being give everything it had to feed itself and its people?" The captain could sense that victory was imminent. "Have we not proved, by doing what no others before us have done, that we are now, more than ever, worthy of what you offer?"

"No," said Haniel. Tensions in the Strappon ship were rising as Haniel continued broadcasting his reply. "If anything, your actions have jeopardized your admission. I told you that we had planned to reassess and return to you one day. Now we must reassess our reassessment. This kind of reckless behavior is unacceptable. Patience is highly regarded in our culture, and we admire those who display it. This, this is unacceptable."

"Patience!" shouted the Strappon captain. "Where was your patience with us? Was it patience to leave us behind and forsake us?"

"Do you even realize the implications of what you've done here?" asked Haniel, ignoring the captain. "You could have endangered countless planets and living species coming so far across the universe without thinking. You have never traveled the way we travel. You do not know the risks involved. What if you were followed? Anyone could have tracked you the way you tracked us. You have endangered our whole mission with your greed and hubris."

"You must take us with you now," said the captain. "You must."

"We cannot. Even if we wished to, which I assure you we do not, we could not transport your people or your ship. We could not divulge the secrets that make our ships untraceable to allow you to follow us. I repeat, we can not."

"You really must," said the Strappon captain as it signaled to its second in command to begin arming the weapons systems. The second tried reasoning with the captain, but the captain simply repeated the order. The second did not approve of this but knew that if it refused, it would be dealt with, and another, more willing officer would take its place.

In Haniel's ship, one of the Angels, known on Earth as Gabriel, gave a status report. Haniel refused to speak with the Strappons, who were now simply rebroadcasting the phrase "You really must" over and over again. "Haniel, we are reading fluctuations in the Strappon ship's power channels."

"Good," said Haniel. "Perhaps they are powering their engines to leave this place. I cannot believe they would do something so rash as to chase us down here. How did they even find us?" he asked, more to himself than anyone else. "We must commence our own launching process as soon as possible."

The fluctuations being read were, of course, the Strappon ship diverting power to its weapons systems. While last-minute calculations were made about firing missiles within the gravity at the edge of Earth's atmosphere and targeting coordinates were checked, the Strappon captain made an announcement to its crew and passengers.

"Brave Strappons," it said, "we have come so far, waited so long for our chance to regain the glory that our ancestors and our elders lost. We have done all that could be expected of us in this respect and have again been denied our great reward. In the name of our people and our pride, what happens next shall be our greatest moment. I thank you for all you have done and all that you are. In what may be the last act of my existence, I hereby revoke the ban on Handjobb. Thank you."

The message echoed through the odd and narrow hallways and cabins of the ship and settled in the odd and narrow souls of the Strappon people. Those still sane enough to understand what the captain had said and the implications of its statement were split in their reactions. Some rejoiced and began forming groups to play the game that had been outlawed for so long. Others mourned, understanding that their entire existence was likely to cease. Many were still so scrambled by their awful trip that they could not follow what was said or what was happening.

After all preparations were made, the automatic weapons systems began their targeting process. A massive payload of explosives and electromagnetic bombs was soon locked onto each of the Angels' Arks. With so few controls to work and so little data to monitor, the crew on the bridge of the ship began to play Handjobb among themselves. The nature of the Strappon rectangles was such that they could play using the minimal excess mass of their bodies. They aligned themselves with the main viewscreen to witness the destruction of the aliens who had twice denied them their rightful paradise.

"Haniel," said Gabriel aboard the Ark with which the Strappon captain had been communicating, "they have fired what appears to be a large cache of destructive projectiles."

The Strappon message, "You really must," was still repeating on the comm channels.

"This is... regrettable," said Haniel.

The first wave of missiles collided with the ship.

The Strappon weaponry was surprisingly effective against the Angels' Arks. Human weaponry would also have worked well on them. They were not built for battle and could resist only the smallest meteorite and space-dust collisions. The Angels' primary intent was to avoid violence at any cost, and they had always been successful in that regard. The primitive nature of most of their technology was offset by their impeccable planning, which typically kept them safe in any situation. This case was the exception to the rule.

A few of the Angels' ships were immediately torn asunder by the impact of the Strappon explosives. The debris began to fall to the planet below, spitting flame and multicolored sparks. Back in the loft of the honeymoon suite of Birch Mountain, Leo initially thought the explosions and light show were some kind of parting ceremony to encourage and embolden the humans being left behind. Within seconds, though, it was apparent to everyone on the planet that things had gone spectacularly wrong.

The ship occupied by Haniel had been hit with the equivalent of several thousand pounds worth of dynamite but was still operational. Haniel ordered his helms to get away as quickly as possible, but after only a few seconds, the Strappon systems launched another wave of missiles. Haniel's ship had ascended about two thousand feet, climbing above the Strappon vessel before the explosives hit, crippling the Ark entirely. As it plummeted, the Ark collided with the Strappon ship, sending both in a blaze to the surface of the planet. The Strappons who used their last moments to play Handjobb died doing what they loved. The others simply died.

The two waves of attack had been all that was required to ground the Angels' fleet completely. Millions of tons of burning metal crashed down, pulled by gravity to the city of Cindervale. The entire town was crushed under flaming chunks of spaceships the size of cruise liners and shopping malls. As they reached their terminal velocity, the ships seemed to fall in slow motion before smashing the ground below and gouging vast craters into the Earth. Spaceship after spaceship fell over the city and the surrounding area for what seemed like ages. At one point, what might have been the remaining Strappons' explosives detonating or a rupturing power core from one of the vessels caused a massive flare-up. White fire towered over three miles into the purple sky, melting or reducing everything inside the limits of Cindervale proper to ash.

Moments later, having exhausted its fuel and oxygen supply, the spire of flame extinguished itself. Every living thing within ten miles of the explosions was now very, very dead. A whirlwind of smoke and debris corkscrewed itself into the sky as air rushed into a space that had all its oxygen and other gases sucked from it by impossibly hot flames. There was a sort of lazy tornado of smoldering ember for a few minutes, then whatever was still capable of burning flared up again. Modest fires started in and around the crater as if to prove that they, too, had been part of something spectacular.

***

After the shock of the Cindervale Holocaust dimmed somewhat, reality began to make itself felt in earnest. Frankie was incapable of crying, as that act required a human body, but she managed as close an approximation as possible in her new form. Unfortunately for those around her, she was still unfamiliar with the nature of her being, and she inadvertently broadcast her sorrow to the others in the room.

Leo felt waves of woe washing over him—deep chasms of despair that he could barely comprehend. He also had a vague understanding of what Frankie was and had been feeling. The destruction of the city and the last remnants of humanity had loosed something in her. The stress of long and awful years flowed out of her mind like a cool foam. Leo felt her hate for the injustice of reality and the loathing of all living things capable of dishonesty and deception. He felt her grief and jealousy and heard the thousands of "whys" and "why-nots" she had played through her mind during her life. A sick sense of catharsis came when she viewed the inferno that took the lives of all the humans left on the planet and those who had been decanted and awaited the paradise she would never have. Following this came the physical illness that sadism causes in those who dabble in it but aren't cut out for it.

It went on for a long time, all this emotion in Frankie. There were feelings of confusion and loss for her body and wishes for a swift death like the countless she had just witnessed. The crushing enormity of what life would be from now on rolled around in her like a huge ball bearing in a stone bowl. Leo felt all this, as did Alphonse and Lois. There were no physical or chemical reactions that could ease the pain in Frankie. There were no endorphins to be circulated—no hormones to be released. There was only hurt and confusion that had to play out for hours. Lois quietly wept as she rocked and petted Frankie in the chair.

Leo, his vision obscured by the afterimage of the explosions and flare-ups he had stared into, looked out onto the ruined city miles away. Several times during the calamity, the lodge had shaken and rumbled, and winds whipped as though a typhoon was coming. In the yard, a few visible trees were uprooted and tipped over. Several others had lost branches or had their tips bent or snapped. There was now a fairly steady breeze outside. The air in the room, which had been chilly when Leo first climbed the stairs, was now balmy. He had turned up the heat a few hours ago, but it felt unnaturally warm now. It was then that Leo thought of something. He reached over and clicked on the bedside lamp. The bulb flared to life.

Though heavy sadness still blanketed Leo, he spoke to whomever would listen. "We still have power," he said. Frankie's silent emotion, interrupted for the first time since the disaster in Cindervale, wavered slightly.

"I was thinking about that too," said Alphonse. "You probably can't see it, but there are some functioning streetlights along the roads out there."

Leo got out the binoculars and attempted to look out at the scene again. Though his eyes were still full of colorful floating blobs and tears, he saw the Angel ship that was to be used as a sort of power generator still lay on the side of the southern mountain. It was severely damaged but still recognizable.

"I guess the ship they left was far enough away from the explosion to avoid getting totally wiped out. At least the part they hooked into the power grids must still be fine. Power to this place must not run through the city."

"Small miracles," said Alphonse.

Leo lay back in the bed. His eyes were sore from the flash of the explosion and the surrogate tears he had cried. He felt Frankie's grief still trickling through him, but it was more bearable now. It was a sadness he understood but had not truly felt. The feeling wasn't his own. It was merely funneling through him. Though it had been a more intense sensation than he was used to, the overall feeling was familiar. He kicked off his shoes, which he had been wearing all day, and closed his eyes. He was tired again, despite his afternoon nap.

He woke up before dawn. Lois lay on one side of the bed with Leo on the other and Frankie between them. They lay above the covers in the now uncomfortably warm room.

"I'm sorry," came the voice of Frankie. She was still broadcasting her melancholy.

"Hmm?" said Leo, barely conscious.

"I'm sorry," she repeated in his head. *"I knew you guys were feeling all that shit I was feeling. I guess I just do that now. I tried to stop when I saw all those... people,"*—her thoughts stopped briefly—*"but I just fucking couldn't. It was too much, and I had to, I don't know."*

Leo laid a hand on her writhing tentacle body and felt her discomfort ease slightly.

"It's okay," said Leo, his eyes closed. He felt the mass of worms that made up Frankie's skin and was surprised he wasn't disgusted by it. It was no longer a strange, alien animal he was touching. It was Frankie. He liked touching Frankie, and this was Frankie, so he liked touching this.

"I saw them all die," she said. *"I mean, I could see and feel them all down there in the town. I could feel the Angels too, and something else. Something went wrong—"* she paused. *"No fucking shit, Frankie."* She had tried to think this last part to herself, but it had still been broadcast to Leo.

"It's okay," Leo repeated, still running his hand along Frankie.

"The Angels were leaving," she thought to him. *"They were packing up and heading off, but there was something else there— something that wasn't supposed to be there, or maybe it was a bunch of things? I don't know. It was alive, though, and it was angry at the Angels. It, they, started attacking the Angels, and then, well, you saw the rest."*

"You don't have to think about it all now," Leo said, hugging Frankie closer to him. A compassion that would typically have required heavy internal excavation and refinement now flowed through him unprompted. The ease with which this emotional connection came threatened to distract Leo and ruin another otherwise pleasant life moment, so he tried his best to ignore it. He succeeded.

"I think maybe I do have to," she replied. *"Everyone down there was already unhappy, or most of them were. Like we are. Confused and pissed off at those lying assholes who were just fucking leaving us here to go off and live in a utopia. Then they all realized*

what was happening, and there was so much fear." She tensed up in Leo's arms, and he squeezed her tighter.

"I guess it's lucky it went so fast," she continued. *"I don't know how much more of that I could have taken, and I couldn't look away. I should have, but I couldn't right then. All those people knowing they were going to die. And I guess everyone knows now that death isn't really the same as we always thought it was, but that's still fucking scary. Getting crushed and burned to death, and..."* she trailed off in her thought.

"Is there..." Leo started without thinking. He didn't voice the rest of his sentence, but he had already thought it, so Frankie had already heard it.

"No," she said. *"There's no one alive down there—no humans, no Angels, no goo-people, not even whoever it was that attacked them from what I can tell."*

Suddenly, Lois spoke, her eyes still shut tight. "We can try to give them a call sometime," she said.

"I'm not sure the phone lines still work," said Alphonse. He had been staying quiet, but he was listening the whole time. He did not sleep anymore.

"Oh, don't have such a sour attitude," Lois said to Alphonse. "There's plenty for everyone."

"Can you tell what she's trying to say?" Leo asked Frankie.

"I'm not sure," she replied. *"I still haven't figured her out. But if she's saying something, it's probably important, or it was, or it will be."*

29.

Something about the fires burning in Cindervale—something about the alien metals and alloys feeding the flames kept Birch Mountain warmer than it should have been. At night, the smoking crater, now a mass grave for billions, continued to glow. Leo found himself coughing quite a bit whenever he went outside, so he stayed in mostly. A thick fog of ash and dust hung in the air, and the view through the lodge's windows became dull and gray with soot. About five days after what was, effectively, the end of humanity, it started to rain. It rained gently and steadily for two days, but the fires in Cindervale would not die.

The rains must have helped clear the air of ash, however. Leo found himself able to spend more time outdoors after the lazy storms passed. The temperature was starting to drop as well. Soon it would be winter. Leo hoped to be able to get close to the town where he had once lived before the snow and ice made travel too dangerous. He wasn't sure why he wanted to go and view the scene where the human race had died. He just felt like it was something he was supposed to do. Knowing he might regret going down there made it more alluring somehow.

Lots of spaghetti was eaten in the days and weeks after the catastrophe. Frankie spent a lot of time with Lois, trying to figure out the secrets of the older woman's past and future. Leo sometimes wished that Frankie would spend more time with him, but, at times, it was also hard to be with her the way she was now. He had feelings about her that he didn't want her to read—pity and disappointment and remorse that he wanted to keep to himself. She needed time to adjust to herself as well.

Life was strange and simple for a while. Leo would spend time playing the games in the arcade or walking the grounds around the lodge or talking with Alphonse about the concerts the decanted human had seen in his youth. The two would also sometimes talk about what had happened, though Leo found himself without much to say about it all. He and Alphonse had theorized, correctly, that whoever had attacked the Angels was some race that had not been allowed to go to Caldo. They would sometimes talk about how they thought the attacking aliens might have looked. They imagined giant scaly monsters and hyper-advanced robots. It was never suspected that the invaders might have been two-dimensional shapes.

One day, about a month after the catastrophe, Leo decided that he was going to try to go to town. Alphonse said he had no interest in going with him, and Frankie's mind now was such that she could see practically everything in the ruined city if she wanted. Leo didn't think it would be wise to take Lois. The terrain would probably be rough.

"Be careful," Frankie thought to him before he left. *"It's really unstable, and there are still fires burning."*

"I was wondering about that," Leo said. "I thought most of them would have burned themselves out by now. But there's still a lot of smoke coming from down there."

"Even though they mined the shit out of those mountains back in the eighteen hundreds or whenever it was, there's still tons of coal in the ground. Those old mines and the mountains around here are probably going to burn for a long time."

"Oh," Leo said. "Right. I forgot all about that."

"It's going to be really hot, so don't go too far into town. Actually, you should probably just not go at all."

"I know I shouldn't," said Leo, "but I just feel like I have to go and see."

"I know."

Leo, carrying a backpack filled with bottled water, a flashlight, a first aid kit, and a few other items, climbed into the water-powered car they took to get to Birch Mountain. He drove down the winding road to the front gate, which he had forgotten about. He was about to park the car to get out and try to open the gate when it screeched and began sliding open. Sometimes the way that Frankie had changed scared him, but he was glad to have her around.

He drove through the entrance, and the gate stayed open. There was no reason to hide or keep others away anymore. There were no others left. Leo kept his speed low and leisurely as he drove down the empty highway. This turned out to be a good idea, as a few branches and downed trees lay across parts of the roadway. Luckily, none of them completely blocked the pavement, and with no other cars on the road, he was able to veer around them. The closer he got to Cindervale, the worse the damage seemed. Road signs had been bent and blown over, and Leo wondered how close he would actually be able to get to the city.

The tree branches on the road started mingling with chunks of masonry and metal, both Earthly and not. About two miles from the exit for Cindervale, the way became completely impassable. Leo parked the car, shouldered his backpack, and began walking down the highway. He had to maneuver around and over larger and larger pieces of spaceships as he walked. It took about an hour to get to the offramp. At that point, there were only stone and metal debris. All the trees and other organic materials capable of burning had done so. The forests lining the roadway had been reduced to sooty stalks. As he continued toward the epicenter of the destruction, even the burnt tree trunks had disintegrated. There was only flat, ashen earth littered with wreckage.

Leo looked around as he walked along the curve of the exit ramp he had driven so many times in the past. It was barely recognizable to him. The road signs had charred and blackened, and the posts holding them up were bent and melted. They reminded him of large metal skeletons doing some kind of yoga. The structures that still stood were burnt and blown out. Many buildings were half-collapsed or missing entire sides, giving views of their gutted interiors.

The ground, itself black and gray, crunched under Leo's feet as he trod into the now unfamiliar city. Traffic lights and posts lay fused to the asphalt or stood doubled over in pain along the main street. Skeletal cars, their tires and innards melted in pools beneath them, lay where the force of the exploding spaceships had thrown them. Leo stopped to take a respirator mask out of his pack and strap it to his face. Frankie had found it in a maintenance closet at Birch Mountain and made him take it along. He was thankful for that now. In the pack was also a pair of gardening gloves from a shed outside the lodge. He pulled them onto his hands. They were too big. He felt self-conscious about his small hands, then remembered that he now had the largest hands of any living human. Lois's were a little smaller.

Hot dust blew through the dead streets, erupting steadily from craters and sinkholes dotted around the town. Leo remembered the commercials advertising "mine-subsidence insurance" that he'd seen years ago. He wondered how much of this town was built on top of mines that were now collapsing into themselves. From what he could see, the tunnels beneath this city were extensive and indiscriminate.

The closer he got to the impact site, which was still a ways off, the warmer it became. Heat radiated from the ground. He would have found the sandblasted streets and sidewalks were warm to the touch from the fires burning underneath if he had felt compelled to touch them. He didn't. Hulking pieces of metal from space vessels, buried unknowable distances into the earth, towered high into the sky. They conducted heat from the fires below and diffused it into the air above ground. Acrid haze ambled lazily about, its sour sulfuric scent mixing with the piercing odors of melted plastic and rubber. Leo's mask did nothing to diminish the smell. He blinked dusty tears out of his eyes.

For hours he wandered, recognizing very little around him and hoping he didn't get himself woefully lost. Ashy darkness blocked out the purple sky and masked the sun, which, when visible, was little more than a rusty nail head in the gray ceiling above.

A building, a half-demolished thing a few blocks away, crumbled the rest of the way to the carbonized ground. It kicked up black dust, and Leo had to turn his back to it and stand still for several minutes before he felt comfortable enough to continue his trek. The heat was becoming oppressive, so he took off his jacket and tied it around his waist. It was filthy.

Deeper into the city, Leo saw a strange, geometric-looking crater. It appeared to be some sort of room or chamber from one of the dead spaceships. It had planted itself into the earth, and its top must have blown away, leaving a crooked box in the ground. Strewn all through the box were half-melted shards of glass. Some of the less damaged bits of glass looked to be curved like jars. This had been a storage bay for decanted humans. Leo looked into the lower corner of the sloping room and saw a mass of boiled, blackened sludge that had settled there. It looked sort of like someone had dropped a bag of blue marshmallows into a gas grill and let them burn for an hour. Leo pondered how many dead humans he was seeing right then. A hundred? Ten million? There was really no way to tell.

He wondered again why he was doing this. The scientific curiosity of seeing the impact area had mostly worn off, yet he continued deeper into the crater of Cindervale. He supposed he was looking for some kind of meaning. If he came here, to the terminus of the human race—of civilization and life as he had known it, maybe there would be some kind of answer to be had. Maybe some absolute truth would find him, and he could foster it into his consciousness and learn from it. Or perhaps, there was nothing to be learned from this burning hole filled with alien machine parts, ruined architecture, and melted glass. That seemed more and more likely to Leo.

He continued walking until he started seeing the oddly preserved, blackened bodies of the non-decanted humans who were left behind. At first, Leo thought he was just seeing more bizarre alien machine parts. As he saw them more and more frequently, he started to see form in the gnarled, black sculptures. Some seemed caught in the midst of a panicked run. Others appeared to have their necks craned back, staring, shocked at what was happening above them. A few, despite the impact of the Angels having shared their empirical knowledge of the afterlife with all of humanity, looked to be kneeling in prayer.

Leo was reminded of photographs he had seen from Pompeii. Bodies there had been excavated and were disturbingly preserved. He didn't know the specifics of why it had happened there, and the nature of this phenomenon as it existed before him was even more foreign. Somehow, the heat or the chemicals or some other thing had instantly hardened these humans where they were, leaving them as statues of coal. It was time to leave.

While he walked back, he saw them peppered about the streets. Coming into the city, he had seen them and mistaken them for inorganic debris. Now that he had stumbled onto a large crowd of them, most lying down but some standing tall, he could recognize them anywhere. Many were broken apart and scattered throughout the town. A length of burnt pipe became someone's leg. An oblong stone became someone's head, face locked in an endless scream. Leo tried to look at his own feet as much as possible as he trudged back toward the city limits.

"*Leo?*" a faint voice called to him.

He looked, shocked to hear a human voice. He called out a few times.

"Yes!" he shouted. "Who is it? Where are you? Hello!" There was no response. He detoured briefly to see if he could find the person who called to him, but he found no one living. He strained to hear the call again, but there was nothing. Afraid of getting lost in the fog himself, he returned to the path he had been taking. His mind had simply played a trick on him, making him hear something that was not real.

"*Leo?*" came the voice again after he had trod another several yards out of the city. Again, he called out and got no reply. He searched more thoroughly this time for the caller but found no one and nothing. There were no survivors here. There could not have been. When he got back to the road heading out of town, he heard the voice again but ignored it this time. He was becoming annoyed now.

It was another twenty minutes before he heard the call again. It was much clearer this time. "*Leo?*"

"What!" he shouted through his respirator mask.

"*Leo? Can you hear me? It's Frankie.*"

"Frankie?" Leo was confused for a moment.

"*You can hear me?*" Frankie's voice asked.

"I, I hear you," yelled Leo. "Have you been calling out to me?"

"*Yeah,*" she said in his head. "*I've been trying to get a hold of you, but I didn't know if I could reach out that far.*"

"Well, you can." Leo felt dumb immediately after saying this. Then he considered the likelihood of someone both surviving this catastrophe *and* knowing his name, and he felt even dumber.

"*There's something I want you to do. There's something I want you to pick up down there if you can.*"

"Okay." Leo wondered what she could possibly want from this place. There was nothing here of any use as far as he could tell. He wondered if she could hear his thoughts from this far away.

"*It's a little ways from here. I know right where it is. If you just keep going back toward the car, I'll let you know when you get closer.*"

"All right," Leo said. He was slightly displeased to have his solitude broken this way but then wondered why he had wanted to retain the dismal, somber atmosphere in which he had enveloped himself. It had seemed right at the time to feel dark and dour, but not for any logical reason. He continued walking and climbing his way back to the car.

After an hour or so, he was back on the highway exit ramp, wondering if Frankie had somehow lost contact with him. He also wondered if he had hallucinated the entire conversation earlier. Who knew what kinds of chemicals and gases were floating around down in the bombed-out city?

"Leo? Can you hear me?" Frankie's voice said.

"Yeah, I hear you."

"I want you to go to your left, off the ramp, and into the trees there."

"Okay," Leo stepped over the guardrail and began walking into the forest of blackened stalks that used to be trees.

"A little more to your right," said Frankie.

Leo adjusted his course.

"Okay, a little more left. Are you wearing two right shoes? You walk crooked."

He took the criticism silently, changed directions again, and followed the instructions to the best of his ability, having no idea where he was going. It was how he dealt with everything in life.

"Okay, stop," Frankie finally said.

"Now what? What am I looking for?" asked Leo.

"There should be a," Frankie stuttered, *"a thing."*

"Seriously?" asked Leo.

Frankie laughed in Leo's head, and it softened his mood slightly. *"Sorry, it's like, a chunk of a robot or something."*

Leo looked around on the ground for a while, nudging odd bits of debris with his foot. Eventually, he stumbled across what he recognized as one of the ghost vessels, like the kind he had seen at Walnut Ridge. He had also, of course, seen them giving interviews on late-night television. It was not intact. In fact, it was only the top of the cylinder with one arm attached. It looked like a shard of a barrel with a few pipes sticking out of it.

"I found part of a ghost robot thing," Leo said. "Is that what we're looking for?"

"Yes!" said Frankie. *"That was kind of fun."*

"Right." Leo had not found it particularly fun to be guided through a dead forest, looking for garbage, but he was happy that Frankie was pleased. "I'm not sure why you want this thing. It's pretty messed up." He lifted the hunk of scrap and examined it. "It's mostly empty except for a few wires and a, a thing."

"Seriously?" came Frankie's voice.

Leo had to smile.

"There's some weird glass bulb or tube or something inside it."

"Is the tube broken?" asked Frankie.

Leo lifted the ruined metal vessel closer to his face. It was lighter than he expected. "It doesn't look like it. I can't believe that it's not shattered or cracked or anything. Crazy. What do you want this thing for?"

"I'm not sure." Frankie's voice was tentative. *"I just, I think we need it."*

"Okay," Leo replied. He continued his journey back to the road toward the car. He placed his backpack and the dismembered robot into the back of the car. Wiping the dust from the side windows, he saw his reflection. He was blackened with soot and coal dust. He tried to pat the dust from his jeans and shirt but only smeared it into his clothes. With a sigh, he pulled the gardening gloves from his hands. They had worn through in a few spots but kept his hands relatively clean. Seeing this, he decided simply to take off his shirt and pants. Stripping down to his underwear felt nice after being in the oppressive heat of the town. Once in the car, he turned on the air conditioner and chilled himself.

The drive back to Birch Mountain was uneventful, aside from when Leo had to stop on the highway to allow a family of bears to cross the road. The largest, as it crossed, stopped and looked at Leo almost resentfully. He wondered if bears could be resentful, then wondered what he might have done to it to make it feel that way. "What's the matter?" he said aloud inside the car. "Look around you. You've won." The beast looked at Leo a moment longer. He imagined it saying, "Then what are you still doing here?" before it tromped off the road.

30.

"Are you sure we got all the right stuff?" Leo asked Frankie.

"I'm pretty sure," she replied, not sounding pretty sure.

Frankie had tried to explain her compulsion to repair the ghost vessel to Leo but could not. She felt a strange, almost external prodding to fix the demolished robot and get it working again. She'd never had any interest in electronics or repair work, and she didn't think she had any desire to talk to ghosts. They were boring. Yet, she could not push the thought from her mind that she was supposed to fix this dead machine.

Leo did not pry about Frankie's desire for him to work on the vessel. Being her hands and feet gave him something to do and allowed him to spend time with her. The two of them had taken a few days to drive around neighboring towns to find hardware stores and electronics dealers. Frankie would tell Leo what to look for, and Leo would do his best to find it. He, not being very handy himself, had very little idea about what any of the parts did, but he was happy to help find them.

They had also found thousands of pages worth of books on electrical repair and machinery. The books were not really for Frankie's benefit. If she were near enough to a book, Frankie could more or less "read" it all at once by effortlessly taking mental photographs of the ink printed on its pages without ever opening the cover. "Near enough" was anywhere within ten miles now, and that distance was growing. The books were for Leo, who would have to do the physical work of crimping, soldering, and connecting things.

The two made drawings together to start the project. Leo had never looked at electronic schematics, let alone drawn his own, but he was going to be doing the repairs, so Frankie needed him to have some kind of guide to follow. It was a terribly time-consuming process. Frankie would say things like, *"Draw a line to the right. Now turn it ninety degrees upward for two inches, then back to the right for an inch. Now make a zigzag for an inch, then make it straight again. Draw a rounded rectangle there and put three vertical lines in the middle of it. Now go back to that vertical line we drew and make another horizontal one going to the left from it,"* and so on.

Leo was a good assistant. He did not ask questions. He did as he was told, and the schematics came out surprisingly well. In the end, they wound up with a dozen or so pages. Leo had used a black pen for the parts of the circuits that were visible in the destroyed vessel and a red pen for Frankie's best guesses as to what the missing parts might be. Presently, these pages were strewn about the floor of the large lobby, along with bags full of small electrical parts and scores of breadboards. Leo had insisted on getting the breadboards, which were reusable circuit boards onto which components could be connected without solder. During his practice with the soldering iron, he had burned his fingertips countless times and made no solid connections.

At Frankie's command, Leo started pushing electronic doodads into the square holes of a breadboard. He pushed the leads of diodes, resistors, capacitors, relays, transformers, and other tiny bits he had never heard of into the board. He'd often put them in the wrong spot, and Frankie had to correct him. It was slow and not always pleasant work, but Leo liked that he got to be around Frankie, who, before this, had been spending much of her time with Lois.

"She's very sad," Frankie said during a break Leo insisted on taking after four hours of mind-numbing work. Leo knew she meant Lois. There were no other "shes" who it could have been. *"When we talk, I can hear a very sad story between her words."*

"Did she tell you where she's from?" asked Leo.

"Not exactly. Somewhere pretty far away, though. It's like I said, she was a scout for her race. They were exploring planets, hoping to find other living creatures. She's been on Mars and Pluto and everything. She was working her way closer to The Sun and, eventually, found Earth full of living shit. That was back when there were dinosaurs."

"Jesus," said Leo.

"Yeah, she's been here, like, forever. I guess she doesn't actually have a real body. Her people are some kind of light or energy or something. But in order to study Earth, she needed to have a compatible body to use. So, when animals or people die, she basically just sneaks in and re-animates their corpses for a while. I think"— Frankie's thoughts paused momentarily—*"I think she said that when she first got here, she became a stegosaurus. Which is fucking cool."*

"That is cool," said Leo. "Why would you ever stop being a stegosaurus?"

"I think she can only hold a body for a certain time before she needs to get a new one. Maybe. I'm not really sure. Anyway, she was supposed to study here for some amount of time. I can't tell how long. Sometimes she gives me an answer like ten thousand years, and other times she says it was supposed to be, like, twelve hours. It's confusing. She talks about trying to send messages to her people to come and get her. The scouts are supposed to explore for a while and then send word back when they need to get picked up, but there's something about the planet—about Earth that makes it so she can't transmit. Something about the radiation from The Sun or the metals in the Earth's core makes it so she can't send the message."

"You said she went to different planets," said Leo. "Why can't she just go back to Mars and send a message from there? Or just from space somewhere?"

"Something happened to her ship. I guess it was really small, like a golf ball. She says something about how it probably dissolved or disintegrated not long after she got to Earth. So, maybe there was some kind of acid rain back then, or maybe it just couldn't take the atmosphere. Maybe another dinosaur ate it. I don't really know."

"So, she's been stuck here for, what, millions of years?"

"Yeah," replied Frankie, *"a long fucking time, and she can't call her friends to pick her up. They probably think she's dead or still studying things, having the time of her God damned life. It's like I mentioned before, they don't experience time the way we do. I think she tried to explain it to me, but I'm still fuzzy on the details. It's not a line of moments like we think of it. It's more like these pockets of moments, all overlapping each other. I don't really get it."*

"Me neither," said Leo. He thought he kind of, maybe, sort of did get it, though—a little.

"I can pick up on other things too, like, I think the longer she's here, the more... displaced she gets. When she talks about stuff that happened a long time ago, at least from our perspective, it makes more sense. The closer she gets to our present time, the more fucked up and jumbled everything is. I think switching bodies might be really hard on her. And she must have done it a million times."

"I guess all this is why she never got decanted. She's not really human."

"I don't think those morons even considered that there might be aliens other than them on Earth." She was, of course, referring to the Angels.

There was a long silence before Leo spoke again. "How are you doing?" He had not really asked about, or even mentioned, her condition since he learned her decanting had gone wrong, but she must have known that he thought about it.

"I'm," Frankie replied, pausing, *"okay. I guess. It was tough in the beginning. I mean, the very beginning, when I finally realized what had actually happened to me. And that, like, that was it. There's no going back now. It's just fucked up, and I guess I have to deal with it. Sometimes I think about my old body, and, to be honest, I'm glad to be rid of it."*

Leo remembered the time he and Frankie made love. He remembered the scars on her legs.

"If there's anything I can do to help, just..." Leo trailed off, knowing how stupid the statement was, knowing that she knew how stupid he thought it was. In trying not to feel frustrated about constantly having his thoughts heard, he acknowledged his frustration.

"You don't have to worry so much about the stuff you think," Frankie said inside his mind. *"I know how it is. I know that when I was... not like this, my thoughts would just appear out of nowhere and bounce around my head. I get it. I'm not going to judge you too harshly for anything you think. I don't like hearing and feeling everything you guys think and feel, but I can deal with it. I guess I'm lucky there aren't more people around. I don't know if I could put up with that shit. I'd turn it off if I could figure out how. I'm getting better at turning it off on my end, I think."*

Leo remembered the sadness that coursed through him when the ships crashed down. He thought of the times since then that, seemingly out of nowhere, Frankie's grief would wrap itself around his skull and sap his energy. Sometimes he was thankful for those moments. Sometimes her surrogate emotions helped him tap into his own sorrow slightly. Other times it didn't. Other times, her ability to allow sadness into her heart made him jealous.

"I can probably help you with that," Frankie said, feeling his thoughts. *"If you want. If I have to be... this forever, I might as well help people if I can."*

"I don't know," said Leo. "Maybe sometime. I guess all we've got now is time."

"I won't make you eat French toast and play Scrabble," Frankie said, *"but if you ever want to try, I'll help you."*

"Want to get back to the circuits?" Leo asked uncomfortably.

"Sure."

He could hear the happiness in her thought. There was a distinct difference, like how someone's voice alters when they speak while smiling but on a different level.

They worked on repairing the ghost vessel for a few more hours until Leo became too sleepy to follow instructions correctly. Frankie sent him to bed. He carried her to the honeymoon suite and laid her on a sofa before climbing the spiral stairs to the loft. The bed in the loft was now his. Lois preferred to sleep in a gliding rocking chair that Leo brought to the suite from the lobby. A few times, she had fallen asleep in it down there, and Leo felt it would be safer to have her in the suite with him. He worried about some crazed animal breaking in and mauling her.

The repair work continued for days. Leo, Frankie, and sometimes Alphonse would sit in the lobby, working on the circuits. Frankie would get annoyed when Alphonse distracted Leo, but she tried to remember that Leo was doing this work for her benefit and also that she had no idea why she had even started the project. So, she let them joke around. Alphonse would say things like, "I don't mean to bother you guys. I just get jealous of Leo sometimes. He gets to hang out with a naked woman all the time." Frankie supposed she could have gotten offended by this, but there was no point in it.

Every once in a while, when Leo would finish constructing one of the circuits designed by Frankie, she would have him test it. Leo had painstakingly soldered wires to the severed leads on the damaged circuit board of the ghost vessel. At the ends of these wires, he had crimped terminal connections so they could easily connect their circuits without Leo having to burn himself or create mountains of molten solder on the floor. He would hook a variable power supply up to the series of breadboards and connect all the leads from the original damaged circuit to the new replacement one. Typically, nothing would happen. Sometimes, one of the fuses or capacitors would fry out on their breadboard, and they would have to assume they had done something wrong.

One day, after one of these failures, Leo asked, "Do you think we'll get a ghost if we get this thing running? I mean, aren't they all probably just floating around the way they used to, not caring about anything?"

"I don't know," Frankie replied. *"I can't imagine why a ghost would want to talk to any of us. I just feel like we need to see this thing through."*

"I'm not sure why, but I kind of think we'll probably get someone, eventually. Those ghosts must get bored of each other after a while."

"Maybe," said Frankie.

It was about a week later that they constructed another circuit. The work had slowed, having become secondary to just spending time together. Leo liked that. He hooked up everything and plugged the power supply into an extension cord leading to a wall outlet. He flicked the power switch onto a low setting, and the glass tube within the destroyed shell of the ghost vessel began to glow orange.

"Holy shit," Frankie thought.

Leo heard it, though he wasn't sure if it was meant to be an internal thought or not.

"A thing is happening," said Leo.

"Yeah," she replied.

"Now what?" Leo asked after a few moments.

"I guess we just wait." Neither of them had thought about what they would do if they succeeded in getting the ghost vessel running.

"How do we know if it's really worki—" Leo said before getting cut off by a robotic, synthesized voice.

"Leonard, Frances, thank you for your efforts in rebuilding this spirit vessel," said the voice of the slightly-less-demolished-than-before robot.

"Um, who are you?" asked Frankie. *"Can it hear me?"*

"I don't know," said Leo. "Who is this?"

"My name is Meng Ji. And yes, I can hear you, young woman," said the ghost vessel.

"Oh," Frankie said. She then added, somewhat dumbly, *"Hello."*

"It took you rather a long time to repair this vessel," said Meng Ji.

"And it would take rather a short time to smash the shit out of it again," said Frankie, sending out waves of anger. *"Right, Leo?"*

"I don't think—" started Leo before the machine cut him off again. Leo was used to being interrupted. He used to get offended when it happened, but he eventually came around to the reality of the situation. What he had to say really didn't matter that much.

"That would be unfortunate for all parties involved, I think. Forgive my rudeness. I appreciate you taking the time and effort to obtain and repair this vessel. Communicating across realms has never been my strong point, but I am pleased to know that my efforts seem to have paid off."

Leo was about to ask what that meant before Frankie answered the question.

"So it was you," she said. *"You're the reason I was so hellbent on fixing this junk without even knowing why."*

"And are you also the reason why I felt the need to go down into the city?" asked Leo.

"No," replied Meng Ji. "That was stupid and ill-advised. You could easily have suffocated, been crushed, fallen into a burning sinkhole, inhaled toxins, or suffered any number of other misfortunes. I would not urge a living human to behave so recklessly."

"Oh," said Leo. He felt his cheeks redden. "I just felt like"— he stopped speaking, realizing once more that it didn't matter.

The ghost vessel spoke again. "Since you did go, and since you did not die, I tried to convince Frances to find the most fully operational means of spirit-to-human communication. She did, and you brought it back here. Regrettably, it was still badly damaged. I never cared for the parlor tricks some other human spirits utilized to harass or contact the living. Maybe I should have studied their methods. As it was, it took everything I could think of just to prod you to keep up with this project."

"Why?" asked Frankie. She seemed annoyed by the outcome of the work she and Leo had done.

"I was working with the Angels in the capacity of an advisor. After arriving, they made a point to seek out spirits with above-average intelligence. I was happy to help and escape the mundanity of my afterlife. I lent them ideas and information about human nature as I understand it. If I had any idea that things would end up this way, I would have never revealed myself to them.

"It is my nature to seek out information. To learn and better myself for my own sake. I toyed with the idea of Caldo but never felt in my heart that it was the right place for me. Seeing how different I was from the other living and deceased humans on the planet, the Angels offered me something else. They said they would take me with them around the universe, so I could continue to learn and grow."

"I'm afraid that ship has sailed," said Frankie. *"Or sunk."*

"Indeed," continued Meng Ji. "Since the calamity that effectively ended humanity, things on this side of the divide have been, well, difficult." The speaker of the vessel popped and buzzed momentarily. "Are you familiar with what is known as The Screaming?" asked Meng Ji.

"Is that some kind of shitty horror movie?" asked Frankie. Her tone dripped with sarcasm.

"No," replied Meng Ji, "It is what happens when—"

"We know what it is," it was Leo's turn to interrupt this time. He remembered the message Alphonse had shown him the day after the Taco Bell trip when they found out Rhonda had died. *She's screaming.*

Leo tried to figure out how to explain The Screaming to Frankie in a way that would soften the horror of the mandatory post-death phenomenon. Tallying up all the worst parts of the brochures he'd read and videos he'd watched in order to intentionally omit them brought them to the forefront of his mind in a sad, abominable swarm. Frankie couldn't help but take it all in. "Shit," Leo said, upset at himself but also glad to have it out without having to formulate his thoughts into something coherent. "Sorry."

"It's okay, Leo. It's… Jesus."

"Well, it is more intense and widespread than anything I have ever encountered. It is"—Meng Ji paused— "annoying."

"I'm so sorry that the agony of the dregs of the human race is 'annoying' you," Frankie said. *"Leo, let's unplug this thing."*

"Please listen," Meng Ji said. The voice synthesizer made it impossible to tell if she was panicked by the threat, but she probably wasn't. "I have been observing your group, and I have taken a special interest in you, Frances, and the one you call Lois. I had not realized that Lois was not of this planet. I admit, it was dense of me not to notice, but the Angels and I had to prioritize our efforts. Lois, as a human to be decanted, was categorized as low priority."

"Nice," said Frankie. *"Really fucking nice."*

"Hearing your conversations has been fascinating," continued Meng Ji. "It is incredibly fortunate that you have happened to find yourself with an outsider—a traveler. As hard as it is to hear, you here are not in the greatest of circumstances. Things are fine for the time being, but your lifestyle is not sustainable.

"I estimate that within two years, natural consequences will claim the life of Lois. She is not built for this survivalist lifestyle. When she expires, she will have no human vessel to inhabit. Eventually, the electricity here will be lost. The Angel ship will produce power, but the lines and cables will fail. The gas and water systems will also fail with no one able to service or repair them."

"I might be able to fix some stuff," said Leo.

"I doubt you have the means to repair a ruptured water main. Infrastructure around the world will fail exponentially every day, and you will be left with only this shelter rotting around you. For a larger, more able-bodied assemblage, I would not have as much concern. But for your motley group, I see a short lifespan. Alphonse and Frances, I am honestly unsure how long you may live now, but I am confident that entropy will eventually work its ways on you."

"Did you just come here to depress everyone?" asked Frankie. *"Did you think we weren't sad and pissed off enough as it is? You had to rub some fucking salt in the wounds? You feel better now, Casper?"*

"Do you fully understand the nature of your new body?" asked the ghost vessel.

"I know that the Angels fucked me up," Frankie's thoughts were carrying waves of anger again. *"I know I can't walk around, or eat, or fuck, or talk anymore. Is that what you're talking about? Because, yeah, I noticed all that stuff."*

Leo felt like an uncomfortable third wheel in this conversation. He excused himself, sat back down on the carpet, and insecurely pulled his knees to his chest.

"What happened to you was not entirely the fault of the Angels. It was their haste and their carelessness that wronged you, not their process. It has taken me some time to piece it all together, but I think that I have a strong hypothesis now. You were infected by an organic, alien entity that was untraceable to the technology of the Angels. I believe it was some sort of tracking beacon sent by the ones who attacked the Angels as they attempted to leave Earth's atmosphere.

"I was given access to details on all living humans prior to their decantation. Most are difficult for me to recall, but yours are far fresher than the others. You are on record stating that you had physical contact with the material that fell from the sky."

"That," Frankie said, pausing, remembering the hunk of space debris she buried with Grady. *"They said that was probably stuff from the Angels' ships coming."*

"They were mistaken. I am fairly certain that element had nothing to do with the Angels. I believe it was some sort of tool sent by the ones who attacked the Angels. It's possible they knew the Angels were coming to Earth and sent some type of scout beacon. I cannot speak to how it worked, but it may have bonded or implanted in your body. If it was meant to broadcast information across light years of space, it might explain your... abilities."

"So, I had some kind of alien walkie-talkie inside me?"

"It is possible."

"Wouldn't I have known or something? How could they have not seen it in all their tests and scans and shit?" Frankie asked.

"If it was alien to them, they may not have even known if they had seen it. If it was designed to avoid detection, there's no telling what properties it may have had."

"Motherfucker!" said Frankie.

"The point I am trying to make," continued Meng Ji, "is I believe you have abilities that may benefit all of us. If we can get more information from the one called Lois about her race, I think we can use your talents to contact them. In short, I think we can send for help."

The conversation halted for a moment. Leo was barely keeping up with what was happening, but he was slowly putting the pieces together.

"You think we can use whatever I am," Frankie said, *"to call Lois's friends to finally pick her up?"*

"To pick up all of us," said Meng Ji. "From your conversations, I gather that they are a race of highly intelligent beings who are likely older and more advanced than the Angels. I think contacting them is in the best interest of everyone involved."

Leo understood this better than what was being said earlier in the conversation. He thought about getting sucked up and taken somewhere unknown by a bunch of aliens he knew nothing about. He thought it sounded somewhat better than freezing to death on Earth.

31.

Frankie and Meng Ji spent weeks trying to get every bit of information they could garner from Lois. They would speak with her for hours and hours at a time, then to each other for hours and hours at a time. They compared notes about what they thought they had gleaned from the nonsense that spilled from the mouth of the old woman-alien-thing. They argued a lot.

Leo hung out with Alphonse. The decanted and non-decanted humans played poker and blackjack against each other. Alphonse could read what his cards were without turning them over, so Leo exchanged Alphonse's cards while they remained facedown to keep the games fair. Alphonse never mentioned that he could also read Leo's cards, as well as every upcoming card in the deck, no matter how well it was shuffled. He let Leo win often enough to keep the man's spirits up. Leo never suspected a thing.

As the weeks went by, the food in the freezers dwindled. Leo and Lois ate peanut butter sandwiches and pasta almost exclusively. Leo had not touched the stash reserved for "FRENCH TOAST SUNDAYS." Sometimes, Leo would go for drives to see if he could find closed markets that might have treats to supplement his boring diet. He was always on the lookout for strawberry cake rolls. It concerned him that some of the stores he entered had no electricity. He wondered how long it would be until the lodge went dark.

After one particular trip, Leo came into the lobby of the lodge with a box of strawberry cake rolls and saw Lois, the ghost vessel, and Frankie in their normal huddle. Meng Ji had not been moved since her vessel was repaired. Leo was afraid that he would break something or undo his hard work if he touched the series of circuit boards. Lois sat in an easy chair with Frankie resting like a cat on her lap.

"Hello, ladies," said Leo, waving.

"Hey Leo," replied Frankie. *"Found some more cake rolls?"*

"Yeah. There's this one store with a bunch on the shelf." Though he knew which stores still had the snack, he liked to search for new places, and he only ever took one box at a time so he would have reason to go out again. Now that there were no other cars on the road, he didn't find driving to be such a chore.

"Would you mind getting Alphonse and bringing him down here?" asked Frankie.

"Sure."

Leo went up to the suite where Alphonse stayed most of the time unless he wanted Leo to take him somewhere else. When Leo got to the living room, Alphonse was sitting on an end table. On his screen, the characters *8===D* were displayed. Leo took no notice as he lifted Alphonse's jar.

"Aren't you going to say anything about the dick?" Alphonse asked in his toneless voice.

"The what?" asked Leo.

"I had a dick on my screen when you came in. I've had it on there for hours so you would come in and see it."

Leo turned Alphonse in his arms and looked at the screen.

"Eight equals, equals, oh," he said, seeing the approximation of a phallus and testicles. He had to chuckle. He liked that Alphonse tried to keep his spirits up. "You should be ashamed of yourself, young man."

"Do I have to stay after for detention, now?"

"I'll be calling your parents." Saying this, Leo thought of his own parents. He'd stopped calling them, and they lost touch entirely after. It had been difficult to talk with them. They had been good to him, and he felt like he hadn't lived up to the expectation of what a good son should be. Whenever he talked with or visited them, he felt suffocated by the undeserved, unearned kindness they gave him, so he backed away from them. It was a selfish way to think, but it was where his mind went. They had been decanted and were now dead. Totally dead. Deader than the ghosts who were floating around, annoyed by the screaming of the freshly deceased. He wondered if they had been in the pit of overcooked blue marshmallow he found in Cindervale. Probably not, but maybe.

He thought he should cry for them—grieve their loss. Though thinking of his mother and father opened up a deep pit in his guts, he did not cry. There had been so much loss and angst these past few weeks, and he already knew that his entire family and everyone he'd ever known was dead. The realization that his parents, who he tried not to think of often, were gone didn't seem terribly important or shocking. Everyone was gone, and so were their parents. Leo felt momentarily guilty for not being dead. It was a feeling he had experienced at various times in his life. This time, it struck him as a silly thing to feel.

Back in the lobby, Leo set Alphonse down on the floor near the others.

"Thanks," said Frankie.

"What's up?" asked Leo. There was a different, more focused air about Frankie today than usual.

"Meng Ji says she figured out a way—a series of questions that might help us find a way to contact Lois's people. She's, like, really fucking smart."

"That's good, right?" asked Leo.

"Yeah, I think it's good. I mean, we never had any kind of official meeting or anything, and you're always so cagey." She paused in her thought broadcasting for several moments before continuing. *"Do you, you know, want to leave the planet? If it's even something we can do, I mean."*

"Well, I was ready to do it before with the Angels, so I guess I ought to be ready to do it now."

"That was different, though," said Frankie. *"You knew what that was all about. You knew there was a big prize at the end of that rainbow. We have virtually no idea what could happen if we get in contact with these aliens. They might suck. They might, like, suck hard. We have no way of knowing. I'm definitely set on going. Lois will go, and Meng Ji wants to get out of here too. Alphonse said that he'd be cool with it. We're starting to make preparations to get this thing going. Have you thought about it?"*

Leo had thought about it a few times. Whenever he did think about it, it made his brain feel heavy, so he thought about other things. "I guess..." he started but immediately trailed off, trying to form the thought he had grown accustomed to avoiding. "Whenever I put a lot of time and thought into something, it seems like there's a really good chance that it goes wrong. Or, at least, it feels worse when it goes wrong. So, I guess I shouldn't think about this too much, huh?"

"Leo, I'm not sure if that's the best way to make a decision like this," said Frankie.

"I'm in," he said suddenly. "That's it. The decision's made. I'll go across space with a bunch of strangers. I don't imagine there's much for me here, especially if all of you are going. So, yeah, I'll come along."

"Okay," said Frankie.

"Would you mind if we began the questions now?" asked Meng Ji. "I would like to keep moving forward."

"Do you need me for anything?" asked Leo.

"No," said the synthesized voice of Meng Ji. "From my observations, I have discerned possible patterns in the speech of the one called Lois. I've designed several logistical algorithms around these hypotheses. Some of her original memories seem to have melded with the memories of the vessel in which she currently resides. I believe I can work around this. This experiment will involve my asking Lois questions designed to elicit certain answers from specific points in her memory. Frances will ask the questions, and I will interpret the answers as raw data. Alphonse will record the information I give him."

"Oh," said Leo.

"Basically, we're going to be chatting for a while," said Frankie. *"And Meng Ji is going to try to make some sense out of what Lois says. She's kind of going to be a Lois-to-English translator."*

"And I'm going to be a sheet of notebook paper," said Alphonse.

"I guess I'll leave you to it," Leo said. He was still uncertain about what was happening, but everyone else seemed to understand. That was okay with him. He took his cake rolls from where he'd left them on the front reception desk and went back up to the loft. He ate one of the cake rolls and lay down on the bed to take a nap. He'd been napping more often.

Following a few hours of dreamless sleep, he rose and showered. Thankfully, the power and water were still running in the lodge. Leo found the showers he took here to be some of the most pleasant he'd ever had. The shower stall was spacious and had a built-in bench seat, and the hot water seemed endless. Sometimes, he would sit under the hot rain for an hour. Today, though, he stayed in for a more modest twenty minutes.

After toweling himself dry, he put on one of the monogrammed bath robes. He wasn't sure why he wore it. Alphonse had repeatedly told him that he ought to take advantage of the current state of affairs and just walk around naked. Leo felt weird about that, though. There were women around, and even though one was an alien in the body of a senile, elderly lady and the other was a lump of meat covered with writhing tendrils, Leo still felt that he needed to remain decent.

Alphonse tried to explain that, despite her appearance, Lois was an alien and probably couldn't be offended by Leo's nudity and that to Frankie, he looked the same whether he was clothed or not. She saw him as a system of organic tissue, a skeleton, muscles, fat, flesh, and hair. Whether or not he wore clothes was irrelevant. Alphonse also pointed out that Frankie was always naked anyway. This perplexed Leo. It also gave him a strange and unexpected twinge in his loins. So, Leo continued to cover himself.

He returned to the lobby and saw the bizarre quartet still about their task. He listened in for a while and heard a conversation he could never have followed in a billion years.

"Where did the square grass connect?" Frankie asked Lois.

After a moment, she responded, "Oh, yes. That was a very interesting thing to hear. Inside the sugar house, we all used to carry on and make leather."

After the response, Leo saw a series of seemingly random numbers scroll across Alphonse's screen. Presumably, he was making note of information being sent to him by Meng Ji. The telepathic connection decanted humans had with the Ether-base seemed to extend to ghost vessels as well.

Following a pause of a few seconds, Frankie asked another question. *"Does the forty-fifth mountain walk around?"*

Lois's face went stony before she answered. "Every time they came to Milwaukee, the spiders flew into mailbox E-17. I sometimes wished that the lake was cooler. It was such a chore to go swimming at the cabin."

Leo sat near the group and observed the conversation for a while. He wondered what kind of information could possibly be learned from such an unnatural exercise. About ten minutes of the back and forth between Lois and Frankie left Leo's mind wobbling. It was impossible to guess what question would be asked next and even more impossible to guess the answer that would come. He stood up and walked to the game room to play the arcade cabinets.

For hours, Leo played games and tried to get high scores, using quarters he had taken from the various cash registers around the lodge. He had gotten rather good at a game called *Teenage Mutant Ninja Turtles: Turtles in Time*. When he was younger, he had been aware of the *Teenage Mutant Ninja Turtles* television show but never cared much for cartoons. The game was surprisingly fun. It was set up so that four people could play at the same time. Four people at once would never play it again.

His supply of stolen quarters exhausted, he wandered the lodge for a while, looking around in the non-public spaces. There were maintenance rooms and laundry rooms and offices, all of which were marginally interesting. The touches of humanity left around the building were beginning to take their toll on Leo. Whenever he walked around the lodge, itself obviously a symbol of humanity and human life, he would see small things that caused pangs within his conscience.

The empty desks where people would have sat to work did not particularly affect him, but seeing things like sticky notes posted on a wall would remind him that actual, *real* people had been here not all that long ago. There was a wine cellar under one of the restaurant kitchens. Leo never drank wine, so the place didn't mean much to him. However, a tiny step stool in the corner stood out to him. He imagined a short woman in black slacks and a white dress shirt, a server. He imagined her unfolding the stool and climbing its two steps, then standing on her tiptoes to reach a bottle of wine on the top shelf of the wine rack. This vision, not the fact that so much expensive wine would now go undrunk, stirred something in him, albeit briefly.

Little things like this appeared more and more to Leo as the days passed. The further the apocalypse faded into the past, the more he realized that real people had inhabited this planet. People like Brock and Miranda and Frankie had spun their small lives into stories and left bookmarks in those stories all around. He wondered if he had left any bookmarks. He figured he must have, and maybe he still was. He sometimes forgot that he was a human like all the other people on the planet had been. The difference between his bookmarks and those of the rest of humanity was that his bookmarks could still be moved. They could be taken from one spot in the story and moved to a new page. No one else's bookmarks could move anymore.

Leo found himself in one of the kitchens, making steaks that he thought were beef but were actually venison. He fried these in a pan and made some lumpy, instant mashed potatoes from a nearly empty box. He brought the plates of food to the lobby and offered one to Lois.

The indecipherable conversation was still going as he delivered dinner to the older woman. While the inane question-and-answer session continued, Leo saw that Lois was distracted and not eating. She would go to cut her steak and then give, or continue to give, an answer to a question that Frankie had asked her.

Leo took her plate and cut her meat into small pieces. He handed it back to her, and she began to fork bits of steak and potato into her mouth between answers. He wondered if the ones running this experiment, who no longer needed to sleep, would remember to let Lois go to bed at some point. After finishing his dinner, he got a blanket from a linen closet and set it next to Lois on the arm of the easy chair. She would likely be there for a while longer.

32.

The inquisition went on for about five days, stopping only for Lois to sleep and use the bathroom. Eventually, Meng Ji decided she had enough data to test her hypothesis. She had Alphonse scroll through his pages of numerical data for hours until she was able to, impressively, commit it all to memory. From that point, the spirit in the ghost vessel asked that she be left alone until she could fully analyze her findings. She was silent and unresponsive for three weeks. Leo checked the tube in the damaged vessel to make sure it was still glowing orange. It was. Presumably, this meant that the thing was still working, though he couldn't be sure.

During the days after the interview, Lois slept a lot. Leo imagined she was tired from the long days of talking. Her voice was hoarse, and she was not eating much of the meals Leo made her. It became apparent that she was sick.

"We should get her some antibiotics," Frankie said one day. *"Just in case."*

"Okay," said Leo. "I know I've passed some pharmacies when I've been out looking for cake rolls. Tell me what to look for, and I'll go and get it."

Frankie made a list of medicines for Leo to find and sent him off that morning. It was a Tuesday, which felt, to Leo, like a Sunday. Every day felt like a Sunday to him now. It took him until that Tuesday-not-Sunday evening to find everything on the list. He checked five different pharmacies and was toying with the idea of finding a hospital at one point. He did manage to track down everything Frankie asked for, though, and came back with bags full of pills and syrups and rubs, and even some canned chicken noodle soup.

They started Lois on a course of penicillin, which turned out not to be a good idea. The confusion in her displaced mind made it impossible for her to access certain information in her human memory. A crucial bit of that information was that the body she inhabited was deathly allergic to the drug. Within hours, she was in acute anaphylaxis and unable to breathe properly. Frail with age and fatigue, her bodily systems shut down entirely while Frankie sent Leo out to find something called an EpiPen. When Leo got back with a handful of the potentially life-saving sticks, Lois was dead.

"God damn it!" Frankie thought. *"We fucking killed her. All we have to do right now is survive, and we killed one of our friends."*

"Frankie," Leo carefully began, "we couldn't have known. With how her brain was all scrambled up, there's no way she could have told us about her allergies or anything like that."

"You *couldn't have known,"* she said. *"I should have thought of it. People react badly to all sorts of things. I had a friend in second grade who got terrible hives from penicillin. I should have fucking thought before I just jammed pills down her throat."*

Leo felt somewhat slighted by the comment, but Frankie was probably right. "None of us could have known," he said again. "I could have fed her something she was just as allergic to. I could have undercooked something and given her food poisoning. She was old, and her body was weak. Maybe she didn't even know she was allergic to it."

"I should have at least thought of it," Frankie said. *"I just wanted to help her. I didn't want anything like this to happen."*

After a moment, Leo said, "I didn't know people could just... die so fast."

Frankie was radiating sadness, filling Leo's heart with cool pebbles.

"I guess I'll, uh." His voice trailed off, but he knew Frankie had picked up his unspoken thoughts. They were thoughts of futility and shame—of sweat and blisters and a shallow grave. They felt crass to him. He wished his silence could have spared Frankie from them, but it could not. He ran his hand through Frankie's tendrils and sighed. Leo knew there was a spade in the lodge's storage shed.

Leo found a spot under a birch tree set aside from a cluster of pines and began to dig. The ground should have been frozen solid, but the heat radiated by the holocaust had kept any frost at bay. Despite this, the earth remained cool and stony. After every few shovel-fuls Leo scraped out, he had to kneel and pull stones from the ground. About a foot beneath the topsoil, the earth consisted of clay, glass, and coal chips. It was a wonder that anything grew on this mountain. He worked for hours under the glaring exterior flood-lights, but eventually, Leo dug a serviceable grave for Lois. He went inside and wrapped her in the sheets from the daybed where she had died, then carried her through the lobby and out to the grave. She was much lighter than he had thought she would be. It saddened and fascinated him.

After laying Lois into the oblong hole, he brought Alphonse and Frankie outside to take part in the ritual. By the circumstances of her nature, the woman had been pretty much unknowable, so no one had anything particularly profound to say about her. Everyone agreed that she had been sweet and friendly and that it would be sad without her around. Frankie remembered the time Lois gave her a decoupage drinking cup. Alphonse and Leo had no specific memories about her to share. Frankie and Alphonse remained with Leo as he covered the older woman's body.

Despite himself, the entire time he was burying Lois, Leo kept wondering what would happen to her. If what Frankie had said was true, the alien that lived in Lois's body was still around some-where. It would have no human bodies to inhabit unless Leo sponta-neously keeled over. He also wondered what this meant for the plan to contact the rest of Lois's alien race. Maybe this meant they were back to plan A—hang around on Earth until they die.

The mood in the lodge wasn't very bright for the next few days. Meng Ji remained silent, caught up in her calculations and analysis. Complex emotions were filtering out of Frankie. Leo knew she was probably trying her best to keep her feelings from spilling out, but it must have been too much for her to handle. She oscillated between anger at herself and grief about Lois. She would also slip into confusion and soul-emptying uncertainty from time to time. It was these notions of uncertainty that affected Leo the most. Hope-lessness and waves of doubt, much stronger than his own, would creep into his mind.

He tried his best to comfort Frankie. He wanted to put her on his lap and pet her as Lois had, but he wasn't sure if it was appropri-ate for him to do. He had thought about it, and since Frankie could read his thoughts, he figured she would give him some kind of nudge one way or the other about it, but he felt no response. He asked her if she wanted to go for walks or drives, but she seemed to just want to stay around the lodge. A few days after Lois died, on the coldest day since the catastrophe in Cindervale, Leo attempted to cheer up Frankie with a joke.

"Hey, Frankie," he said. "Have you heard the one about the two muffins in the oven?"

"What?" Frankie thought to him.

"The one muffin looks to the other and asks, 'Is it getting hot in here?' And the other muffin goes, 'Holy shit! A talking muffin!'"

Frankie was silent but radiated a wave of anger so intense it made Leo's eyeballs ache. He decided to go for a drive. He went on a lot of drives in the days when Meng Ji was calculating. Alphonse would come along sometimes. He needed breaks as well. Even the decanted weren't immune to Frankie's projections. They would explore the surrounding towns, looking for food to augment the supply at the lodge, which was running lower and lower. On this particular drive, Leo and Alphonse were returning to the lodge with a few bags of canned goods when it started to snow. The squall enveloped the car and made it nearly impossible to see. Leo had been waiting for this. He knew that once the first snow fell, it was unlikely he would be able to drive off the mountain for the rest of the season. There were, of course, no plow trucks.

Leo parked the car, gathered Alphonse and his bags of cans, and started trotting to the front entrance. Alphonse made a strange and abrasive noise that Leo had never heard him make before. It was some kind of warning buzzer, and it was loud.

"Whoa, what was that? What are you"—before Leo could finish, he saw the reason for the warning. In front of the lodge doors stood a hulking black bear. Leo stopped in his tracks. The bear had seen him. It heard the noise Alphonse made. Leo and the bear froze where they were—about fifteen feet apart.

The beast, snow clinging to its fur, stood there, staring at Leo for what felt to him like an eternity but was probably closer to a few seconds in actuality. Then the bear grunted, adjusted itself, and plopped down on its rear. It didn't seem to have any intentions of going anywhere. Leo remembered the other entrances to the lodge and slowly began moving his feet. He couldn't remember what a person was supposed to do when confronted by a bear. He remembered something about not climbing trees because bears are good at climbing. Leo was not good at climbing, so that was not an option anyway. Were you supposed to stay still? Were bears like the Tyrannosaurus rex? Could they only see you when you moved? No, that was stupid. Was Leo supposed to play dead, or was that only after one attacked you? As panic drilled its way into his head, he suddenly heard Frankie's voice.

"I think it's Lois."

Leo was momentarily flabbergasted before his mind began to process what he'd heard. He guessed it stood to reason. Frankie said Lois started her life on Earth as a series of dinosaurs and other prehistoric creatures. Leo looked at the bear, sitting placidly. It was gigantic, or at least, it seemed that way to Leo. It must have lived for a while to get to be so big, so maybe that meant it was old as well. Maybe it had died, and Lois slipped into its body.

"What should I do?" asked Leo in a whisper.

"Try to get to a side entrance, and I'll distract it somehow. I really think that might be Lois. She might remember enough to come back here."

Carrying Alphonse in the crook of his arm, Leo began to creep away around the corner of the front entrance to the lodge. He wondered if it actually could be Lois. It was possible, he thought, but it also could be a regular, old, maul-you-and-eat-you black bear. Maybe Frankie's guilt was distorting her judgment. Maybe this was some bear that hung around the ski area every year, getting fed by tourists or groundskeepers or something. That could be why it was so big.

As Leo began to hear Frankie's voice "distracting" the bear, he started to edge his feet along the stone pathway. Frankie seemed to be speaking to the animal as if it really were Lois. She was directing thoughts toward it about decoupage. Once around the corner and out of the bear's line of vision, Leo ran to the side door and raced inside.

"That was pretty spooky," said Alphonse.

"Why didn't you tell me there was a giant bear at the front door?" asked Leo.

"I'm sorry," he said. "I just wasn't looking, I guess. I didn't notice until we got closer. I can see a lot of things that you probably can't, but I'm not always looking."

"Well, I'm glad I didn't get eaten," Leo said. "Thanks for the heads up, anyway."

They went to the lobby, but Leo stayed near the rear, far away from the front entrance.

"I think it's okay," said Frankie's voice. *"She's just sitting out there."*

After a few moments, Leo began to walk closer to where Meng Ji lay in her robot body.

"I know you think I'm just making shit up or that I'm losing it, but I honestly think that bear is Lois."

Leo toyed with the idea of lying but knew that Frankie would see through it. "I just don't think it's safe to jump to conclusions right away. Based on what you said, there's a chance that Lois went and found a new body and came back here. Would she be able to do that, though? I mean, how scrambled is her mind?"

"I don't know," said Frankie.

"When she was at Walnut Ridge," Alphonse began, "she acted like a human for the most part. She did human stuff. What if she just does bear stuff now that she's a bear?"

"I don't know!" Frankie's voice rang loudly in Leo's ears. *"I don't know anything that you guys don't know. I can't really communicate with her or get a sense of her thoughts. It's just a gut feeling I have that whatever lived inside Lois remembers us and knows what we're trying to do."*

"I guess it doesn't matter too much right now," said Leo. "There's not much we can do about a giant bear hanging around the lodge. I mean, I'm not going to mess with it. Presumably, if it really wants in here, it will find a way. I guess we'll deal with it at that point."

"Yeah," said Frankie. *"We'll just have to wait and see what happens. I hope it's Lois."*

"Me too," said Leo.

It snowed throughout the night and into the morning. From the window in the loft, Leo could see that about halfway down the mountain, the precipitation had fallen as rain and sloppy slush. He wondered if it wasn't the best idea to isolate themselves on a high mountain during winter. From the window, he also saw the bear that might have been Lois waddle its way into the woods on the property. Perhaps it was simply a curious creature confused by the strange, recent changes to its environment.

Even though Lois had not spoken much and had spent a lot of time with Frankie, Leo still found that the lodge felt lonelier without her around. It also felt strange knowing he was now the last living human on the planet. Lois had been an alien, but she looked human, and that counted for something. It counted for more than Leo thought it had now that she was gone. Alphonse and Frankie were humans, but they looked like aliens. Leo felt set apart from them.

The bear came back later in the day. It sat outside the windows at the front entrance to the lodge. Though she still thought the bear was most likely Lois in a new body, Frankie had taken the liberty of locking all the doors. If it was a regular bear, it might accidentally find a way inside and eat her or Leo. Alphonse would probably be okay.

Over the next few days, the bear would return for several hours during the morning and afternoon. It sat or lay outside the lodge, just looking through the windows. Eventually, it would rise and tread off into the woods, but it kept coming back. If Frankie was right, she hoped Lois had somewhere warm to stay until they figured out what to do with her. There was more snow in the days that followed, and if Leo drove down, he doubted he'd get the car back up the mountain before spring. Although the trio had not planned on leaving the lodge, the snow gave a strange sense of entrapment.

No one knew if Meng Ji's vessel was still operational. There was no reason it should have failed or shut down, but the time she was spending on her calculations was concerning. Frankie wished the ghost would give some kind of signal that the vessel was still working or that she had not abandoned them. Meng Ji was so strange, so aloof. It was possible that she may have met with failure in her project and just drifted back into the afterlife without saying anything.

A little over a week after the bear had started visiting, Frankie grew impatient with the state of things and made a decision. She was going to let the bear inside. She was almost certain that it was Lois. If it tried to eat her, Frankie was pretty sure she could blast it the way she did that murderer-Angel. Leo had not come downstairs yet, and the bear was sitting outside, gazing through the sooty glass into the lobby. Frankie used her projection abilities to unlock the front door and pull it open.

Snow swirled into the lodge, and the bear looked through the open door. For a long time, it sat, just staring at the entrance to the lobby.

"Come on," thought Frankie. *"Come in. It's okay. I hope."*

After a few minutes, cold air filled the room, and Frankie was about to close the door again. The longer the bear didn't enter the lodge, the more likely it was not actually Lois, or that's what Frankie told herself anyway. As she was about to close and lock the door again, the bear stood and slowly walked through the entrance.

"Okay," Frankie thought to herself. *"I guess this is really happening."* The bear curiously looked about the interior of the lodge's main entrance, sniffing around and staring at seemingly random objects. It knocked over a coat rack. Frankie lay prone on the floor, hoping she would not have to hurt this creature, wondering if she even *could* hurt it if she needed to protect herself or Leo.

Eventually, the beast made its way over to where Frankie was. It reached out with a paw and touched the wormy lump of flesh that was now Frankie. She allowed the animal to touch her at first. The claws, large and pale with age, scraped against Frankie's body painfully. There was no aggression behind it, though. It was merely an unintended consequence of the bear's touch. It prodded at her, more carefully this time, seemingly trying to figure out what she was. The bear sat down and stared at Frankie for a while longer, then reached out a paw and placed it on top of her. It ran its paw down over the tendrils of her flesh but barely scratched her with its claws this time.

The bear leaned down, sniffed deeply of Frankie, and snorted loudly as the tiny tentacles tickled its nostrils. After this further exploration, it clumsily lifted and flipped Frankie over, then flipped her back. It then placed a paw on her again and held it there, not applying much pressure. Suddenly, it grasped at Frankie with both arms. The claws poked her body. The bear drew Frankie into its chest and leaned onto its back, hugging Frankie to its belly. After a moment, it began to gently stroke Frankie with one paw while holding her with the other. It seemed very careful not to touch her with its claws now. It lay there, petting Frankie. She was now certain that this bear must be Lois.

Leo was coming down now. He had heard the coat rack fall over and wanted to see what had happened.

Frankie sent him a thought-message. *"Leo,"* she said, *"don't panic. The bear is inside now. It's holding me and stroking me like Lois used to do. I'm positive this is her now."*

Though he had heard what she said, Leo still stopped halfway down the stairs to the lobby, frozen in terror. It was difficult to see someone he considered a friend in the clutches of a huge bear.

"I don't know what to do," he said quietly.

"Maybe just give us some time here," Frankie thought to him. The bear accidentally dropped Frankie from its arms, groaned, and picked her up again. *"I'm pretty sure it would have eaten me already if that was what it wanted to do."*

"I still don't know what to do," Leo said.

"Go upstairs and eat a strawberry cake roll," said Frankie. *"Maybe come down in an hour or so. Unless I tell you to come earlier or... something goes wrong."*

Leo slowly backed up the stairs again. He trusted Frankie, but this was somewhat insane. He went back up to the honeymoon suite and looked at his box of cake rolls. He did not eat one. He was worried about Frankie. He kept thinking at her and saying aloud, "Are you okay?" She continued sending him messages that she was fine. It still didn't feel right.

After about an hour and a half of sitting in the living room of the suite, being reassured by Alphonse that Frankie knew what she was doing, Leo was starting to feel slightly better. If the bear hadn't eaten her by now, she was probably safe. She was also probably right that this was Lois, or it was just a really peculiar bear.

"Okay, come down now," came Frankie's voice.

Leo took Alphonse to the lobby, creeping very slowly down the steps.

"I'm still really scared and unhappy about this," Leo muttered.

"It's okay," said Frankie. *"Come down."*

Leo finally got to the foot of the stairs. The bear sat up, turned, and looked at him, clutching Frankie close to its body.

"It's okay," came Frankie's voice. *"That's Leo. You remember Leo. He's a nice guy. He's a milquetoast."*

Leo took a step closer to the bear. It made a low groaning sound in its throat, not necessarily a threatening groan, but still scary to Leo. At Frankie's instruction, he took another step closer and then another. Soon, he was feet away from it.

"Put your hand out, palm up so she can see you're not a threat."

Leo did as he was told, holding out his arm to the bear. He closed his eyes, certain the giant beast would rip off his arm. It did not. He felt its fur on his hand and opened his eyes, expecting an attack. Instead, he saw that the bear had leaned itself into his open hand. His hand lay on the shoulder of the bear. Its face seemed uncertain, but Leo lacked confidence in his bear-face-reading skills. Maybe that look was "hungry."

"Pet her," said Frankie.

Leo slowly moved his hand down the coarse, black fur once, then again. Perhaps this wasn't just a bear. Maybe it really was Lois. Leo continued to pet the animal until it lay back on the carpet.

"I think she wants you to rub her belly."

It was strange to Leo to refer to the bear as "she." He hadn't been able to tell if it was a male or female bear, and he wasn't sure if that mattered. He supposed Lois would always be "her," simply based on the body she had when they met. He wondered if her alien race even had different sexes.

Leo rubbed the bear's stomach as it lolled on the floor. He had never anticipated that his life would end up this way. All things considered, he had adjusted fairly well. The bear, Lois, made contented sounds as she received pets and belly rubs. Leo felt momentarily strange to think he was scratching the chest and stomach of the sweet, old, crazy lady with whom he had watched the apocalypse. The feeling passed as he saw how much pleasure the bear seemed to derive from the contact.

"I have discovered what I believe to be the location of the one called Lois's home planet." The voice of Meng Ji's vessel suddenly splattered through the room like sonic acid. "Why is there a bear in the lodge?"

***

As Leo kept the bear in good spirits, Frankie explained what had happened while Meng Ji was lost in herself, doing calculations. It didn't take long. The spirit of the ancient Chinese woman tended to be very quick on the uptake.

"We were wondering if you had gone away or if the ghost vessel was broken or something," said Frankie.

"I prefer to have no distractions when I work," said Meng Ji. "How long has it been since we finished our information gathering?"

"Um," said Leo. "About three weeks or so."

"I see," Meng Ji paused. "I knew it would take me some time, but I thought it would be four days at the longest. I lose track of time as the living experience it, you see. I apologize if I worried you in my absence. I did not anticipate being in thought for so long. I also did not anticipate that you would kill the vessel containing the one called Lois."

"We didn't fucking kill her!" came Frankie's voice loudly.

A spark of pain flickered behind Leo's eye.

"She got sick. We were careless. It was an accident."

"Well, either way, we must still attempt to move forward with the plan. How certain are you that this beast contains the Lois-entity? Its behavior is certainly abnormal enough."

"I'm one hundred percent sure it's Lois," said Frankie.

"I'm," started Leo, "I'm ninety percent sure. Maybe ninety-three percent."

"Well, I trust your judgment, Frances," Meng Ji replied as though Leo had not spoken.

33.

It took a while for Frankie to grasp the concept of what Meng Ji was trying to explain. In basic terms, the deceased woman had worked through the subtext of Lois's answers from their interviews. From the jumbled information, Meng Ji thought she had gathered enough real data to formulate where Lois's race was located in the universe relative to Earth. She wanted Frankie to send a message in a very specific direction with as much effort as she could muster.

"I don't know if I can do that," Frankie kept saying.

"I want you to try," said Meng Ji's ghost vessel. "I went to a lot of trouble to get here and to sift through that being's idiosyncratic thought processes. I'd appreciate it if you could attempt this for me. If my theory is accurate and your body merged with an extra-terrestrial object meant to transmit information across vast distances through space, it's possible that you can send a message to these beings."

"You just gave me a string of random numbers," Frankie protested. *"I can't just think about a bunch of numbers and know what they mean. I know it's, like, coordinates, but that doesn't mean I can just know where it is I'm supposed to... think."*

"We should meditate on this," said Meng Ji.

"I told you," Frankie said, *"I don't know anything about that shit. I tried to do yoga, but I couldn't stop fidgeting. I don't know what you want me to do."*

"Can you manage being quiet and keeping an open mind?"

"Can you manage not being a bitch?"

As the conversation went on, Leo felt increasingly uncomfortable and decided to go up to the loft in the suite. Alphonse was up there, and Lois was outside doing whatever bear things she did now that she was a bear.

Frankie radiated frustration as Meng Ji continued to speak to her. "I would like us to stop talking and simply be for a while."

"Fine," Frankie thought at her.

They sat in silence. Eventually, when Frankie cooled down a little, Meng Ji spoke.

"I would like you to envision that you are in a very dark cavern," she said.

"Oh, please," Frankie scoffed. *"Are we going on some kind of spirit journey?"*

"In light of all you have experienced, what reason do you have to remain closed off in so many ways?" After another moment of silence, she repeated herself. "I would like you to envision that you are in a very dark cavern."

The woman had a point. Despite her reservations, Frankie conjured up the image of a cold, dank cave. *"Now what?"* she asked.

"Simply remain open and follow suggestions."

It was difficult, but Frankie did her best to follow Meng Ji's prompts. Frankie envisioned herself in her human form, crawling through a dark tunnel. The tunnel went on and on, sloping downward ever so slightly as she progressed. She groped around, feeling her hands and feet take purchase on cool smooth stone.

"The moisture in this cavern increases as you travel downward. You can hear the occasional drop of water fall from the cave ceiling and hit the stone floor."

The more Meng Ji described the environment, the more Frankie allowed the vision in her mind to become real. She had never been in any kind of natural cave system, but she had seen enough photos and movies to create something that felt real to her.

Frankie descended into the cave for what felt like a half hour. She was beginning to enjoy the experience. The farther she went, the more the walls were illuminated with a ghostly glow. It was dim, with only enough light to make out the vague shape of the stone walls. Her feet fell into shallow puddles. The water was a pleasant temperature, and even though her imagination had constructed this reality, Frankie was surprised. For some reason, she felt it would be cold.

"The tunnel now opens into a large, natural chamber," said Meng Ji. "The floor becomes the stony bank of an underground lake. You feel the chilly mist envelop your skin, though there is no breeze here. There are many droplets of water falling unpredictably from the chamber ceiling." Meng Ji's prompts had wormed into Frankie's mind in such a way that they no longer existed as spoken words. They were, in essence, Frankie's own conscious thoughts and observations.

An impossible ambient glow danced in the chamber's every nook. Frankie gazed upward and noticed thousands of quivering droplets on the ceiling. She watched, waiting for the shimmering drops to swell and fall into the pool below, but they remained, trembling in place. The longer she looked up at the twinkling, blue-white pinpricks, the more she saw. The ceiling of this cavern was endless, peppered with millions of what now appeared to be stars.

Frankie began to hear water sloshing as she gazed at the never-ending night sky that was the cavern's ceiling. When she lowered her eyes, she began to make out a silhouette gliding across the surface of a lake before her. The figure grew closer and closer until features began to appear. It looked to be a girl much smaller than Frankie. She was standing on a shoddy raft, pushing herself with a long pole across the lake's glassy surface.

The girl's hair was pulled back into a braid. Her eyes were narrow and upturned, and her cheeks were full. She slowed the raft to a halt at the bank where Frankie stood.

"Join me," said Meng Ji. She did not speak in a robotic, synthesized voice now. Her voice was that of a teenage girl.

Though the girl spoke a language Frankie could not have known, Frankie somehow understood what she was saying.

"Let's gaze at the stars."

"You're so young," said Frankie as she took the girl's tiny hand.

"Not as young as I may appear," said the girl—said Meng Ji.

She assisted Frankie onto the raft, then pushed it off the bank with her pole. They floated away, the sounds of the pole splashing through the water easing Frankie's mind further.

"I think this is far enough," said Meng Ji after they were a long way from shore.

She took Frankie's hand again and had her lie down on the old planks of the raft. They stared up at the ceiling, which was the sky. Meng Ji pointed up to a tiny, twinkling star above them. Frankie instantly knew to which dot of light she was pointing, though there were hundreds in the vicinity. Meng Ji told Frankie the name of the star. Although that name was a long string of numbers, it still sounded pretty, somehow. She pointed to another and named it as well. Then another.

Frankie began to realize the ceiling had wrapped down the walls and connected with the lake's surface and that the raft was no longer floating on a plane of calm water. It was now suspended amid the billions of stars. They stayed in this world for what seemed like hours to Frankie. They turned and lay on their sides, then their stomachs, as they looked all around, naming the stars and planets they saw.

"How did you learn all this?" asked Frankie.

"I spent my life studying the stars," replied Meng Ji. "And I spent much of my afterlife doing the same. I've gazed farther than humankind would ever have seen. Now you shall as well."

"This is so much to take in," Frankie said doubtfully. "How can I ever name all these stars? How can I ever understand everything I'm seeing?"

"You will," said Meng Ji. Frankie believed her. "We can stay here for as long as we need to."

"Okay." That idea seemed nice to Frankie. She was enjoying being in this cavern that held infinity. They continued to look around themselves, identifying every element they could see of the universe. In time, it began to make sense to Frankie. She began to be able to name the galaxies, stars, and planets on her own without prompting from her guide.

"What you've received in exchange for your life and body is a gift," said Meng Ji. "It does not feel that way and may not for a long time, but I believe you will see this. You are unique in this universe."

Frankie gazed farther and farther out from the raft, seeing and identifying new stars in faraway galaxies. She saw the echoes of stars that had lived for billions of years and died, and she named those too. "Lois," she said. "Where is Lois?"

Meng Ji spoke to Frankie in a series of numbers and letters, which now made perfect sense. Frankie turned to her left and looked out into the blackness. She found the planet that Meng Ji said would house the beings of Lois's race.

"That's it?" asked Frankie.

"To the best of my knowledge at this time, yes. That is it."

"It's so small and far away."

"And so are we," said Meng Ji. "Yet we house one of their own. Would you like to tell them?"

"I'll try." Frankie focused on the tiny dot of reddish-purple light that might have been Lois's planet. "How do I...?" she trailed off. But she knew what to do. She thought hard about the name of the planet as she knew it. She thought about the distance between it and herself as a straight line. She imagined two cans connected by an impossibly long string. But that wouldn't work, would it?

"You know where it is, and you know how to get there," said Meng Ji.

Frankie imagined throwing a ball to the planet so far away. In her mind, she saw a long, rubbery cable connected to the ball. If she could put her message into the ball, she could throw it and guide it where it needed to go with the cable. "What do I tell them?" she asked.

"The truth as you know it. Tell them what you feel."

Frankie thought of all the pain and fear she'd endured over the course of her life. She thought of the moments of happiness and love she had locked away for fear that they would make her soft. She poured those into the ball she was going to throw. She thought of the Angels and their promise to take the human race away to paradise. She thought of the great lie that had been and how everyone was now dead because of it—because of them.

She then thought of Lois. The poor, displaced woman who was now trapped in the body of a black bear, living in a ski lodge. Though she had never entirely understood the broken tongues in which Lois had spoken, she tried her best to put the woman's thoughts and feelings into the ball. Frankie added to this ball the story of how she and Leo had tried to cure the older woman's sickness and had accidentally killed her body.

Unfamiliar images of Lois came into Frankie's mind—images she could never have seen or imagined. She saw Lois as a sphere of light coming to a young planet Earth. She saw misty, dreamy scenes of that light entering different living creatures, studying them and their surroundings, always with a growing sense of dread. This ethereal light that was Lois had known all along that it was becoming fractured and rearranged, but it still clung to a baseless faith that if it kept going—kept trying to move forward, it would, one day, return home.

The scenes continued through the entirety of Earth's history, becoming ever more disjointed and harder to follow. These were images that Meng Ji had gathered and translated from the conversations with Lois. She now gave them to Frankie. These were memories from Lois's life that she could not grasp or articulate. Frankie put them all into the ball. She felt herself weeping with the enormity of the alien being's seemingly infinite life in her tiny hands.

"If I may," said Meng Ji before adding her own finishing touches to the message. She added all the information about herself and some general details about the human race. She added a request that Lois's people, if they could return to collect Lois, might also take herself and a few others away from this planet. "I think that will do," said Meng Ji.

Frankie pressed the ball into the palm of her hand and hurled it outward into the stars. Gripping the cable connected to the ball, she pulled and whipped it so the ball containing her message would not crash or fly off course. She guided the message around burning worlds, collapsing stars, and in wide arcs around vortexes and wildly spinning galaxies until, at last, it reached the red-purple planet that was so far away.

"I think we should release the cable now," said Meng Ji.

Frankie looked down at her hands holding the tether. With the apprehension of one grasping a dangerously stretched bungee cord, she let the cable go. It eased away from her, slowly at first, then with increasing speed. It sped through the course Frankie had created for it until it bunched up and collided with the message ball she had thrown, effectively completing the transmission.

"Did I do it?" asked Frankie.

"You did."

"Now what?"

"All we can do is wait now."

"I like it here," said Frankie, lying on the raft, exhausted. "Can we stay here?"

"I would like that," said Meng Ji before adding sadly, "Your friends are probably worried about you by now."

"Okay," Frankie replied. Meng Ji stood and used the pole to push the raft back to the lake's rocky shore. As they traveled, the sky above, once again, became a dripping stone slab. The stars turned back into glittering water drops. At the shore, Frankie rose and stepped off the raft's wooden planks and onto the bank of wet stone. Meng Ji pushed the raft away from the shore, and Frankie waved as the small Chinese girl faded into the darkness of the lake.

While climbing back through the tunnel that brought her to the chamber, Frankie became vaguely aware, on some level, that she was actually still lying on the floor of the lobby of Birch Mountain. She stopped her ascent of the cool, rocky ridge and closed her eyes. She did not—could not open them again since, in reality, she no longer had them. But she quickly returned to three-dimensional reality. It took her a while to gather her bearings. She surveyed the surrounding area, and it began to seem familiar. She was still lying on the lobby floor but in a slightly different spot than she remembered. She was disoriented from her mental journey and couldn't perceive who was near her. *"How did I get over here?"* she thought out to anyone who might be there.

"Hey, you're back," said Leo. "I was worried about you. Oh, and you're over there because Lois moved you a few times."

"Lois?" Frankie was almost fully back to reality.

"Yeah. She picked you up nearly every day and petted you. I tried to get her to stop a few times since I figured you and the ghost-lady were busy, and I know we're pretty sure she remembers us and doesn't want to eat us, but she's still a bear. So, I pretty much let her do what she wants."

"Wait," said Frankie. *"Every day? How long has it been since we talked to each other?"* As she gathered the visual information about the room, her vision of Leo clarified. She saw that his hair was shaggier than she remembered and that he had a scruffy beard.

"Um," said Leo. "About a month, I guess. It's been kind of lonely. I was afraid something had happened to you. I didn't know if you died or if the ghost-lady took you away somewhere and left us here."

"Jesus, I'm sorry. It felt like I had only been away for a few hours. Well, not away. Here but... not here. "

"I think I understand," Leo said. "You guys were in your own world, I guess." He couldn't help but feel envious of Frankie and Meng Ji's ability to seemingly check out from real life for a while. "So, how did it go?"

The exact details of the journey in the cave were fading as though it had been a dream, but the important parts stayed. *"I think it went okay. I sent a message to another planet. I guess. "*

"That's cool," said Leo.

"It was"—she paused—*"nice. "*

Leo smiled. Frankie radiated warm, contented feelings, and he was reaping the benefit.

"I'm glad to hear that."

"I can't be sure I sent anything that will make sense or if I even sent anything to the right planet. I can't even be sure if anything I experienced in the past month was real. I believe that it was, though, and I believe that we did it. I think I sent a letter to Lois's planet. "

"You did very well," said the voice of Meng Ji's ghost vessel.

The sound jarred Frankie. She had grown accustomed to the voice the little girl had used in the cavern.

"I have no reason to believe we achieved anything less than success."

"So, we just wait for a response?" asked Leo.

"Yes," said Meng Ji.

Leo was somewhat surprised that she had acknowledged him. Perhaps she was in good spirits.

It was late morning when Frankie came out of her trance state. By evening, she found out her message had been received. A blinding light from out of nowhere overtook her vision. She panicked at first. She'd never experienced anything like this in either of her forms. The light faded to a fuzzy, green static, and she began to hear a hum in her mind. The hum warbled and swirled for several minutes as though she was slowly inserting fingers into her ears and removing them again. She, of course, had no ears, but it was similar to how she remembered that sensation.

"Do you hear that?" Leo asked, walking down the stairs to the lobby. He had been in the loft when the noise started.

Frankie sensed Leo walking unsteadily toward her, his vision affected by the peridot haze. *"Yeah, I hear it,"* Frankie said to him. *"I don't think we're the only ones, either."*

The Lois-bear was on its belly, flat to the carpet, looking around unsurely.

"Go get Alphonse."

Leo went back up to the suite, grabbed Alphonse, and brought him to the lobby, where they joined the rest of the group in waiting awkwardly for whatever would happen next. Leo's vision began to clear as the green fuzz dispersed. Leo wondered if there was some sort of gas leak causing them to all have a simultaneous hallucination. Frankie caught this thought and responded to it.

"I don't think we're seeing and hearing things," she said. *"Well, I mean, we are, but I don't think we're being poisoned or anything. I think this might be a reply to the message we sent."*

"Already?" asked Leo.

"What is happening?" asked the voice of Meng Ji. "What are you all experiencing?"

Frankie told her about the static and the warbling hum.

"It's really weird," said Alphonse. "It's like someone plugged a wah-pedal into my ear."

"I am not sensing any changes in my perception. Perhaps they can only communicate with living creatures on this planet," said Meng Ji.

They sat for a while, waiting in the lobby as the bizarre occurrence assailed their individual senses with all manner of strange sensations. Leo had convinced himself that he was hallucinating. The shapes and colors of the world around him changed and distorted. He smelled things that were simply not there, like cedar wood chips, bananas, and Aqua Velva aftershave. His flesh went cool, then warm, and back again. He got goosebumps and sweats. His penis stiffened. At one point, he thought he tasted an earthy, grassy flavor. All the while, he heard bizarre tones and hums and knocking inside his head.

Occasionally, Meng Ji would ask for a status report, and one of the others would attempt, if they were able at that moment, to explain what they were experiencing.

"Is this what I did to them?" asked Frankie at one point.

"It's entirely possible," replied Meng Ji. "With our two races so vastly separated—so uniquely evolved, I'm not sure we could ever predict, with any certainty, how any sensation would translate. We can barely accomplish this with members of our own species."

After more than an hour, the strange hallucinatory event seemed to calm and focus. Lois appeared to be the first to catch on to the message being transmitted to them. Leo glanced over and saw her sitting on the floor, staring forward, looking as rapt as a bear could look to a human. Lois, being of the same race as those sending the message, was interpreting it the fastest.

Words began to form out of the aural mush. Or rather, there were sounds that seemed to be words but made no sense. Leo, who had taken German in high school, was reminded of a time he tried to read an article on a German website years after he'd graduated. He could pick out words and a general tone, but the overall story was incomplete and made no sense.

The abnormality had cleared from Leo's vision almost entirely, and he no longer felt any changes in his sense of taste or smell. His temperature was also back to normal. All that remained were the strange noises in his head.

"What is happening now? Are you all safe?" asked Meng Ji.

"I think so," said Frankie.

"Yeah," added Alphonse. "There's just weird noise now. It's almost like talking."

Over the next several minutes, the noises became more and more recognizable, their meanings gathering together like oil droplets in a bowl of water until the message was perfectly clear. Lois let out a slightly unnerving growl, but it wasn't menacing.

A voice spoke in the minds of the former Walnut Ridge lodgers. "We have received your communication and are replying," it said. "Acknowledge your understanding of this message. We have received your communication and are replying. Acknowledge your understanding..." and so on.

"We hear you," Frankie thought out to the voice. It seemed to be able to hear her method of speech because it ceased the repetitive message.

"Good," the voice said.

In Leo's mind, it was an authoritative female voice. To Frankie, the voice was gentle, like a grandfather. Alphonse heard it as the deep, smooth voice of the singer and musician Prince.

"We have received and analyzed your communiqué. Your story is quite harrowing. For a long time, we assumed the one you know as Lois was lost to us. It is joyful news to hear that this one still exists and was able to find a way to contact us."

"We kind of just stumbled into all that," said Frankie. *"Thank you for replying to us. We didn't know if we had sent the message correctly or if you would bother to talk back to us."*

"We value the lives, as you call them, of all of our own. We would like to have located the Lois much sooner than this, but it was, unfortunately, not possible. I can sense that the Lois is there now but cannot communicate?"

"Yeah," said Frankie. *"She's in a bit of a weird spot right now."*

"The story you told in your message to us was compelling and powerful. We send our deepest condolences to you and your race. It is a terrible thing when a civilization perishes. We know of the ones you call Angels. We feel no desire to enter the fantasy world they offer, but it is certainly tempting for most beings.

"It is important to us that we obtain the Lois, and it seems that this must be achieved through physical means. We have other means of travel now, but it would not be safe to use them with the Lois in its current state. We also wish to provide you, humans, with travel if you still desire it. Based on the information we received in your message, we are confident that we can quickly construct adequate life support for you on the ship we will send. It will be necessary to keep alive the vessel in which the Lois is trapped as well."

"We've talked about it," said Frankie.

She seemed to be the default spokesperson. Leo was thankful for that.

"We would like to join you. There's nothing left for us on this planet. We don't want to just sit here and rot. So, if you're willing to

take us somewhere or bring us along to your home, then we're willing to go."

"It will take time for you to decide what you wish to do, but we will assist you in whatever way possible. It is a small repayment for your help in returning the Lois to us. We have your location logged and can reach you rather quickly. We do not wish for you to stay on a languishing world any longer than necessary."

"Thank you," said Frankie. *"Please come as quickly as possible. I don't actually know how long bears live or how to tell if Lois is an old bear or not."*

"Bear?" asked the alien voice.

"That's what we call the animal that Lois is now."

The voice continued, disregarding what it couldn't translate. "We have no way to express to you the amount of time it will take us to get to you into units you will understand, but we will do our best to arrive without delay."

"Thank you," Frankie said again. Then the voice was gone.

"What happened?" asked Meng Ji.

Frankie explained to her the parts of the conversation that she had not been able to hear.

"This is good news," said the synthesized voice of the ancient ghost. "This is good news for us all."

34.

With snow falling and piling up higher every day, Leo was stuck in the lodge and getting a little squirrely. It had been three weeks since the aliens contacted them, and supplies were beginning to run low. Leo didn't know much about bears, but when Lois's ribs started showing through her fur, he realized she was not finding enough food when she went out.

He started making meals for her. It was mostly just thawed raw meat, but when that ran out, he switched her to canned goods and soup. There was also rice, which he figured wasn't great sustenance for a large mammal, but it would keep her going. He wondered how long it would take for the aliens to arrive, "soon" being such a relative concept.

There was no meat left, and the dry goods were dwindling. Leo decided it was time to go to the small freezer in the offset pantry. It was time to make the French toast. He dug out a few loaves of frozen bread, set them under a heat lamp, and ran hot water over the cartons of dipping mix until they thawed enough to be poured into a bowl. Then he set the bowl on a burner to melt the mixture the rest of the way.

Once the bread was warm and soft to the touch, he ran it through the bread slicer and brought the sliced loaf back to the stovetop's flat griddle section. He looked at the bowl full of slimy, milky-egg mixture and felt his appetite start to ebb, but he knew this may be the last opportunity he would ever have to try this dish that everyone told him was so good.

He grabbed a slice of bread, still slightly frozen in the center, and dropped it into the bowl of primordial chicken muck and spices. He was about to reach his fingers into the slop when he felt the blood drain from his face. It was too gross. He remembered the sets of cooking tongs that hung above the range and plunged them into the egg mix. Even with the tongs, it was revolting to have to dig around in the large bowl to dredge the soggy slice of bread from the bottom. He lifted it, and it dripped viscous globs of yellowish ooze.

Trying to avoid looking directly at it, he slapped the piece of bread onto the griddle. He took another piece of bread and, after psyching himself up, dunked it into the bowl. He repeated this process until he had four slime-coated, disgusting slices of bread cooking on the flat top. Begrudgingly, he used the tongs to lift the first piece of bread and flip it over. It splatted grotesquely onto the griddle and sizzled away. Leo had to step away for a moment before he could flip the other three.

After he flipped each slice until they were browned on both sides and appeared to be fully cooked, he piled them onto a clean plate and stared at his creation. He had cooked French toast. The worst of it was over, wasn't it? Having endured the nauseating process of making it, he should easily be able to eat it without a problem, right? Yet he couldn't bring himself to take a bite.

As he poured maple syrup onto the slices, the walls of the Lodge began to shake. It felt like an earthquake. Leo wasn't sure that was even possible in central Pennsylvania. He'd never heard of it happening before, but maybe some of the mines were collapsing. Perhaps the collision of those spaceships with the surface of the Earth had ruptured something. With an impact and an explosion like that, Leo supposed anything could have happened. Some plate could have shaken loose.

"They're here." It was Frankie's voice.

"What?" Leo called, though Frankie, lying in the lobby, could have heard him even if he'd whispered.

"The aliens, Lois's people. They're here. Their ship is shaking the ground. They should touch down in a couple seconds."

As Frankie said, the earthquake stopped after a few moments. There was a hum in the air, though—an electrical buzz that shot through the atmosphere. The same voice that had spoken to the lodgers weeks ago came back into Leo's head.

"We are sorry to have taken so long and to arrive so suddenly without warning," said the voice. Leo took his plate of French toast and walked to the lobby where Frankie and Meng Ji were. He set the plate on a coffee table.

"I'm going to go and get Alphonse," Leo said.

"Okay," said Frankie.

There was tension and excitement in the air but also apprehension.

Through the large, dirty windows of the lobby entrance, Leo saw part of a hulking ship. It was not like the Angel's ships or anything he'd seen, even in movies. He saw more of the ship through the honeymoon suite's windows. It was an oblong sphere of pearlescent white, and it was about sixty meters wide. Color danced across the smooth material of its surface as though the entire ship was slick with iridescent oil. There were three claw-like protrusions near its base. It used these to support itself while in Earth's gravity.

"Time to go?" asked Alphonse.

"I, I guess so. Yeah." Leo's voice was thin.

"Don't worry," said Alphonse. "This is the best chance we've got now. I think this is going to be okay."

"I guess it's still just a lot to take in. These past few months have been a roller coaster. I don't really know what to expect anymore."

"I hear that."

Leo grabbed the backpack he had used to transport Frankie when the Angels exiled them, and they made their way back down to the lobby. Through the glass door, Leo saw a glowing humanoid figure. Its form was watery and incorporeal. It spread its arms and spoke into Leo's head.

"We do not wish to risk leaving our ship or attempting to find suitable vessels, so this projection will have to do."

"Okay," said Leo.

The projected image walked through the closed door into the lodge. "We appreciate your efforts to contact us and return one of our own," the figure said. "Based on the information we received from the ones called Frankie and Meng Ji, we have constructed suitable living quarters in our transport ship. We have also manufactured an apparatus to house the one you call Meng Ji. You need simply remove the glass tube containing her and insert it into the vessel on our ship.

"Right," said Frankie. There was a degree of awe in her thought, even through mental projection. *"We're going to have to unplug you for a little bit Meng Ji."* Frankie relayed the message to the ghost, who could observe what was happening but could not receive the alien's telepathic messages.

"I see," said the voice of the spirit vessel. "Thank you for all your help, Frances, Alphonse, Lois, Leonard."

"Thank you," said Frankie, who then redirected her thoughts and nudged Leo to carry out the instruction. *"Leo?"*

Leo walked over to the mess of circuit boards and wires. He leaned down and reached into the open shell of the ghost vessel. When he felt the glowing orange tube within, it was not warm as he'd expected it to be, but rather, it was cold to the touch—almost frosty. He twisted the tube out of its socket and buttoned it into the breast pocket of his shirt.

Lois, in her mixture of confusion and understanding, had padded over to where the alien projection stood. She pawed at it affectionately, her large feet passing through the glowing, misty thing without touching anything real. She groaned in her throat as if with longing.

"We are ready to have you board our ship at any time," said the alien figure. "We can discuss the logistics of your travel once you are aboard if you still wish to come along."

"We do," said Leo.

Outside, the ship had lowered a ramp to allow passengers to enter. Leo walked to the front entrance and propped the door open so Lois could exit. Cold wind blew into the lobby, and dusty snow particles peppered his face. The alien projection led the way to the ship, and Lois trotted eagerly after it, knowing that she needed to go with it but not knowing why.

Leo lifted Frankie from where she lay on the floor and hugged her tightly to him.

"Thank you," she thought to him.

He didn't know what he had done to be thanked. "Thank you," he said to Frankie. Then he slipped her into the backpack and slung it over his shoulders. He lifted Alphonse and carried him in the crook of his arm. Leo looked around the lobby. He wasn't sure why. He supposed it was maybe for some kind of closure or maybe because it was just a cliché thing to do. His eyes fell on the plate of French toast on the coffee table.

He walked over to it, picked it up with his free hand, and trod out of the lobby into the blustery wind, carrying his friends and breakfast. He looked down at the French toast.

"Are you bringing that along?" asked Frankie. *"Are you going to eat it?"*

Leo looked down at his breakfast and stopped, hesitating for a moment. "I think so." He continued walking up the ramp to the otherworldly ship. "I feel like I have to now."

"I hope you like it," Frankie said as the door closed behind them.

"Me too," said Leo. "I think I will."

The End

Afterword

Walnut Ridge, an outgrowth of an unfinished short story entitled "Bucket People," was initially written between February 11 and April 27, 2019. Like many fictitious tales—despite how fantastical—the themes of this book are rooted firmly in reality. The pain, malaise, confusion, and dissatisfaction exhibited by these characters are familiar to many, as are the joy, friendship, love, and acceptance. It's my belief that as humans, we are eligible for all the despair and all the contentment that human existence has to offer, granted that we are willing to adjust our expectations and attitudes to whatever that might mean…

As the world becomes smaller and smaller, I think there is a temptation to recede deeper and deeper within the self, and not without sound reason. It's rough out there. Some of us are better equipped to handle it all than others. I, myself, have a relatively low tolerance for existence in general. For this reason, I try to count it as a blessing that the world has shrunk to the point where I can fairly easily reach outside of myself if I choose to do so. A lot of times, I do, and it works. Sometimes, I do, and it doesn't feel like it works, but I get through the day. Sometimes it doesn't work. But if I don't try, then I've got no chance.

Though neither I nor the publishers of this book wish to imply representation for nor endorsement of any official organizations, there are resources for many of us, should we choose to make use of them. One such resource is the Suicide and Crisis Hotline, available by calling or texting 988 from your phone in the US. Sometimes it's easier to barf your words out to a stranger than someone close to you.

AA.org is a great site to get some quick info about addiction and recovery if booze is part of your story. AA meetings are good places to learn about yourself and meet people with whom you might relate if you allow yourself to do so. Sometimes, they have free coffee, too. If you ever get really jammed up with static in your head, and nothing seems to be working, pick up this book and read it again. I'm sure it's even more excruciatingly boring on the second read. It'll put you right to sleep. When you wake up, some time will have passed, and you may have a chance to get a fresh perspective or make some positive choices! There's no need to feel ashamed about getting help (as much help as it takes). Frankly, based on what I've seen, there's very little to feel ashamed about in general these days. Huzzah!

I do hope you've enjoyed this book. I'm really not certain it's any good, but it is a book. It has words and pages and a cover and shit. So, there's that. You could use it to swat a fly or an angry wasp. I mostly wrote it in hopes of making sense of some of my own personal experiences over the past few years. It is my selfish desire that someone will read it and relate to it in ways that ultimately benefit them, whether they enjoy it or not. Many of us are looking for some form of connection or validation, egotistical fiction writers, perhaps more so than others. I sincerely thank you for reading.

About the Author

Dan Scamell (Daniel Vincent Scamell) is a writer of weird and speculative fiction that takes place in a slightly less pleasant version of the world in which we live. He is the co-author of the novella *Stuck Together With You*, and his short fiction has appeared in the Dead Star Press Anthology *From the Dead, OOZE: Little Bursts of Body Horror, Coffin Bell Journal,* and *The Molotov Cocktail.* Dan likes cats.

He currently lives in Pennsylvania, USA, with his robotic creation/pal Winston, where, in addition to writing, he also creates artwork, plays drums, and watches too much professional wrestling.

Dan's works are available at DeadStarPress.com, DVSfiction.com, and Amazon.com.

www.ingramcontent.com/pod-product-compliance
Lightning Source LLC
Chambersburg PA
CBHW070449200726
48293CB00007B/2149